Perrywinkle

The Story of Morning Runs and Peanut Butter Dreams

Eric Herkert

ISBN: 979-8-9878274-1-3

To Mom for always encouraging my creative side

MARTIN 1

Something curious happened to Martin when he crossed the bridge from a spry and lively twenty-something into a mature and wise thirty plus father of two. Things that he took for granted would continue forever without any problem needed more and more incremental effort to maintain. Metabolism gradually decreased. Poor eating habits that were easily taken in stride in youth have now taken to the waistline. Energy levels also had taken a hit. The magical three-oh wasn't just a changing of one day to the next, but it represented a whole scale shift in life. This, of course, occurred over time, but it surely snuck up on him. To get back to the virile twenties, while impossible to do mathematically yet possible mentally and physically, the requirement was an enormous amount of time and effort.

Martin found the quickest way, albeit most painful, to bring his current self back to his more life-infused previous version would be to strap on the training gear and lay feet to the street. He had competitively ran track for the majority of those adolescent years and was even the captain of the track team throughout high school. Yet once he had entered the career portion of his life, most available time and any enthusiasm for such endeavors waned considerably. While shorter and faster distances were his forte, distance running was the best way to shred the build of layers of poor life decisions. This was how he decided to get to the slimmer former self, as Martin determined that would equate to nearly thirty pounds removed from the waist. While it sounded completely reasonable, being quite the impatient individual, he wanted to accomplish it as soon as humanly possible. The safest time period, he figured, would be to one pound a week. Sounds perfectly reasonable and would take him right until the heart of the summer to accomplish. Just in time for beach season, which Martin didn't care for anyway.

The year started out challenging, as anyone who lacked the required endurance can certainly attest. That, along with the typically unpredictable New Jersey winter season, made getting off on the right feet, figuratively and physically, quite the chore. The bitter Winter's cold required many layers when exploring outdoors, but not as much if a runner wants to avoid overheating (which in itself sounds illogical but is indeed possible while exercising in the freezing elements). If Martin could persevere through those harsh and adverse conditions, then the thirty pounds should be a walk in the park.

But that is what he did. Each week passed with clear and tangible progress being made. Every time the trusty running shoes were strapped on, he pushed his limit slightly further. A training magazine once read that a person should only increase the distance run each week by ten percent. Martin stuck to that mantra religiously, and his slacks continually felt more and more complementary. As an added bonus, the time it took to run some of his favorite courses around town began to contract.

During all of this, Martin found it easiest to fulfill his cardio intake before the twins, wife, and hell, even the sun was awake. Something felt cathartic about watching the sun rise as his heart rate kept being elevated, feeling its loving warmth cut through the chilly winter darkness. On a few rare occasions, he would even enter the fabled runner's high, which he can certainly attest to its existence. Everything in one's mind melts away. There are no thoughts or concerns for the day. Any of yesterday's troubles feel like fading dreams. The entire process of running becomes completely involuntary, as one's breathing syncs perfectly with the beat of one's steps. Hills that may be daunting at other times are but anthills. Entering this quasi-hypnotic state is nearly addictive as the strongest opiates. This feeling can push a runner further than normally possible. Pain, physical and mental, ebb as one approaches exercise harmony. The mere afterglow of its occurrence will fill any motivation for weeks if there is any issue keeping that cup filled. This cycle certainly eases any frustration with slimming down.

On all the other times when he ran, Martin let his mind wander. On some of the mornings, his mind went through all that on his plate at work. That was generally on Mondays, considering shortly after he was back from his run and washed up, it would be not that long before the twins were at pre-k and Martin was square at his desk. Other days, actually most other days, his mind drifted to his family. Not Sasha or the twins, but the few others in his life. He always worried about his sister and her well-being. Above that was always Perrywinkle. Every single time he saw her, Martin couldn't help but be in amazement at how she had turned out. Martha was far from the most caring or most attentive or the most anything mother in the world. In the end she was still his sister. Given how some of the unfortunate events had transpired in their past, who the hell knows how either of them would have gotten this far. Between Martin and Martha, they seemed to be on the two different sides of the coin that flipped their lives upside and down. But in the end, both were still above ground. Both had steady jobs and managed in life. Both had another generation in this world. And at the end of the day, they were both siblings.

Months passed like this, and Martin continued to march along his path towards his personal achievement. He constantly pushed the journey forward toward the elusive thirty-two waistline. The cold winter mornings slowly softened as days marched onwards towards spring. Each day and week, the challenges kept fresh, whether it be choosing to add more elevation or the additional mile or even simply a faster pace.

"If you aren't pushing yourself with what you can do, then you are not gaining a goddamn thing," Martin repeated to himself every morning as he got through the double knot of his shoes. "Or losing a goddamn thing, if you consider what the goal is!"

As he continued to push along, results followed close behind. After the calendar turned thrice, Martin was already outpacing all of his goals. Miles and pounds piled up and shed off. Every pair of last year's khakis loosened. Tone and definition took shape. Attention at home once the kiddos were snug in their beds also increased. Energy levels hit highs that hadn't been seen since college, which caused early bedtimes for the boys (the Daddy monster came out in full force after work and would typically outlast the fierce five-year-old energy capacity). The only negative that could be found was the added mileage and wear on the expensive trainers. That itself would only require moving to the new pair earlier than expected. All things considered, that would always be a good trade off, even if Martin's top shelf shoes could cost as much as a monthly payment on a decade old midsize sedan.

One of the most difficult aspects of training was always the course itself. The little quaint town of Hex Point had enough main drags and side roads to start out training, but his biggest bugaboo with training was the redundancy. The same course could only be of interest if he was to improve upon any mile splits or even overall time. If there was failure at either, motivation could quickly or immediately be zapped. In a slight variation of the age-old adage *"Varied courses are the spice of running."* That also made Martin chuckle as he scoured the road map to figure out new places, new routes, or anything to keep his morning routine fresh and interesting; anything but routine. The courses that he had planned and ran seemed to fully encompass the new part of the town in its entirety, which is where the family and Martin staked a claim to one of the many new construction Cape Cods. With that, he began making his way down Main Street and into what the original locals labeled 'Old Town'. The only difference he could ever ascertain between the two was that Old Town was the locale of Hex Point's beginnings and New Town was simply that. Martin also didn't claim to be one of the unoriginal natives as he laid claim to New Town later in life.

By the end of April, Martin was still going full force, marching ever so closely towards his personal goals. With the sun rising earlier each day, it became increasingly easier to rise and shine on the streets. Each week that passed saw added miles and lower bulk. The mysteries that Old Town held dear to itself slowly appeared with each passing run, as he pushed the routes further into the side streets and winds and turns unknown to him. And this was being done in record times, which equated to over eight miles in under an hour. Each daily course took him progressively deeper and deeper into the other side of town and through the meandering streets. With no real reason to explore previously, save for the occasional kid birthday party, everywhere he went brought new sights and sounds. The added wear to his shoes weren't much of concern, as their accelerated demise signaled quantifiable progress. The progress itself was undeniable as told by the scale not screaming at him as much (down a full twenty by that point) and the lung burn stage of training was far in the rearview mirror. And the cherry on top of the cream was that occasional runners high, which kept the motivation tank at full.

As the second quarter of the year marched along, the unknown expense of Old Town shrunk rapidly. Martin consistently managed to keep mile times around seven and a half. The journal that he kept, which detailed miles, times, notes, or anything else an obsessive person may track, grew with unwavering consistency. While the average pace continued its slow assault downward, the weight loss had officially plateaued. This eventually happens to everyone in worn shoes at one point or another. While he tried to reassure himself at every turn that it was a normal part of the process and would need to be dealt with soon, it was hard to gloss over. The month of May was coming to a close and he was still ten pounds away. The problem arose from May starting out the same way. Each and every day, Martin desperately tried to convince himself that all of the pain, all of the struggles was indeed worth it. Not working in his favor was the fact that the work pants still felt tight on the sides, and these ones were not even his goal slacks yet his thirty fours. Yes, the mile splits and overall times were still lessening, but it appeared that the pace at which his pace was increasing was decreasing. All the while, the one item that wore the truth of plateaued training was his shoes, as they were the only items that were progressing in wear at a constant rate. By the end of May, even the newness of Old Town had lost its sheen.

When things often appear overwhelming, grim, and dour, there is always the hope of the sun's rays bursting through the gloom. Often, this can be reinvigorating and inspiring, breathing new life into one's path in life. Martin never knew where the phrase 'the night is darkest before the dawn' had come from, but, out of sheer survival it seemed, he clung to the meaning as close as possible.

PERRY 1

The first telltale sign was right below her nose. A slight, but definite sign of what might have befallen her. It was only a few droplets to start, but she was sure the flow might pick up at any moment. It was an unmistakable sign, but that was the least that concerned her.

When Perry opened her eyes, her surroundings left her completely confused. Not even a mere five minutes ago, she was having a slice of birthday cake in her living room, next to her mother on the couch. Then again, Perry uses that description loosely, as it was the only thing that her ol' drunken mother could muster up using the limited food items in the house between her waves of medication time. The more she thought about it, she couldn't really know what ingredients were put in the batter, but somehow it was a lot better than what was produced in many years. For the two of them, this was the closest they had to what a normal family might call a tradition. Their other traditions were more like side effects of an addiction.

Birthday party at the Shiner household aside, Perry tried to get her bearings to her current location and predicament. Her knees buckled slightly with each gentle breeze that passed over her body. It didn't appear as if it was the wind making her unsteady, but the fact she was smackdab in the middle of a lake of some kind. She glanced down to see what was holding her afloat. Only a partial piece of what appeared to her to be plywood was under her feet. Then again, to a thirteen-year-old not well versed in the ins and outs of construction material, it could have been the inside of a barn for all she knew. Strangely enough, Perry found herself without any shoes or socks. As she glanced upon her bare feet adjoining her faded painted toes, she didn't feel any sensation of water or cold that she should have, considering the moon was chasing the sun past dusk. What was even more perplexing was that every aspect of her body felt unsolid. Instead, she felt as if her being was more like that of a cloud, taking shape over a meadow field during the heart of springtime.

Perry tried her best to look around her, being careful not to tip over whatever was keeping her dry. She figured it was a lake, and that the slight rocking she felt wasn't just the wind, but a bit of the small waves caused by it. Still couldn't figure out how she was able to be above the water line and not the opposite, but that wasn't here nor there. Trees appeared to line the small shores on most all sides that she could see. The dusk light of the setting sun exacerbated her plight, all the trees blended together in a way that would make even the great Bob Ross jealous. There were no distinct features as she slowly rotated her body to see behind herself. A small break of the green monotony around her six played tricks with her mind.

"Is that a bridge?" Perry wondered. Too far to tell, but the shade of green that lined the structure did appear to be a result of years of wear and growth escaping the water.

"Bad time to forget your binoculars, kiddo," she muttered to herself, in her best Uncle Em voice. That cheered her up a bit. She always held a warm spot for him in her heart and she was sure it was the same reversed. She wasn't close to many people in this life, especially those her own age. Most thought the way she escaped into a book was nerdy, or even worse. Family, for the majority of the small numbers she had,

was a great retreat. Most family except for the most important, that is.

She slowly twisted her torso back to the forward position. When she was back to the right side, the far side of the lake and its tree residents choking away the shoreline were even smaller than before. The sight didn't bring much suspicion to Perry, as she, as an apparent cloud-like figure, was already adrift in a nondescript lake in a place that she couldn't recognize even if it was one of her earlier haunts. The sun continued its descent behind the forest line, and, in a few short minutes, Perry figured nothing but the water would be seen. The moon must have been hiding off in the distance, going through one of its own cycles.

Perry brought her sight back to the water beneath her. Even with the dimmest of lights from above, she couldn't make out any objects or shapes below. The water was a solid mass of color, trapping any clues to its hidden treasures to itself. The harder she tried to peer into the lake, the harder it became. The water and all it had encompassed was held tightly together in a deep abyssal black, no details were allowed to emerge. The purity of the singular mass produced very relaxing hypnotic feelings. Of course, floating out in the middle did not lend itself to admiring the side effects of this phenomenon, so Perry snapped herself out of her trance.

With one of her five senses failing her, she tried to focus on another to figure out her location. She closed her eyes tightly, took a long deep breath, and pushed all her sights she took in out of her mind, and let them float away. This was the same exercise she had mastered growing up when she encountered something unpleasant or even downright horrifying. Not all thirteen-year-old girl lives strike the same path as Perry's, but those who have might have gotten off at an exit a while ago. She was able to push many visuals out in this manner throughout her relatively few years of existence. Anything from her mother passed out in the hallway before their bathroom, and with the collection of the previous night's festivities to the typical white-tailed deer split in half on the side of the local county road so common to these parts of New Jersey. Another deep inhalation, and all was clear. The only thing she could see in her mind with the colors dancing around behind her eyelids.

After a few moments in this stance had passed, Perry could hear something. It wasn't until that moment that it became evident that, despite the breeze blowing over the surface of the water and through the trees that took root at the edge of the water, that the unnatural nature spot was completely silent. There wasn't a whisper, tweet from a bird, leaves moving amongst the wind. Nothing. But a sound that was slowly making its way into Perry's ear didn't sound like the nearby forest was putting it forth. It seemed out of place, extraterrestrial to the landscape for sure. A distant twanging that kept up an even rhythm. The pulse of sound increased in volume slowly. Perry, intently focused on the sounds coming from what appeared to be out of nowhere, began to piece it together. Besides the rhythmic twang, voices began to sound audible, and behind them came a beat in lock step with the twang.

"Music...I can't hear a damn thing out here except music..." Perry whispered to herself. *"Oh wait, hold on..."* Perry recognized the music, because she had been listening to the same album nonstop ever since she got it as a Christmas gift this year. Uncle Em and his lot exchanged with Perry and her mother a few weeks before the most holiest of days of the year. The holiday season had never truly been uplifting for Uncle Em and his sister, considering it was on Christmas day many years ago that their parents' case was officially closed despite the lack of bodies. Perry would never refer to them as Grandmom and Grandpop or anything like that as there wasn't any relationship since they left this earth long before she came around, and neither her mother nor Uncle ever have really talked about them. So, in order to avoid that low place where the grieving drunks go while wallowing in their sorrow, thinking about what could have, should have been, Uncle Em (actually it was more of Aunt Sasha, she was the more considerate and thoughtful of the two, no disrespect to her favorite Uncle) suggested celebrating a bit early, and more non-denominational. As early as she could remember, the first gift they gave to Perry was her

own turntable. As a youngin', it was such a mystery to her, given the massive advancements in technology since her gift's heyday. But Uncle Em just kept reassuring her the quality would be second to none, and boy was he right! Every year since that first gift in her memory banks was another album, different genre, different era, but always the same quality. It was a few years ago that he snagged a European metal band, which Perry wasn't too keen on at first as it was her first real exposure to the foreign sounds, but it did grow on her. Every year since then, the genre was the same, but the bands changed. It was In Flames that really got Perry up and about. The lyrical messages matched with the sometimes heavy sometimes mellow rhythm of the instruments had her hooked. A few weeks ago, she received their latest offering as her gift. She was careful not to listen to it all the time so that the grooves would get worn down too fast. The sound in the distance was the third track from the band's thirteenth offering.

Perry brought her right hand to her lips. She gently pulled her index finger over her top lip and onto the bottom. A tingling sensation followed a step behind her finger. It wasn't surprising as now the leaking from her nose was more of a stream than a drip.

"It is one of those kinds of dreams," Perry surmised. Everything, from the hazy forest to the unnatural murkiness below the water's surface to the mysterious flotsam that held her afloat to her own shadowy presence, was askew. It had been a long time since she had experienced this kind of dream. She knew enough that she could help herself in this scene, she could make things happen here. Perry forgot the exact name, but that didn't matter. What did was she could do her best to explore what her mind was showing her. There were occasions where happenings in these dreams had affects in her real life, but Perry chalked that up to her inner mind reminding her of things that she may have glossed over. The mind was funny like that, just when you might have given up, it unlocks one of the doors that the answer was behind.

Perry concentrated, visualizing an object in front of her to let her step on top. She closed her eyes tightly and let her mind's eye work. After a brief second of going through the myriad of different options, she let her eyes open. Directly in front of her wooden flotation device were a seemingly endless number of shiny lily pads, each one a strides length away from the other. All of them formed a makeshift row and led in the direction of the forest ahead of her.

The music continued on around her. There really was no specific location of its source, it was just there. She continued onward, having the warming chorus helping her along the way.

Perry stuck her right foot out, being particularly careful not to rock the boat, so to speak. She was quite confident that the wood below her would not move, but it is best to concentrate and do your best. She placed the big toe of her right foot slowly and steadily onto the first of the dream lily pads that was laid before her. Once part of her foot was stably onto the next step, Perry shifted her weight from her left foot onto her right and brought forth her second foot. She couldn't feel anything from the footing. It felt as though she was not on top of the pad but hovering above it. She studied the next few, and found each had complete uniformity in color, sheen, and texture.

"Beggars can't be choosers, as my dearest Uncle would say," Perry said, only she didn't. While her mouth was moving, the only sounds were heard inside her head.

After the first step was behind her, Perry made her way swiftly yet cautiously across the lineup of lily pads. Even though she was positive that what was going on was one of the dreams where she could control some aspects, the last thing she wanted was to fall into the murky depths while her sleeping body wets itself.

As she moved, she had tried her hardest to keep count how many she had traversed. When she hit double digits, Perry paused and lifted her head. The far-off forest seemed to appear closer, but there wasn't any good way to tell. So, she continued onward. Twenty. Thirty. Forty. Fifty. She was going at a pace that would have made her breathe heavily, but this wasn't gym class. Perry paused once again so that she could make a new assessment. For as many strides she made towards the lake shore, it seemed to her that she only advanced a few yards.

Rather than continue to hop across the lily pads that seemed to move in the opposite direction, Perry stopped. There was some reason for this dream experience. Her mind must have been trying to tell her something, but what it was was completely lost on her. Could it have been something she forgot about for school? The calendar was close to summer break and there were a few assignments that she had to take care of, but Perry was pretty sure all were completed. It was her freshman year of high school, and, having skipped a year due to her advanced smarts, she has been trying extremely hard to impress her teachers and classmates. So definitely not schoolwork. Did she forget to put away the clothes from the dryer? Her mother wouldn't care as much (she was never really a mean drunk, more of a crying-your-heart-out or whoa-is-me type of drunk), but maybe John Doe 32 would be back. Perry lost track of what was coming and going in her homestead but gave each a number and tied a personality description to said number. JD 32 was a neat freak and a yeller. But, no, Perry was pretty sure that one moved away last year.

"If this is a dream then there should be some meaning to things," Perry thought to herself. When she was asleep and had to relieve herself, the dream always had some pond, faucet running, Niagara Falls, or anything that would make Perry zip to the bathroom. But this didn't have the same feeling. It was a lake for sure, but it wasn't at the same time. The opacity of the water below her reminded Perry of a scary movie she watched with JD 19, he was one of her favorites if that was possible, when her mother took one too many sips. The movie was just all short clips, but one had a group of teens on a lake that each got eaten by what looked like an oil slick in the water. The entire mass of this lake looked like that oil slick.

Perry tried to make any association with what she could see. The tree line was still a smeared green coating the landscape. After a quick pivot, she saw the greyness of the bridge behind her, as it was when she spotted it initially. The moon now had completely chased the sun. The only sounds that could be heard were the guitar and heavy drums of her Euro Metal obsession, but even that faded to the point that she couldn't decipher the track that was filling the air. The lily pads were unlike she had ever seen, but nothing about them stood out. Nothing around her caused any ah-ha moment, no long forgotten memory had been washed ashore.

In a sign of frustration, Perry dropped her head down towards the water, completely exhausted mentally. Nothing made sense. There were no connections between reality and this reality. No signs that meant anything. Most of the time, Perry was able to make sense of her dreams. She often had dreams that had a red dog in it, often ripping apart a stack of papers. That always reminded her to put her homework into her bookbag in the morning. The evil looking garden gnomes from old Mrs. Callaway's yard tearing up their front yard? It was garbage pickup the next day (sometimes pneumonic alliteration worked well). But what connection could be made by being in the middle of a lake, no distinct trees or landmarks, lily pads that looked more like landscaping decorations than foliage, water colored a solid ebon below the surface…Perry glanced around again. While before the uniformity of the mass like water was undeniable. Now, shapes slowly danced and formed around each other like a paint can when the surface is stirred around. The solid black in the water was now being invaded by thin lines of grey and white. Something was moving below the lily pads and below her feet.

Lines started to slowly make their way around through the murkiness below. Appearing to not follow any pattern or shapes, the grey and white invaders traced lines through the mass like a snail across the sidewalk. The number of them creeped up, as everywhere Perry glared under her cloudy feet the lily pads appeared more and more out of the darkness. Curves and sharp angles began to form. Wild lines showing no true definition littered the abyss. Perry's mind tried its hardest to focus and matrix something, anything below.

"Could this be some hint at why I am here?" she dream-talked to herself.

Like staring up into the beautiful blue during a nice spring day, Perry's mind drifted between making different shapes fit the ever-moving tracing below. An elephant appeared riding a motorcycle to the right. A clown making a grilled cheese sandwich. A skull with flowing hair wrapped around it. A cartoon rabbit popping out of a hole. The sun setting over a snow capped mountain. A skull with slight remains of decaying flesh and jagged and missing teeth. A dog with elongated teeth protruding from its jawline. A skull with one eye smiling back at her.

Perry gasped. The randomness below had truly been taking shape. Not shape, but shapes. Every which way she looked different macabre scenes came to life below her. Different scenes of layered decay and rot of humanity spun slowly around her spot. Each one directed its attention to her. Some had enough flesh remaining to show lips. To Perry, they appeared to be in abject horror, exactly the same way she felt inside. Her stomach turned to a great pain, with vile churning pushing the tastes of cake and stomach acid up towards her mouth. The sights were vivid and disturbing, even for a dream.

"This isn't one of those dreams," Perry thought to herself. *"This is something different."*

It felt like she had been staring below for ages. In the dream world, time was tough to judge. Perry did all she could to divert her attention. Something, anything else, had to have details she could focus on. Once again, she took a deep breath while squeezing her eyes shut. Rather than trying to make her walkway appear, she tried to force her mind to push away those below her. Another deep breath, with more focusing. She was not going to risk it and was giving all that she could to make things more palatable. One last deep breath, and with an exhale, she opened her eyes. Her nerves were on high alert in the event that the grey and white lines that traced out nearly living shapes peering at her still were in existence, and her powers did nothing to drive them to where they came from.

To her surprise, and definitely not to her chagrin, everything was back to the way it was once again. The water was still, and now her vision could peer deep down under the surface. She could make out the shadow shapes of assorted freshwater flora and other denizens of the lake. Every slight ripple of the water top distorted the visions below, but only in a more natural way. Not menacing at all.

The lily pad steps were still in front of her, directing her towards the land's edge. The forest, even illuminated by the moon only at this point, appeared different. Perry could make out actual features of the trees and bushes. The smeared mass of green had given way to the more natural sight of branches and leaves. Even the slight sandy shore of the lake could be seen, along with various rocky outcrops. Bats had taken to the night sky, seeking their nightly insect intake. The mid spring breeze brought out different sounds and movement out of the surrounding nature view.

"Okay, this I can work with," Perry sleep whispered to herself.

As she began to tip toe from step to step, this time she could have sworn there was a feeling from the bottom of her feet, sensing a rough yet slimy top of each pad. To her surprise, Perry could make out the outlines of her feet, enough so to see her nails were in dire need of attention. All her senses seemed to be within her grasp. Her dream world was back to what she had grown accustomed to over the years. What had previously happened, while brief, was not like anything she had ever experienced, and Perry hoped would never happen again. She was about half right on that hope.

As she continued her path off the water's surface, she kept checking her relation to the edge. This time, the more she traveled the more she traveled. That was a good sign. Perry picked up the pace, hoping to figure out why she was here sooner rather than later. With her speed increasing, she focused on each step at a time, slowly looking ahead further foot by foot. Her right foot caught an extraordinarily slimier footing, and she was on her backside, legs halfway submerged in the water. Perry took a moment and placed her head down into her cupped hands.

The music was back, barely audible at first, up to almost boisterous by the end of the stanza. Perry instinctively picked up her head. It wasn't just one of her favorite songs from the album, but one of her all-time favs. Sometimes when friends have abandoned you, the one thing that won't abandon you is getting lost in a good tune. There are times when Perry thought the lyrics of a song had some meaning to her and her life, but most of the time it was just strictly coincidence. "If you boil down to the theme of all the songs out there, over ninety per cent are either generic, sell a million albums, take the money and the groupies kind of horse shit or ones that make as much sense as those paintings with a single line across the middle," one of the smartest things Perry heard her mother say to her after getting her own turntable when she was eight for Christmas. Surprisingly enough, it was said when she was sober and for some reason, Perry could completely relate. That is one of the reasons radio, as archaic and fragile a business could be, did nothing for Perry. She opted for vinyl first, streaming second. Perry could find anything on Spotify, but the quality just wasn't the same.

This song was different. Hell, the whole album was, but this one spoke to her, and Perry knew it was part of the other ten percent. If anything could possibly encapsulate her being into a nearly five-minute interval of melodic Swedish heavy metal, then "Follow Me" was it.

A part of her perked up, and Perry found herself up and onto her bare feet once more. One step at a time, she made her way towards the side of the lake. Left, right, left, right. She paced herself to not end up on her ass again. As she was around a dozen steps away, something caught her eye in front of her, and halted her dry land pursuit.

With the trees and tickets now in clear focus, even despite the sun having lost the battle with the moon, Perry could make out shapes and objects in the forest. Everything looked like it had its place, a peaceful scene of nature's beauty. Greens and browns mixed together under the moonlight. Shapes of leaves danced as the gentle breeze returned to bring movement to the living forest. A faint, yet bright blue stood tall between two solid oaks.

Perry rubbed her eyes in her dream, while in reality she sleepily brushed them over her face. What she saw in front of her, it didn't appear the same as the dancing skulls found in the water. She tried to close her eyes tightly and give herself a few deep breaths. The process that had helped her countless times before could not be of any help.

As hard as she could peer, Perry could not make out anything more than the hypnotic blue hues emanating from between the trees. It appeared to be swaying slightly, side to side, like it was adrift on the sea. To her, the shape looked almost human-like, with a head leading into broad shoulders and a stout lower. If there was anything that a person can come up with to stand out and catch an eye while standing relatively still in the woods, Perry couldn't think of anything more eye-catching.

Slowly, features came to her vision. A fuzziness of outside lines blurred the object, mixing green and blue. An arm raised on its right side. Perry thought the worst and hoped for the best.

The otherworldly blue being was beckoning to her to come closer. *"Perry…...winkle…."*

With that, Perry sat straight up from the living room couch where she was passed out and released a shriek. Her clothes were drenched with what seemed like sweat, and hopefully not lake water. The television was still on, and loud, which has always been a way for mother dearest to not hear Perry's snoring, whether it be a result of deep sleep or a reaction of some type. At least she had made it to her room, so Perry didn't have to bother helping her back.

Perry caught her breath, relaxed her arms down from her face where she found them when she was overly scared, and sat back down. Half a slice of cake was laid on a plate on the coffee table in front of her. She had half a mind to finish the rest and see what happens, but she wasn't tired at all and didn't wish to tempt that fate. That is normally not a wise choice if one wishes to continue their way in this world. Perry was pretty sure of her limitations at such a young age, so discretion won out again against valor. She retreated to her room, changed into fresh clothes, and laid down. She fully knew that not a wink would be slept for the remainder of the night. It was past three in the morning, so the loss of sleep really wouldn't matter.

The whole experience kept playing back like Muzak in her mind. Nothing made much sense to her at that point. Everything would come full circle in time. Not that night, not for a while. She couldn't come up with any reasons for the rhymes. But the whole ordeal seemed too real to be one of her normal dreams. If it was a run of the mill dream, there would be a great deal of linking to reality. But the one thing that didn't sit with her that night and stayed with her for the rest of her life wasn't the morbid scene that unfolded below her feet in the aquatic depths below. That blue monstrosity in the forest knew her name.

ALEX 1

Stepping out of his studio sized apartment turned office, Alex took a moment on the stoop, surveilling the parking lot. Force of habit he thought, but it was always a good thing to ensure personal safety. It wasn't because the town was a hotbed of arsonists, rapists, and murderers. It was far from that. Hex Point had always seemed like the most nondescript location around all the fair state of New Jersey. But Alex always got feelings. Not premonitions, just feelings.

His biggest worry was always, and will continue to be, the numerous John Does that he had outed over the years. He had built quite a reputation around the area, not just the town or county, but the whole state. Being so close to the city, an enormous epicenter of wealth, opulence, and extravagance, many of the assorted executive Johns tended to grow a feeling of invincibility and invisibility. With a city with millions of people traversing like ants in a colony, Alex could see how that mindset could be developed. But nine times out of ten, they were sloppy. Not obviously sloppy like booking a motel room under their name and their landline as the contact. Slightly sloppy, like not double checking for people watching in parked cars. Alex had developed a fair level of what ordinary people might deem extrasensory perception, but to him, it was just a whole lot of logic.

Alex didn't find any of the vehicles of those prior client requests in the parking lot. They would have stood out to a layman as most had cost more than some of the locals in Hex Point might have been lucky to make in a few years. It was a comfortable blue collar type town that still had larger celebrations than other towns with larger populations.

Nothing suspicious, so he continued on his way. It was a relatively brisk June day, a crisp touch in the air. Alex was in between cases at the moment. If he went through the academy like his father wished when he was growing up, the constant income and benefits would just continue to inflow, not to mention the work. But he knew it really wasn't for him. Alex always had his reasons and was quite comfortable given the two options. The police chief in town was one of his neighbors growing up, and they had always been friendly throughout the years. Even in his earlier days, he would try to lure Alex into the force. Not that they really needed the help, it was just apparent to the outside that Alex was good at what he did.

So, in the beginning of June and the summer around the corner, Alex found himself with some downtime. He often found himself wrapped in some mystery, ranging from the most mundane local questions to the most grandiose, national level murder cases. Not that he had access to anything, Alex simply dug into the available details. Any good investigator could connect some of the dots, and most of the time he was able to make the right call. Call it a hobby that helped him focus his skills when they might be needed most.

Before he was able to step down, Alex reached into his pocket and grabbed his phone. The aged phone, not even as old as a thoroughbred but as technology goes it might as well have been an antique, occasionally gave him slight shocks the moment a call might be incoming. He didn't program any client numbers into his phonebook but could associate a number with a face and a name. This one was the rare exception.

Incoming Call – RUS

"Hola, jefe!" the voice sounded after Alex picked up. "Got any work for your best recruit?"

Alex couldn't help but smile when he heard Rus's voice. There were many cases where a simple phone call to the self-proclaimed PI guild member in the middle of the night would bring him back to reality and lighten up a bit. Quite often, it ended with a case closed.

"I never really know what the hell you are saying half the time, but I got nada," Alex replied. "You know the deal by now, if I have a case, I will give you a call." He waited a moment to think, before continuing. "The parents putting pressure on you?"

"Not really. Just getting on my nerves. I am a spry and energetic stud in my early twenties. So, I live at home still, it happens. That is the way this country is going. And they still don't think this is a real job."

"You put it on your resume, right?" Alex retorted.

"Hell yeah! C'mon, Pee Eye Pee, I have been your sidekick for years, I know it is a real job," Rus shot back. Alex never really liked that nickname, but with the last name of Peters, he couldn't argue. "Trying to convince my current landlords, well that is a different story."

"Agreed." Alex paused. "Why don't you meet me for lunch? I'll call it a business lunch."

"If you are buying, I won't be lying. Meet you there in five."

"Want to know where I will be?" Alex questioned.

"Mr. P., you go to the same place every lunch that you are in between cases. I will give you ten. Five will be for me to drive there, the other five will be for you to make some time talking up Ms. Reynolds at the front desk. It is a Tuesday, and she won't be on schedule at Morey's Diner until the end of the week, Friday or even Saturday. Given the circumstances, you are probably all dressed up in that purple striped button down that she had used as an ice breaker before asking you out on a date a few years ago." Rus stopped, and gave Alex a moment to take it in. Alex was sure Rus could hear the smile coming across his face.

"Well goddamn it, my boy. You must have a great teacher. Give me fifteen, I haven't caught up with Lisa in a few months."

Morey's was a place that all the locals tended to hang out at one point in their lives. The occasional out-of-towner would drop by, and they were welcomed just as well. Those working the business have been for years, and they knew everyone by name. That was their easiest way to make new customers into repeat customers into regulars. It didn't hurt that the menu was a typical Bible sized Jersey Diner menu, and if a first timer couldn't find something that would satisfy their hunger, well they might have just stayed outside. It was situated on the corner location of Hamilton Square, eastbound side. That made it easiest for Alex to drop by, as his business was one of the spots on the second floor. The only impediment to getting a quick bite was that he would need to walk around the back of the plaza and to the front. It doesn't sound like much, but on one of those cold winter storms, it was easier to opt for whatever leftover he hauled out of the fridge.

Rus's intuition was spot on. Lisa Reynolds was working the front desk on that Tuesday. As guests arrived, she greeted them by name, exchanged pleasantries and showed them to their table. But whenever Alex Peters came in the front, the other wait staff knew to help out if any other patrons followed. She was in the same boat as Alex was at that stage in life. Borderline old enough to be a grandparent, and yet living single and working hard to make ends meet. All the years that she worked hard to get through didn't have a way of showing on her appearance. Lisa was one of those lucky individuals that, no matter what life had thrown their way, outward appearances looked a cool twenty years smaller than reality. That is why old man Morey had pasted her on the front, and, when he was long gone, his son kept her there. On a bad day, sometimes people just need a familiar, smiling face.

Alex didn't even notice that Rus had parked his new old car in the back and found his way around. To no surprise, there were Alex and Lisa off to the side of the diner, chatting like high school sweethearts.

Rus took a minute, learning against the outside window, staring gently their way. After a few more tender moments, he caught Lisa's eye, and she finished their conversation and beckoned Rus to follow them to an open table.

They both took seats across from each other. Rus shot a quick smirk over towards Alex, partly for walking in on the two of them and partly for his call on Alex's wardrobe choice this morning. For being a private detective, he was sometimes quite predictable.

"So how is the new ride?" Alex inquired.

"Well, the woman ain't lining up to hop inside, but it beats the hell out of riding the bus still," Rus replied, showing a bit of pride in the decade old Honda that he managed to push a few pennies together and buy. Still having the weight of student loans weighing on his back, he was lucky enough to have gracious parents letting him live at home rent free until he made his way a little into life. "It is better than the alternative, Mr. P. That is all I am saying."

"Your parents are still not approving of this paid internship?"

"Well, they are happy it is getting me out of the house and gaining some life experience," Rus said the latter part using his best old man, fatherly advice voice. "I just think they are worried. Pretty soon I can apply for my own license, and with that I can carry. That is why they are worried."

A waitress stopped by to drop off the menus. She told them her name was Nora, and that she was new to the Diner. Alex could never figure out whether people stated that to others they just met to not ruin their expectations when the service is subpar. She was nice enough and went off to get their two cups of coffee.

"If you want me to talk to them again…"

"Nah, that won't help. They know all they need from you. Just is the business side of it. I tried to tell them I could always become a member of the force. Or even one of those Turnpike patrolmen. Man, that is much more dangerous."

"Understood," Alex confirmed. "I cannot argue with the protection of a parent. Well, you have made it this far. I hope I haven't led you too far astray."

"Nah, you have shown me the ropes pretty damn well these four plus years. Am I ready to go out on my own? Hell no," Rus said plainly. "I can learn all I can by reading manuals and books that go through every situation imaginable. None of that holds a candle to riding shotgun with the best damn private investigator dick in the Garden State." Rus could feel Alex cringe without looking at him. All the slang for the job in the world, that was the one Alex never liked. "Let me back this up, the best damn gumshoe this side of the grand ole Mis-sus-sip!"

"Not much better," Alex retorted, but with a sly grin. Rus always knew how to read people and the room very well. Sometimes Alex thought he was much better than he was at that point in his life.

"Annnnnyway...you don't have to pay me for times like this, considering you are in between cases. I just thought that I can use this time to see what happens in between."

"And you are seeing it. Not sure I am following you, Rus."

"See, I have been around for the past years, learning on the fly. Case by case, I have absorbed tons from my time with you. Every time we ride around, I take mental notes, try to learn at least one thing every time. But those mental notes are now past a mental five subject notebook. So, I was thinking the other night, I am pretty sure I have learned as much as I could to be on my own. Now, I am not saying I wouldn't be the best, or that I would know anything, but think if it was sink or swim, I wouldn't need my floaties. Does that make sense?"

"Crystal clear." Alex had actually thought of the same thing recently. Rus had been riding along and working cases with him for years now. Every time back from college, he would opt for more work time rather than party time. He had always been a sharp kid. If he wanted to make a name for himself, and not be making calls and researching for his mentor, he very well could. And considering he was rapidly approaching twenty-five, nothing could hold him back.

"Coffees gentlemen," Nora announced as she had returned to their table, placing their mugs on the table, along with cream and sugar.

"Have you had a chance to look at the menu?" In fact, they hadn't. They had been in conversation the whole time, and the food never crossed their minds. Also, it was partly because the answer to that question was never in question.

Rus deferred to Alex. "Can I have the French Dip, add provolone and a side of fries, Nora?" Alex ordered politely, without any second thought.

"Of course. And for you, sir?"

"I will take the pork roll, egg, and cheese on a kaiser roll. Salt, pepper, ketchup, por favor," Rus replied confidently.

"You are two gentlemen who know what you want," surmised the newest of the wait staff. With a brief smile, she was off to put through their order, and they were back to this conversation.

With a thought of what was to follow, Alex inquired, "So what else do you need to know?"

"Well, the other things. The down times. You have been so good to teach me what you could when we are on an active case. But I have no clue what you do when you are not. Zip. Nada. Nothing. I imagine it is like any other small business, with the ups and downs. But that is something that I cannot prepare for. What the hell is your life like when the times are slow?"

Alex hesitated for a moment and leaned back in his chair. He wished to be as guarded as he could without sounding defensive. The truth was that ever since Marianne filed the divorce papers, the down time was the hardest. He had his hobbies and interests, but he decided to keep it strictly to the business.

"Mostly paperwork. You'd be surprised how much minutiae that goes into small business upkeep."

Rus, sensing a level of defensiveness, relented.

"Oh, speaking of paperwork, I have an extra check for you to pick up."

"Extra check?" Rus raised an eyebrow. "I thought we were settled after the Vinland case?"

"Yeah, we were. But the client was quite appreciative on how everything went down, she passed along some extra."

"Old lady Ginny? Man, you had better odds squeezing wine out of a rock than getting a single buck from that woman!"

"Well, Rus. It just goes to show how professional and courteous we can be on the job."

"Hell yeah, but you and I know, there isn't a check. Captain By-The-Books only takes the payment in the amount that he was contracted for, give a bit for additional expenditures. Every single receipt is itemized and filed away. You are more to the books with your business than the damn book itself. So, again, you and I know there isn't a check."

Alex stirred a bit more cream into his coffee and placed his spoon back onto his napkin. "She gave cash. You should come back to the office after we are done."

"Oh sweet. A little under the table action. You aren't going to report me or what you want to give me, right?"

"Not your slice. Mine, I may. Depends on how the books look at the end of the year. Anyway, she mentioned that she wanted you to have half. You must have made quite an impact on that nice old lady."

"Shit, I will dress up as Mother Teresa for work every day for a cash tip. Man, I would show up in my birthday suit for a nice compliment."

Nora was behind with a fresh pot of coffee to top them off. Rus couldn't tell what she heard, but by the blushing he could see, it must have been long enough. She appeared to be around the same age as him, and looked put together nicely to Rus. And there weren't many twenty some year olds, or even older as Ginny Vinland might confess, that couldn't help being attracted to him.

"If you are done, then we will swing upstairs to the office and I will give you your share after we eat," Alex stated as Nora retreated to the kitchen.

He was and was a little bit embarrassed. Despite being a smart, sometimes loud and outspoken twenty someone, Rus's bravado often hid some aspects of his insecurities.

At this point, the food had arrived, and both received it in silence.

Neither of them could figure out how many times they sat in the Diner, let alone ordered the same thing. There never was any degradation in the quality of their usuals, and, considering that the Morey family always placed a premium on loyalty to their employees, it wasn't that much of a surprise.

They sat in silence while each other finished their meals. The only sounds coming from their table were chewing hungrily and thirsty sips. Not a single crumb was left on their plates, as they made short order of their meals. They didn't take time to sit around and get a fresh cup of coffee, as there was business to attend to. Before Alex could get out his wallet, Nora stopped by for one last time.

"No worries, Mr. Peters. This one was on the house."

Curiously, Alex raised an eyebrow. It didn't take long before he noticed Lisa smiling from the front desk. The smile came back to his face.

He turned his attention back to the newest member of the Morey's family and finished attending to his wallet. He presented her with a twenty and a smile. "This is for you. Welcome. I am sure we will see you around."

Quite tickled by his generosity, Nora turned and attended to her next table with an obviously happy gait to her step. With that, Alex and Rus rose from their chairs to retreat back to the office. After a brief, friendly exchange with Lisa on the way out, the two started their stroll around the building. Even for a midday Tuesday in June, each of the shops that were open for business, and they all were, had a healthy number of customers. Mostly familiar faces. Some new ones sprinkled in between as well. During the wild economic swings that the country had seen recently, the small businesses that were the heart of downtown survived.

"So, take me through your day," Rus stated plainly, trying to reopen the conversation. Alex had known Rus for a while and had him working for him for over four years. When he had his mind set on something, he would get his answers.

"I am assuming we are back to your question from earlier.

Honestly, I just try to keep my mind sharp," Alex replied. He realized that the statement was technically correct, but, on the other side of the coin, it was quite loaded. "Sometimes I look back through my notes on old cases. Most of the time I just look for connections that I could have made at the time. There is almost always a different way to look at things. A different angle. It can be a good exercise to try to relive how things went to find any mistake or misstep that might have occurred, so it won't in the future."

The men turned the corner of the Square and were making their way behind. Alex was looking down at the sidewalk with his hands in his slacks. Normally he would have them in his jacket, but he left it in the office today. Didn't want to risk wrinkles.

Rus stopped. "That's it?" he inquired, expecting to hear something ground shaking.

Alex stopped along with him. He took a moment to gather his words, still looking at the ground. He picked his head up, looked at Rus and replied, "Yes, that is about it."

Rus looked at him back eye to eye. He felt there was more but didn't want to rattle Alex's cage for the fear that he may lose the last less than year of experience needed to apply for his own license. Cocking his head to the side the way a parent would do to a child that told them nothing was wrong despite the lamp being in pieces on the floor, Rus gave his boss a side eye.

"Is there something wrong, Rus?"

"Something just doesn't fit. I have been working with you, alongside you, for years now. I am pretty sure I have developed my own good sense of deduction, not to your level, but pretty damn good. When I first started, the cases came in and out like clockwork. The one thing that is constant in this world, in this area, has always been a level of infidelity. Your services have been in demand since Beatlemania as far as I can tell," Alex grimaced at that one. "The point is that the world hasn't changed. Men are even more assholes and pigheaded than before and making a shitload more money. If anything, our prime suspects should have risen exponentially over the past few years. The thing that doesn't add up is the workload. You are only in your fifties, so I sure as hell don't think you are winding down the biz. But last year, we," Rus stopped for a moment while debating his words, "I mean, you. You had taken half the cases from the year before. I never hear you complaining about your health. You treat your body like a temple. Nah, actually you treat it like Chichen Itza. So, you shouldn't be worrying about that. Your mind? Keeping your mind sharp, finding missteps in past cases? You and I know that is just a load of stinkin' pile of manure."

Alex always knew he had found the right person to take over when he did step aside. But, as Rus had most eloquently pointed out, he wasn't retiring anytime soon. In fact, the toll the job took on was quite minimal at this point in his life. Alex figured he could go on for a solid twenty years if he wanted.

"That is my story, and I am sticking to it. If you push me on it again, I will plead the fifth," Alex retorted.

"Fair enough," Rus once again relented. The two restarted their walk and made the turn behind the building. "You want to know what I have been doing when you give me the silent treatment?"

"Shoot."

"I have been following the local stories. I try to pull up all the research I can on the going-ons around town and the county," Rus answered.

"Going-on?" Alex interrupted.

"Yeah, that is something my professor in Criminology would use. Going-on wasn't just a felony or a petty offense. It was something that just wasn't right. Something that didn't stick well in your mind. He would say that sometimes a few different going-ons wouldn't just be that, but something bigger. Sometimes everything just might be connected. Sometimes a going-on is just old Missus Smith really losing her cat. The thing might have been up in age and just got lost, and not brutally murdered by a group of teens worshiping the occult. Most things are just plain things. But sometimes, a few of the going-ons can get put together, and the real story will rise to the surface."

"Your professor is a smart man," Alex responded, both now at the stoop of the office. "So, what did you find?"

"You remember that time a few years back when that kid was found in a creek up in the Catskills?"

Alex provided a blank stare, helping along the conversation.

"There was a big amount of press on it for a few days. Kid was a sixth grader with his mother, a single mother, on a little camping trip in North Jersey. One morning, he goes out to find some kindling or something, and never comes back. They find him a few days later a mile downstream doing the dead man's float. Autopsy comes through and it turns out he drowned, go figure. But the report also mentioned the kid had an asthma attack because of the cold water and of all the excitement of the possible way he ended up face down in the running water of God's country. The mother did some interviews with the press, everything was standard. Few days pass and the world moves on like it does."

"Sounds cut and dry to me," interjected Alex, both still standing near the office door.

"Yeah, to most people. But the moment I watched the first interview with the mother, something was just not right. A single mother just lost her only child to a freak accident. You would think she would be emotional or something. Nothing. Not a single bag under an eye. Not a goddamn tear could be seen. For all I know that kid wasn't hers."

"So that is the going-on? She murdered a pre-teen that wasn't hers?"

"Not gonna lie, it crossed my mind," Rus continued onward hastily. "Couldn't find a way that would make sense. It would be hard to make it look like that and have the autopsy not find foul play. After a few months, after the world moved on, I did some digging. Found out that the mother moved away, must have been too much to stay in the same place with her dead son's bedroom. I can see that. After doing some quick searches via the old internet, her name popped up in a real estate transaction. She bought a nice two mill ranch up in a ritzy part of North Jersey."

Alex interrupted again, "Did the kid have a policy on his life?"

"Not that I can tell. In order to get a face value high enough to live comfortably in a damn near mansion is impossible. So, I filed that away in my mind. Sometimes if you just let things progress naturally, the answer may just pop up and smack you in the face. You ready for this?"

"Ready as I'll ever be."

"Small time pharmaceutical off Route One near Princeton got slapped so hard by the FDA two months ago that they had to shut down. When I say small time, I mean small time. How they got any meds out to the public is beyond me, but I can't say I have a background in that field. As far as I can tell, some of their R&D budget was mostly spent on paying off officially. What they put out was those cheapy drugs that only those who can afford it get. One of their main product lines, can you guess?"

"Inhaled medications."

"Annnnd bingo was his name-o. Thanks for coming, please take a parting gift on the way out."

"So, Mr. Going-On. Where is the connection?" Alex probed him. He knew the link that was coming but wanted to see how his protégé would get there.

"Kid didn't have an asthma attack after he hit the water. He had it before he went into the drink. Meds he was on either were faulty or caused the attack. He had no chance. Small-Time Drugs puts two and two together, gets to Miss Now-Relatively-Wealthy-Former Mother before anything comes to light. This time they dip into the janitorial budget to pay the lady off. All things clean and over," Rus concluded. The look on his face showed pride brimming from inside of him, hoping to impress his boss.

A few seconds passed, as Alex pushed the proposed scenario through his mind's eye. He rolled his head around as he usually does when his calculating-self debated the answer. He brought his eyes back to Rus's.

"Interesting theory. Let's go inside and get your money." He turned and unlocked the door. Alex proceeded to start up the stairs, with Rus still stuck on the stoop.

"Theory? C'mon, everything is there. Cut and dry!" Rus followed Alex up the stairs and into the cramped office of Peters, Investigator. He took a seat in one of the two chairs in the office, the one usually reserved for potential clients before they signed off on the contract to bring all the dirty secrets to light. "And that isn't the only one."

Alex settled into his well-worn chair behind the desk. "Oh, there are more?" As he finished, he grabbed the envelope marked FOR RUS from the top drawer, hoping to move the conversation to something different. Rus was nearly oblivious to the white envelope containing a stack of twenties inside.

"Yeah, there are. The one that I can't figure was about…"

"Mrs. Crosby," Alex finished his thought.

"Exactly. I didn't bring it up because it just never sat well with me. I figured you felt the same thing. The richest lady in this town. Could've bought the entire town a round every day for a year. Got half from her even richer husband after his indiscretions were brought to light. Both of us saw it, I know. Her story had more holes than Swiss cheese, and his checked out. His never seemed fabricated at all. Mr. Crosby was the nicest guy in town, money or not. But he is the one that 'fessed up to her story. Made no sense. And that heartless bitch seemed happy to crush him and his reputation around town."

"I agree. In the end, the case was over the day David wrote all the things down on paper. Memorialized her story," added Alex.

"But that isn't what hasn't sat well with me. She was the one to off herself. She had no remorse for anything she did. But he is still around and kicking."

"And his stance around town jumped up a bit the day the police found her body hanging in the park."

"Exactly. I didn't put it on her to have any second thoughts. She was damn near a sociopath."

"So, what is the connection between poor Mrs. Crosby and the

Ellison boy?"

"Not a real connection outside of the going-on aspect of both. Plus, I can tell you are holding things back. I never mentioned the kid's name, so someone was just as interested in that case as me."

Alex sat back further in his chair. Once again, he found more and more confidence in his potential soon to not be sidekick. When he took a deep look into Rus's face, Alex saw Rus had him.

"You got me. That Ellison mother had something off about her. You can tell that sometimes by people's facial expressions. If you follow their eyes for some time, deceit is easy to spot."

"So, something bigger is going on. Why else would you have ten new voicemails on your work line? The one that you do not put out to anyone except to clients. The number that seems to be passed on around the group of jilted wives, you know that one. If I check the missed calls log on your phone, I guarantee that all the area codes will be 212, 332, 646 or 917."

Alex didn't have to check the missed calls on his work line. He knew that Rus was completely correct. The cases were there if he wanted. That was never the problem. There were times that the line just had to stay off.

Placing his arms on the desk in front of him, looking Rus directly in the eyes, Alex started, "There are things that are really hard to explain. You call them going-ons, some people call them coincidence. To me? They are just clues. You see, Rus, not everything is as it should be. You know this. You understand, that is why I brought you along. Things will make more sense as time goes on. There is something coming. What it is, I am not sure. I have that feeling. But the feeling ebbs and flows like the tide. Most of the time, it comes and goes, and life goes on. Every now and then, the tide grows and damages the seawall. Sometimes the tide rolls in and is out before you can even see it."

"Okay, I am following," lied Rus for the first time to Alex. He was pretty sure it was obvious.

"For the past year or so, the tide had been going out. But rather than come back in, it kept going further and further out. You know what normally comes next?"

"The water comes back in with force. A tidal wave."

"Exactly. I think the water is coming back towards the shore."

Alex sat back deep in his chair. He didn't continue with his analogy. He could see that he conveyed what he intended.

"Have you felt anything different around town?" asked Alex.

Rus put his hand to his chin. He took a moment to debate the question sent his way.

"Something seems a bit askew. Can't put my finger on it. I think that is why I called you, Alex."

"I know that is why you called me. I have a weird question. How does it feel around town? Not just downtown, but New Town, Old Town, all of Hex Point."

"You know what? I felt a bit different riding out to the highway yesterday.   I had to stop at the old church on the other side of town this morning. When I got out, the air around me.... I couldn't put my finger on it."

"Thin."

"Excuse me?"

"The air felt thin."

PERRY 2

Like clockwork, the sun slowly pushed its illuminating fingers through dark blinds, sending revealing rays across the carpet. Textbooks, still stuck on the same pages as they were left, were strewn over the floor, cascaded around study material and sticky notes. A systematic madness patterned itself over the various texts. Everything from Spanish to Algebra to European history was present and accounted for. There was not much room for anything else, especially on the floor. The desk was not much different either, as assorted science papers were laid out in an extremely meticulous yet scattered manner. Pages full of scribbles, calculations and shorthand notes could be found everywhere.

The light rays continued to make their metered approach across the room, and finally found their way to the makeshift blankets that were hanging delicately off the bed. Tufts of hair started to reflect the morning sun and shone brightly against the cluttered room. Hidden within a swath of hair was yet another textbook, but its contents couldn't be seen.

As the sun's rays soaked the entire room, the blankets slowly shifted around. The long, curly locks shifted around, with the side of a face finally poking out of the blanketed cover. A tired, yet determined eye searched around the room for the clock. With the iris adjusting to the early morning sun, the eye strained to find its footing with the turn of the new day. Eventually, it locked onto the digital clock set atop the bureau. A quick squint couldn't help determining the time, so an arm followed out of the covers to search blindly on the chair masquerading as a nightstand next to the bed. With a pair of glasses in hand, the arm retreated to its beginnings, along with all of the tufts of hair.

Perry popped her whole head out and peered across the room. The time flashed an even twelve o'clock across the face. Another blackout must have come and gone in the middle of the night and reset the clock. By looking at where the sun was set in the morning sky out her lonely window, Perry pegged it around seven in the morning. At least it gave her time to rise and get somewhat ready for the day ahead. And the Lord and Perry knew it was going to be a long one. She was definitely not disappointed in that.

Today was the start of many important exams in Perry's studious career. The stars aligned and brought her three major exams on the same day. It would be understandable if it was finals week, but that lovely time was a full two weeks away from now. The stars and fate decided that this first Tuesday of June would be the most stressful of Perry's thirteen years on the great blue world. Tests and exams, well that was her forte. She could always rest on her systematic processes to help guide her from start to a solid A. No, tests and studying and classroom questions were where Perry found the most comfort. That had allowed her to escape from her sometimes sour sometimes haunting reality and delve straight into the world of academia. She advanced to the point where she was on the verge of being two grades ahead of the normal early teen. A few bumps were in her way, namely anything that required a higher level of creativity. Logic made sense. History could be memorized and interpreted. Creative writing, well that was mostly a lost cause.

Perry rose from the bed and onto her feet. She was still a little bit wobbly from the events that transpired the night before last. She was still trying to wrap her mind around what had happened and how it happened. What a way to end a birthday. She lucked out that, with each day that passed it was another day closer to her grandparents' anniversary. That left her mother in quite a mess of emotions. And whenever she was left in a mess of emotions, she turned to her self-medication. It was easy for Perry to take the day off, which required her calling the absence line and giving the only real impression she could make, and she had mastered it over the years. And, in Perry's mind, it was just and deserved after having her sole birthday present shot histamines all through her body. It had been a while since she was down and out like that. Anytime it had happened, Perry reassured herself it wasn't going to be the end, but a small part of her was always rooting the other way.

All during the previous day, Perry debated whether to call her Uncle Martin. He was the only one that she truly could trust throughout all those tumultuous years. Granted, he was the closest she had to an actual caring family, but that wasn't the fairest assumption. Perry fully understood Martha was provided with such a tragic turn in life that it would be understandable if the average person packed their bags, called it a day, and found the nearest building to try to fly off of. Every life came with adversity, as far as Perry could tell. It was just what happened next that would define a person's true self. That last part Perry had paraphrased from her Aunt Sasha during one of their much beloved dinners together. Uncle Martin provided the no nonsense answers to some of her questions. Aunt Sasha was the high level, no bullshit lady that Perry very much respected.

In the end, Perry couldn't really frame the conversation with her Uncle Em to relay her experience and not have him calling the looney bin the moment they hung up. As much as they had true, connecting talks, this one would just be off the reservation. She thought she could make it sound like her mother was having some illusion playing through her mind, but it wasn't fair to bring her into this. In the end, while her mother indirectly brought her smack dab in the middle of the dream lake with dancing skulls, blended forests and, above all, cognizant blue shapes hanging out in the woods, Perry couldn't bring herself to letting the truth out to anyone else, so Monday was set with resting and studying.

As she made her way around the room, Perry collected all of the textbooks that she packed away for each Tuesday at East Stone High. With an Algebra test in the first period, she couldn't afford to be late for school. At this point in the morning, she could afford to scrape together whatever to eat for breakfast and get changed before she risked missing the bus. With a quick change of clothes and a refresher in the bathroom, Perry made her way into the kitchen area, not forgetting to pop her headphones into her backpack.

As she crossed through the hallway towards the kitchen, Perry's foot caught something lying on the rug. Her body shot forward before she could get her weight back under her legs. With a moment she looked around to make sure she didn't break anything. An empty bottle was still rolling back and forth on the floor. She scanned the rest of the area and couldn't find anything else out of place. The size of the vacant bottle usually would lead the normal person to knock over items, bumping into each and every thing, and leaving a trail of destruction to where the person might have laid to rest that night. Not in this household, as the living room area, which is something that only Perry had called it, was very thoroughly organized with not a thing out of place. This time of year was always a strange time for Perry, and more times than not, her mother surprised her for better or for worse.

Perry had a pair of white bread slices in the toaster, when she heard rumbling in the room adjacent to the living area. Quickly grabbing a swatch of butter from the fridge on a knife, she spread what she could, pressed the two into a sandwich and grabbed her backpack. Rather than face any confrontation on a day like this, Perry opted to get out of Dodge before the dust got kicked up through the town. She watched as the doorknob jiggled a bit before the door slowly creaked open. With a seamless continuous motion, Perry juggling her butter sandwich, backpack, house keys, and the front door, swung the position to lock as she escaped. It was best to avoid potentially distracting situations on mornings like this one.

Given that she was a solid twenty minutes earlier than when the bus would cruise by her house, it was best for Perry to make her way to school by foot. The last thing that she wanted was to be seen by her mother, and whatever conversation that followed. That kind of conversation could range from a sobbing remorseful confession to a stern and berating lecture. Both sides of the spectrum and everything in between were entirely avoidable in Perry's eyes. School was not too far away, and her house was close to the beginning of the bus course, so it made sense if she had to make a quick escape out of the house.

The quickest way to school was a shortcut through the woods to the ritzy area of town. This part of town was closest to the school, and it was where all of the executive transplants from the city found their way to plant their roots into a place where their bratty kids could have a backyard and a tree fort and whatever the hell else they wished for. Perry didn't like walking through the area, not because those kids that were associated with this place never talked to her yet literally stuck up their noses in her presence. To Perry, it was more like walking down Fifth Avenue, looking through all the fashion and wares that even the more affluent could only dream about having experienced. But she could rest assured that there would never be confrontation when she decided to make her way through her day along this route because all the high schoolers in this area would never dream about either walking to school or taking the plebeian bus. All these monetarily blessed offspring took their individual chariots of Mercedes, Porsche and even Rolls Royce, and they definitely weren't slumming it at East Point High.

As she made her way out of the woods and into this emerald city, Perry couldn't help but wonder what life would be if things had been different. It was hard not to find her mind wandering and wondering. Would things have been much better if she had landed in a different home and a different upbringing? Surely, she wouldn't have to worry what kinds of men paraded through the house. Well, in all honesty, she wasn't even sure of that. Perry had heard stories from school about the children that hailed from this affluent part of town. From all she could ascertain, problems still existed with money. Just not completely the same problems. From all the rumors and tales told throughout the high school halls, the common themes tended to be the same. Father works long and hard hours. Typically played harder, too. Sometimes played hard with others outside of the family. Mother looks after the house. With kids in teenage years, responsibility had shrunk over time. More time for Mother with others. Others outside the family. Daughter and Son appear to have been well put together. Appearances are deceiving. Daughter likes to party and get away with murder. Son has developed a nose candy problem before going off to college but is awesome at hiding the symptoms. If Perry heard it once, she heard it many times. While the extent to which the rumors were inflated, she couldn't tell. But when there is smoke, there sure as hell is fire somewhere.

Perry continued onward through the development, passing mansion after mansion, each with a yard full of ornate decorations making her feel like she was on a movie set. To help the time go by a bit quicker and to help keep her mind from daydreaming over what could have been, she threw on her headphones and flipped on the music from her phone. The sound filled her head, it was right around the same part when she fell asleep the night before.

Track six of <u>I, the Mask</u> was "(This is Our) House". It brought a chuckle to Perry, the whole irony of the situation. And the more she had the newest In Flames album on repeat, she could completely and utterly understand the marked difference in sound quality between vinyl and digital. She put the sound up all the way and put her head down to continue along.

At this point in the morning, all the Fathers were far off at work or the golf course or wherever they conducted their business. The Daughters and Sons that had their licenses were already at school, or at least that is what they led their Fathers and Mothers to believe. Those that could not drive themselves always had other Daughters and

Sons to drive them on their way. The lonely Mothers must be planning out their days attending whatever or whomever they must attend to before others return. In the end, Perry could walk assured that she wouldn't come across another living soul at this time.

She exited the winding development and made her way to Stone Drive, where the high school was located. It wasn't the largest of schools in the district, but it was surprisingly adequate to maintain the number of students that attended. It wasn't always like that, as the demographics recently changed, with more and more of the upper-class moving in. Their children were not to be allowed to mingle with the common folk. They were fast tracked to their respective Ivy League schools by way of high school at the closest private institution. They might as well be colleges considering the tuition was just as high. Perry, being the academic that she was, always kept her finger on the pulse of higher learning. She was more advanced than those in her classes despite being the youngest by far. She had come to the realization that she could find a way out of this town and it would be up to her learning. She pegged her chances to get into any college at around ninety percent. This subset was large enough for Perry to have one of her top choices to be included. And the money side, well her mother didn't make or have much so that never crossed her mind.

Perry made her way into school with a few minutes to spare. After a quick stop at her locker, she turned her way towards her homeroom. She was going over all the algebra problems she practiced the night before. That was the first on her agenda because once the bell rings for first period, it was game on. She kept her head down, music still blaring in her ears. Normally a typical high schooler would be gossiping and making the most of the time before the bell rang, but Perry wasn't like the rest of the other young adults. She was convinced that no one outside of her teachers had noticed her absence. Perry, while not exactly a loner, chose to focus on other things.

She kept her head down as she turned the last corner before she could duck into homeroom, Perry went headfirst into another student coming the other way. Both took the brunt of the impact and found themselves slowly reaching the ground. Textbooks and notepads were strewn across the floor as passersby tried their best to avoid the accident. Perry reached out to grab her things when an unsuspecting flat came down onto the back of her hand. She let out a quick shriek of pain and had her hand retreat to her side.

"Oh man, are you okay, Pee?"

Perry looked up to see who she had recklessly run into while trying to mind her business. And there she was, Lucrecia Avendale to her parents but Lucy to everyone else, taking a break from reassembling her materials for the day to look at her.

"Lucy, I am so sorry. I…"

"It's okay. I hope your hand is all good," Lucy replied.

Perry felt the throbbing pain emanate from her hand, and she took a moment to inspect the damage. Everything pointed to skipping the hospital visit on this lovely morning.

"Yeah, I'll be fine. Thanks for asking."

"No problem," Lucy answered as she rose to her feet. The one-minute warning bell alerting the students for homeroom echoed through the hallways.

Perry got up, and, with the way the two were positioned, they were eye to eye. The moment, however fleeting, felt overly awkward. Here stood Perry's best friend for the majority of her time on this earth, and yet they could not find any words to say. For endless days and nights, they had been inseparable. Perry and Lucy had an innumerable number of things they could talk about, that they could bond over, that they had in common. They had even developed imaginary friends throughout the years together, and they were even the closest that imaginary friends could be. They had bonded over the vast similarities within their own family units. If Perry was ever to have a sibling in this world, God would have created Lucy.

Yet here they were. Staring blankly into each other's eyes, Perry and Lucy couldn't be further apart. Perry knew that people came in and out of life from time to time, but she always thought the two of them would be together for many years. They shared so much intertwined history, heartache, and growing pains for two early teens both could fill volumes. At one point that Perry couldn't peg a finger on, Lucy desperately tried to shed her life of any remnants of her early childhood. As far as she could tell, Lucy couldn't accept what she perceived she was. Maybe she wasn't happy with what other kids were saying about her, and kids, even early on, can truly be mean. The two of them had instantly bonded at such a young age because of the broken homes they were coming from, and the same thing seemingly pushed them apart.

As they both awkwardly shifted to go their separate ways, both seemed to be searching for the right words to find. They had their mouths agape, half expecting the words would start coming out on their own. Nothing came out. The look of both faces could show that each was holding back some quite raw emotions.

As the girls were searching for the right words to say, the bell for homeroom blared throughout the halls. Both were late, but it didn't matter now. For the first time in a long time, Perry and Lucy shared a moment, even if it may have been a fleeting one.

Perry turned her head to make her way to class. If she was quick enough, old Mrs. Penny would not report her tardiness. As she started away, she felt a hand on her upper arm.

"Perry, wait a second. I know it has been so long," Lucy started. "I am sorry for ignoring you all these times. I want to make it up to you."

Perry's eyebrows raised. She had felt slighted for a while now, with all the passings in the hallways with eyes shooting the other way when Lucy fiercely wanted to be a part of the high school upper crust. Every memory together was metaphorically trampled in Perry's mind. But all of that anxious energy borne from the invisible divide was appearing closer to the metaphorical water under the bridge. Perry couldn't find the nerve to respond.

"I am going to a get together after school in Essex. Some friends that go to Perry High got a pirated version of the new slasher film that just hit the box office. They would be fine if I brought a friend." Perry felt shocked and optimistic about being called that. Lucy continued, "I dunno what you are doing. I mean it is a Tuesday night, but I thought it would be fun."

Perry was dumbfounded. It must have been fate that brought the two souls together ten years ago as well as two minutes ago. As tough and strong Perry made herself out to be, she desperately yearned for a friend.

"Umm, yeah, I don't know. My mother…"

"I understand. But maybe it would be a good break. I mean, I know what time of the year it is. A few hours away from home might do you some good."

Lucy always knew how to convince Perry to do anything. In this case, the fact that she remembered that this particular stretch in June was always the worst.

"You know what, I can probably sneak out for a bit."

"Awesome! We can meet at the entrance to Essex, you know where that is?"

Essex was the name of the development that Perry had traversed through to get to school this morning. She was quite aware. "Yeah, I'll be there."

"Six sharp, and I will bring you to the place."

"Okay." Perry had a bit of trepidation. As elated as she was to possibly reconnect with a friend of over a decade, which in itself is insane to say for a thirteen-year-old, the thought of mingling with girls that have nothing in common with her and more than likely looked down on her made the butterflies inside come to life.

Both gave the other a smile and hurried along, hoping not to get written up for being late. The rest of the day for Perry went as she had planned. Algebra test posed no problems. Lunch was yet another lone meal, not making eye contact with anybody in the surroundings. The afternoon continued as any other day. Once the bell rang to mark the end of the school day, that is when things went awry.

***

Perry made her way back towards the opening of the Essex development. It felt like she was retracing her path from the morning. Anxiety was at its all-time high. The feelings that were running throughout her body made her skin tingle. She hadn't felt this way in a long time. Part of it was due to the fact that Perry wasn't seen as anywhere close to the popular crowd, so she tended to be on the fringe of high school society and part was she hadn't even tried for some time. So many scenarios ran through her mind, from the most mundane to the most outrageous. Nerves had made her sick when she was younger. Over time Perry found ways to keep things under control, but that was more of a necessity as everything was in a state of continuous flux.

In times when the nerves had come, Perry turned up the volume. She had on her headphones and tried to push the world away. When she was able to do this, she could let the music truly come in. A few deep breaths with her eyes well closed, and she felt the nerves melt away.

As track number seven from her favorite album continued, Perry was in a deep trance that she didn't even notice when Lucy approached her from the side. A quick tap on the elbow and Perry was off the ground.

"Holy shit, I am sorry, Pee! I thought you saw me coming," Lucy shot out, clearly unexpecting her old friend to be so alarmed.

Perry collected herself and pulled off her headphones. She looked at Lucy, and both had a true smile across their faces. Just like it used to be.

"Lucy, it is okay. I was just in the zone, I guess."

"Are you still rocking out to that metal stuff?" Lucy asked.

Perry, now back to herself, replied, "Lucrecia Avendale, you know very well that it is not metal, it is euro rock."

"Honestly, Pee, it is Swedish heavy metal, you and I know that," Lucy answered as-a-matter-of-factly. That brought another smile to Perry's face. The two of them spent hours sticking to Perry's room, listening to all her vinyls when Martha was at work. Even though Lucy preferred whatever pop was on the hot station of the radio, being a friend, she got to know and appreciate Perry's preferences.

Both girls giggled lightly. Once they composed themselves, Lucy turned and led Perry down the road. She kept close to her old friend, keeping a pace behind. The two strolled silently down the way and turned into one of the community's many dead ends. The destination was close at hand, Perry could grasp.

She stopped in the middle of the road before the two got to the mansion at the end of the street. Lucy had continued a few steps, only stopping when she didn't hear the second pair of footsteps near her, then turned around.

"Everything okay?" Lucy asked.

"Yeah. No. I don't know." Rather than ask a follow-up question, Lucy gave her friend a moment to continue. "Lucy, can I ask you a question?"

"Yeah, of course."

"Why now?"

Lucy was quite caught off guard. "What do you mean?"

"I mean, like, we have passed each other how many times in school, between classes, through the halls, walking home. And there were all those times that we passed, and I was just so confused. And I think you felt that too. We were such good friends for so long. You were the only one I could talk to when things went nutsy in my life. I was the only one you could talk to when things went uber nutsy in your life. There wasn't anything that could come between us."

"Uh huh…" Lucy added gingerly.

"There were like thousands of times that you could have said something. Then we crash in school, and that was the time you wanted to say something?"

Lucy couldn't help but look at the ground near her feet. She seemed to be hiding something from Perry, but she couldn't figure it out. Feelings and hormones coursing through the veins and hearts of early teen women tended to make things tough to determine the root cause of issues.

"I have been meaning to talk to you," Lucy started while still not making any eye contact. "I feel bad. I have felt bad. Things have just been complicated."

"Uh huh," Perry retorted. Lucy looked up and looked her in the eyes. Complicated was something that Perry knew quite intimately. Lucy seemingly realized that, and her eyes retreated downward.

"Ehh, never mind. I am just, I don't know. I'm sorry how things went."

Perry couldn't pin a specific event or incident that had transpired between the two of them that could have possibly compromised their kinship. It would have been different if some insane course of events took place that involved the two of them changing the directions of their social lives. But nothing. Not a single thing that Perry could think of had come between the two that forced them to go their separate ways. It seemed like Lucy had woken up one morning and had enough of being there for her.

"Let's just go in and have a good time, okay?"

Reluctantly Perry obliged. "So which house is it and what are their names?"

Lucy realized at that moment that she hadn't filled in any of the details to Perry. "Ah, sorry, Pee. It is the house at the end of the road. The girl that lives there is Tania and her best friend is Missy. Tania is a spitfire, you will really like her."

"And the one that is named after a cat?"

Lucy chuckled and held her hand to her face. "Oh man, get that out now. Missy, well she is a bit of a wildcard. I dunno what meds she should be on or what meds she is on, but those two aren't the same." The smile dropped off her face as quickly as it had arrived. "Be sure to be square with her. Unpredictable is an understatement."

"Tabby cat acts like a house cat, hissing at the dark and running around the house aimlessly. Check," Perry quipped.

"Seriously, Pee. She is not one to mess with. And your tone can be, well you know. Not the most personable."

"Roger, over and out."

The two continued on their way to the end of the road. While each of the mansions had sat alone on their own large plot of land, the one they were heading towards was on a different level. The sprawling yard more closely resembled a noble estate. The driveway winded up and around the hill where the building laid. From the outside, the exact enormity could not be understood. The immense mansion on the hill held a looming and sordid look to anyone who approached. Ivy climbed up the red brick face of the front, hiding the individual facets that seemingly brought the house alive.

As Perry got closer with each step, the details of the monstrosity became clearer and clearer. While most houses that Perry had known throughout the years had distinctive features that transformed the house into a home, she couldn't put a finger on it. There always seemed to be the personality of the homeowner shining through that an observant bystander could easily distinguish. From the various lawn ornaments adorning the dwelling of a bright and bubbly retired high school teacher to the lawn with the exact clean lines butting up to the sidewalk of the mechanical engineer recently out of school, every house had its differing characteristics. Even Perry's house had its features, while unkempt and wild, and reflected the chaotic and unpredictable insides.

This house was devoid of any features. It felt lifeless and worn. Whatever experiences that those inside might have had didn't make it feel welcoming or at all friendly. Everything from the wrought iron fence that traversed around the borders to the gigantic oak standing half alive half dead on the side of the house to the overly worn aspects of the fascia boards on the top level didn't seem right. For a house of this size adorning the crest of a hill overseeing the wide expense of the property, it should have provided some redeeming features. It more resembled the setting of the slash'em up flick the girls were there to see than the warm and cozy home it should have been.

Both stopped at the end of the driveway and peered up at the house. Perry assumed that Lucy had been there before considering she led her this far. But she took a glance at Lucy, Perry could see the same feeling on her face that she felt in the pit of her stomach. Short, quick breaths between the two were completely synchronous, showing the level of anxiety was off the charts. While the sun would still be hung in the sky for some time, it might as well have been the middle of the darkest night.

"Um yeah." Perry muttered under her nervous breaths.

"You can say that again," Lucy responded, even quieter.

Perry slowly turned her head to find her friend next to her. "Honestly and be square with me. What are you trying to do here? Why am I here?"

Lucy tried to gather herself, but the nerves were too much for her. Her eyes welled up with emotion. Something was there, but she couldn't find the words to express it. The tears rolled down her cheeks, streaking towards her chin. Slowly, Lucy brought her eyes up to meet Perry's.

"Pee, I just." Lucy took another moment, wiping her nose with her sleeve. "It is complicated."

"I am not sure how complicated it is. Seems like something is under the surface. Just wish you would tell me, let me know what the hell I am getting into." Perry trailed off as the tears of her own followed suit over her cheeks. They shared sniffles between the two of them but didn't have the time to finish their conversation.

"*LUUUUUCCCCCYYYY,*" came from the front of the mansion. Perry could see someone standing in front of the door, waving hands over her head. "*COME THROUGH THE GATE!*"

As soon as she finished, the overly sized iron gate started creaking open, giving an entrance into the estate. Despite the impressive length of the driveway, there was only a single vehicle that Perry could spot. The extensive length of the pavement could have fit an entire fleet of commuter buses and still have room to put a three-ring circus at the end. Both sides of the driveway were left unkempt, which caught Perry a bit off guard. For a location like this, the inhabitants were certainly not getting out the mower and weed-wacker themselves, but it appears they were too busy to see the shoddy job the landscaping crew must have been doing. The meticulously spaced shrubbery was seeing its fair share of browning and death. At some point in the not too distant past this path must have shown visitors a wonderful and inviting trip towards the house. All of that was in the past and now it was neglected and dreary.

The lone car sat idly in the driveway, but Perry could see what appeared to be a five-car garage. Of course, she could count five bays so there could be yet another fleet hiding inside. The closer the two got, the car came into focus. It was an older Mercedes but wore some very hard years on its body. The driver's side door was pocked with dents, and three lines stretching from the front bumper to the back panel. The only thing that Perry figured in her mind were keys. The side of the grey Benz was littered with pin stripes that were the result of the owner not playing nice with friends. The rear-view mirror hung low and lifeless from the windshield, and once Perry and Lucy were along its side the passenger seat was littered with burn holes in the upholstery. Whomever was behind the wheel had the wheel moving but the hamster was long dead, and half rotted in the corner.

Lucy pulled close to Perry, and whispered to her, *"That* is Missy's car. If you thought I wasn't being serious before, well you see that. Serious shit with her."

Perry tried to swallow but the nerves got it caught in the middle. The severity of the situation, if it wasn't clear before, was crystal clear now. She kept her eyes on the vehicle, half expecting to see a limb popping out from under the seat. As she passed it, the overwhelming stench of rot and musty staleness hit the back of her throat. Perry had to clench hard to stop any gags from traveling up her esophagus.

"Lucy! C'mon girl! The movie is all set in the theatre. Got popcorn all ready too!" Tania bubbled towards them. "Oh, you brought the famous Perry with you!"

At this point, Lucy and Perry were at the front of the house, standing toe to toe with one of its inhabitants. Compared to the decrepit nature of the estate, Tania was, at first glance, a striking opposite. She bore a warm smile across her face, every part of her was brimming with energy. Her large blue eyes were deep pools of azure. Perfectly curled, blonde locks laid a few inches below her shoulders. Every facet of her outfit seemed to complement the rest. Being a beautiful blonde mid teen like this, she surely had her pick of the varsity football team.

Perry put her hand out towards her. "Hi, I'm Perry. Thanks for having me." She held it there for a second. And another second. And another second. Tania didn't reciprocate. But she did keep the smile from ear to ear pasted on her face. Her non-blinking eyes kept staring forward towards Perry's direction, but not at her. Tania appeared to be stuck in time as if someone hit the pause button on her.

That is when Perry saw it. A thin line of blood started out of Tania's right nostril, slowly fighting its way down towards her candy apple lips. Her left hand was quickly twitching back and forth like hummingbird wings. The blood started poking out of the left now. This stream was a flow, and it quickly fell to the ground, splattering on the top of her right Louis Vuitton. Her eyes still peered out into the distance, oblivious to the guests at her house.

"Hey Tania," said Lucy. "Earth to Tania."

Nothing. While it wasn't more than a dozen seconds, to Lucy and Perry it felt like an eternity. Moments of heightened stress and awareness tended to do that to people, and both the girls at the front of the house had seen their fair share of tense moments in their so far short lives. They had been through a lot, maybe not something like this, so they were not too shaken.

Lucy put her hand out and grabbed hold of Tania's left hand. The instant that they made contact, the hand stopped dead. Tania brought her eyes back into the world and down to the two of them.

"Oh hey, Lucy! Glad you made it! The movie is all set in the theatre. Popcorn all ready too!" Tania turned her head towards Perry. "Oh, you brought the famous Perry with you!" The bubbly texture was back in full force. Like a record player that had a worn-out album skipping over, Tania had rewound a bit.

"Tania, your nose," stated Perry skipping the second introduction and trying to push the evening's events along. She held out some of the napkins she pulled from her backpack. For a brief second, the everlasting smile disappeared from Tania's face.

"Oh, lord me. Why, thank you, Perry. That is a very kind gesture," as Tania put the crumbled napkins to her nose, unfazed.

"No problem."

Padding her upper lip thoroughly and believing she cleaned up herself, Tania brought her smile back to her face. Below her nose, the blood was now smeared all the way to her cheek. The contrast between the over-the-top smile on the well put together blossoming woman in front of them and the clearly disturbing underlying sourness boiling right under the surface was striking.

"What am I doing to you gals, having you stand outside. Please come on in!" With that Tania turned around and started off into the foyer of the mansion. Lucy and Perry, with the risk of being left behind and lost, kept close pace behind.

The foyer opened towards two matching curved staircases. The floor below them was decorated with alternating black and white tiles, shining so bright Perry could see her reflection as she looked downward. A smattering of pictures adorned the walls, mostly stock pictures of the family, some hanging cockeyed on the wall. More wrought iron lined the staircases up and around to the second floor. An oversized chandelier hung down halfway towards the floor. A number of lights and crystals were either blown out or missing.

There was a door at the base of one of the staircases, and Tania beelined straight towards it. Perry and Lucy followed closely, watching to avoid any of the small blood droplets that preceded them. As they walked through the cavernous foyer, every one of their steps echoed off every open wall and structure. The complete lack of details made every sound deafening. Perry looked around at the nearly barren walls. Outside of the family pictures, there was nothing ornamental or decorative holding place in the area. She could see the occasional stripe of paint peeling off the walls, showing wear that was hardly unexpected given the condition of everything that she had laid eyes upon so far.

Perry ran all sorts of scenarios through her mind to help her mind find the most reasonable explanation for her current predicament. To her, it could be the difference between life and death, or at least total and utter embarrassment.

"All the details speak to a family or person that rushed into a stagnant, abandoned house, to get out of the weather. Paste a few frames on the wall, get a fresh cut on the lawn, put your head down for a month or two and pray no one notices. It was possible. But the asking price on a behemoth like this one had to be well into the seven digits, especially considering the high-end neighborhood it was settled in. And on a dead end, too, that should boost another ten percent up at least," Perry continued her inner monologue. *"So at least someone has the money...or had. Every time I overhear the rumors around school, these houses are chock full of dirtbags. Sleezy rich dads, not paying much attention to their neglected family."* That made Perry pause and look at her friend next to her. That hit home. There was a reason Perry and Lucy had developed a bond as tight as thieves. No family was completely perfect, and Perry knew they were far from that.

The doorknob turned, and Perry was brought back to reality in an instant. The large, oaken door swung open slowly with Tania putting all the force her ninety-pound body could muster against it. The entrance going downward was gently illuminated near the steps, showing a dated red carpet wrapped around each step. The feel was like that of an old movie theatre, with the darkened steps leading down to the audience seats. Perry could even smell popcorn emitting from below, almost beckoning the girls down into the unknown. At least something about this house was not a complete surprise to her, considering that the whole reason they were here was to catch a new flick.

"Welcome to the theatre!" Tania exclaimed.

"Pretty cool house, Tania," Perry complimented.

Instead of responding to the nice attempt to break the ice, Tania stared blankly at the two, holding the door open as a proper host. The blood returned to its perch on her upper lip, despite the large toothy smile that was molded across her face. She seemed more of a mannequin than a real person. Except her left hand was once again fluttering like a butterfly. Only this time it was joined by a rapid tap-tap-tapping from her right Louis Vee.

Lucy grabbed hold of Perry's arm tightly and brought her close. "I hope you are not expecting an answer from her," Lucy whispered. "When she gets like this, it is best to just roll with it."

Tania still held the door while staring out into the blank abyss.

"What the hell, Lucy," chirped Perry back, not caring about the volume of her voice or the subsequent echo that reflected around. "This is seriously messed up. What the hell is with her? Where the hell am I? Where the hell are we going?"

The sound of her discontent brought forth a bellowing from out of the depths of the basement theatre.

"Holy shit, Taaaan! You have 'nother episode?! Dammit, you must've! Off and on, off your ass and on your feet, you fuckin' coke fiend! Get my shit and get the fuck down here!"

Lucy, still grasping Perry's arm, squeezed a lot tighter. The two caught each other's eyes. Lucy mouthed the name *Missy*, and Perry nodded understandingly.

Tania was brought back to reality in an instant. The moment she came back, with her smile unwavering on her lips despite the blood flowing down her chin, Tania made eye contact first with Lucy and moved to Perry.

"Welcome to the theatre!" Tania re-exclaimed.

This time neither Perry nor Lucy bothered to inform Tania that her nose was leaking blood like a worn-out faucet and she was skipping like an old worn out 45. That was a fool's errand, as the person that was warmly hosting the two in her house was not truly here or there. Whatever was flowing beneath the surface of this human being in front of them, it was caked over with cocaine and misery, amongst other things.

"Let us go and enjoy a super wonderful time together, shall we?"

bubbled Tania, pointing with her left arm down towards the faded abyss beneath them. Part of Perry thought it would be wise just to call it a day, cut her losses, and get the hell out of there. Not kidding herself, it wasn't a part of her, it was the majority of her. Everything about this place, about this girl, about the throaty she-demon inhabiting the floor below perked up every hair follicle on her body to a perpendicular. The electricity flowing over her skin made it completely impossible to move her feet. Both felt cemented onto the tiles below. In fight versus flight mode that settled into her being, flight was beating the hell out of fight.

Tania peered at the two of them intently, hoping that either one would take the lead so that she could finish her hosting duties to help them along and close the door behind. Neither was budging from their spot in the foyer. To an outsider watching the scene unfold, everything appeared to be more intense and stressful than the actors might have fully experienced. The drip, drip, drip of the blood repeated on the floor, slowly forming a pool of red onto the white and black tiles below. Splatters continued their assault on the only high end heels gracing the porcelain flooring.

But then, a part deep down inside Perry beckoned her to continue on. Her entire life on this planet, Perry managed to keep her head above water. Most of her energy was spent trying to avoid devastation at home or pushing forward in her studies. She never put much time into adventure, into the darkness. Lucy and she had developed such an unbreakable bond throughout the years, but they never put themselves in situations like this before, probably because life itself dropped them into the deep end of the pool without any flotation devices. They were little kids, and they did what little kids could do given their home atmosphere. Yet, they drifted apart, and Perry could sense that Lucy knew a lot more than she was leading on this day, but that was neither here nor there. Here they were, on the precipice of potential disaster, and facing down what they didn't know would set a drastic shift in their lives forever. With all of the bells and whistles that were reverberating through her being, all the danger signs that were flashing bright neon colors, every single instinct that was pushing her away, there was something deeper that was sitting counter to everything. Deep in the jowls of Perry's being, she could feel something sitting down, watching her, gently coaxing her onward, assuring her that everything would be alright. She couldn't explain it in the years to come, but the feeling that she went through at that moment was unlike something she had ever had before.

Perry closed her eyes, took a deep breath, and opened them. "Find me. You will find a better place," she encouraged her friend. With that she led the way in front of Lucy and descended into the depths of the sublevel of the mansion, not knowing what was lying ahead of her or her friend Lucy, but, in the end, she felt comforted by the feeling she would be fine and make it out to fight another day. She walked with confidence that whatever may come, it, in a way, was meant to happen, and was not fighting against her instincts anymore. She didn't even notice that she planted one of her feet in the ever-growing crimson puddle near the doorway. Lucy followed nervously behind, clearly wondering what predicament she had gotten the two of them into and hoping against hope that everything would work out fine. As they stepped down a bit, Tania spun towards the opening, and brought the door closed behind her and she attended her visitors downward.

ALEX 2

It had been a few hours since he left Rus at the Morey's, but Alex couldn't stop thinking about their conversation. He knew that Rus would turn out to be a fine detective one day, and it seemed that day was a lot closer than he anticipated. When that day came, it would hurt his business and his circle. Those that surrounded Alex in his life were typically a small amount, and that was on purpose. Not that he was a loner or not friendly. On the flip side, he was actually an amiable people-person. That always came in handy when he was on the case. It was quite easy to work people over if you had a smile on your face and not have a fist in your hand. But as good as he was at it, Rus was light years ahead of him in that regard.

Alex settled back into his chair behind his desk, giving himself a little more room to help his oversized lunch to continue its digestion. His eyes scanned around the small office in which he took root decades ago. It was a force of his habits, whenever Alex was looking for some answers, or in a general direction, he turned to those that had provided that same thing in the past.

The walls in his office were littered with dated pictures of family and friends. The old, sun-faded memories on the wall included many of the good times with himself and Marianne. They had their fair share of good times and an even better share of great and wonderful times. But as time went by something changed, and no more additional pictures became adorned on the office walls. She had often provided Alex with the most rational advice during times of stress. The problem was that he typically didn't listen to her during those times. When he was locked in, or in Marianne's words 'full blown dick mode', he took to staring and calculating more than the day to day listening that a marriage desperately needs. They had their fair share of problems, but the married couple that had no problems tended to end up either with one on the front page of the local news due to a lifeless body in a pool of bodily fluid or constantly refusing police support while wearing sunglasses indoors. There was more to it, deeper down, but Alex tried not to bring up those buried memories.

The newer selection were pictures of himself and Rus, mostly on the job. When Alex chose to be busy, they were on the job most days and nights. But Rus was dead right about that. He hadn't been taking on all the jobs he could. In this day and age, the supply of significant others that were seeking out the truth, along with the multimillion-dollar settlements that may accompany the aforementioned truth, had more consistency than the sun rising in the east and setting in the west. And with Alex's reputation, he would even have his pick of the litter. He could not only be living high on the hog, but he could also have broken ground onto a dozen pigs stacked high. Only on a few occasions were there any follow-up altercations from the multitude of outed John Does, but never did it result in a hospital visit. Alex figured most of them deep down inside felt the day would come, and who better to crack the case than the one and only Mr. Peters, grade-A private investigator.

Instead, here he sat, slowing down physically and occupationally. It had been a few years, but Alex felt the metaphorical water start to recede. For his whole life, he had noticed things. Not the five-car pile-up on Route 1 leaving a twisted metal menagerie of flesh that the average bystander would stop and ogle. It was the way certain people avoided eye contact after exiting a high brow designer clothes retailer or the precipitous decline of the local feral cat population during an economic downturn or the way items seem to change location without any outside interference. These things had happened around town that didn't fit into any profile, and always had a way to pique his detective ears up. And there were a lot of those little things in Hex Point. To borrow a phrase from his trainee, this little town seemed to be brimming with going-ons.

Alex had seen many odd occurrences come to life in town, only to be forgotten about once a logical explanation was provided to the public. The only problem with it was that the logic that was applied really didn't fit the event. The local population seemed content to accept logic if it sounded smart and could be the answer to a question even if the logic itself stood out as illogical. Herd mentality, it is best to be ignorantly blissful and go about one's day thinking everything around was hunky-dory rather than to peel the layers of the onions back to fit the bruises and rot under the surface. Alex occasionally found himself settling into that trap when he was not on an active case, but luckily for him either he or Rus would snap him back to reality.

Alex continued staring from picture to picture in this manner, hoping one of the photographic eyes would answer him back. Sometimes all he needed was a hint, something to make the synapses in his brain align in just the right pattern and he would be off. Looking at his connections of the past and present helped to bring him formulate their responses to the questions he had on his mind. Being able to simulate what his Uncle Louie's rationale was when proposed with a dilemma had actually helped Alex make a break in whatever case he might be on. Unfortunately, when he was working, he rarely needed to go this route, and when he did it the time needed would be less than a commercial break. But right now, he wasn't on a case per se. The air was thin, and he needed to figure out what the upcoming tidal wave was to be bringing towards the town, and whether there was anything he could do to help. Uncle Louie would have simply shrugged, took a sip of his Budweiser, and answered, "Life's a bitch sometimes, Al."

Realizing the answers were not coming from his logic inspirations that adorned him, Alex brought his head down on his arms that were folded on the desk. Normally this wouldn't have been a problem, his finely tuned detective mind would be able to figure it out. The pressure would eventually build, and he knew it. The times that he wasn't able to figure it out, things tended to go sideways, strange, and, above all, dangerous. He couldn't let history repeat itself, but he knew that every time was different, nothing seemed to be the same. He knew that there were others around town that, while not truly understanding what it was that was going on, would be able to provide more eyes on the ground. It could be a break in Alex's personal case, but hopefully it wouldn't come to that.

An hour passed before Alex got back into a prone position. An outsider looking in would assume that he had just risen from a food coma, something the Diner was quite famous for. The truth was that he probably wouldn't be able to fall asleep later that night. His mind was on full charge, and rest would not come with the absence of a lead. Alex thought of pulling out the file safe that he kept in his jacket closet, but its contents may not help him at this moment. He kept copies of all the documents revolving around his business itself, along with his handgun. That work item had only left the safety of the safe less times than an average person can count on their hand. He used to keep his notebook labeled "Downtime Notes" in it, but he opted to keep that back in his bedroom. Adding lines into that made it more essential than anything in his office, and recently it changed residence to his residence.

Coming to the realization that sitting in his chair as the day was slowly making its way into evening was not helping any cause, Alex rose, and made his way outside. Rather than head to his car to retreat to his house, he opted to hit the streets. Many times, he found a nice walk back home to be a great way to clear his mind and let his brain do its thing. The distance wasn't too great either. Adding in potential for being sidetracked around town, it was typically less than two miles to home. Add in the refreshing weather that had rolled into Hex Point, and Alex left his car in the parking lot behind the plaza for the night. Only once did he receive any call from the police regarding this infraction, but it was from one of the newer officers on the force. All of them knew him and knew him relatively personally considering him and Chief Williams had a long history.

Once out in front of Morey's, Alex hung a left turn and made his way down Main Street. It wasn't but a few hundred strides and he was crossing Point Lake. The place had always given him the chills. The surface of the water was typically glass smooth, which, coupled with the deep and thick hues that made up below said surface, caused the unknown factor to be off the charts. This was just one of the many things that Alex tended to pick up on when on surveillance, which was for the most part all the time, that the typical lifelong resident would not give a second thought. It was just Point Lake, and the neighborhood kids would spend the hot summers on its accessible banks, the annual fishing derby would always take place on the first day of spring, and even the local scout troop held their pseudo regatta that always raised a fair amount of funds for the Old Town church. In the end, it was just another overlooked item on the long list of things that everyone knows but no one had really known. Alex had his fair share of experiences around, and unfortunately inside, the lake, but those were generally the lumps and lessons of growing up that helped shape his upbringing. Outside of the fact he was more aware of the unnoticeable, he also knew parts of the truth that made it more than just a memory.

Alex peered down at the water as it slowly made its way under the bridge and continued to the Run. Whenever he felt the air becoming thin, the water in the Lake seemed to do the opposite. The viscosity of the water appeared to be that of something closer to molasses than freshwater. There were times when the lake played the role of soothsayer in town, with occasional rough waves seemingly originating from mysterious sources followed in short order by dramatic events coming to fruition around town. Just as the ocean peels away from the beach before the tsunami hits, as he had explained to Rus earlier. While the unnatural murkiness below was quite unnerving, the stillness that surrounded the body of water helped to calm Alex's nerves.

"That could be a disaster averted," Alex thought to himself. He had found there appeared a positive correlation between rough Point Lake and dark times to follow.

Content that location number one was not the smoking gun he was searching for, Alex continued his way over the bridge to the other side of the lake. What laid past on the other side of town was mainly the restricted woods and the rest of Old Town. The restricted woods were another one of the locales around town that those in close proximity really didn't know what had lied inside the trees but knew enough to stay away because if anyone was spotted trespassing would have a visit by an officer of the HPPD. That was enough for the vast majority of the locals to keep their heads down and move along. For the small percentage that were daring and adventurous or simply ignorant or dumb to the potential legality associated, well they typically had their wild expectations quashed. The truth of the matter was that the restricted woods remained a government owned span of nature with the occasional broken-down shell of a previous homestead littered throughout. The most surprising aspect of the restricted woods was the pure serenity that could be found inside even as it was adjacent to a bustling little town. That was the most surprising to an outsider, while Alex had his own thoughts and experiences.

Instead of passing the woods from the sidewalk, which both the woods and sidewalk in this area of town were quite unkempt, Alex stopped momentarily to check the traffic in town. Jaywalking wasn't really enforced in Hex Point, but as the crossing party, anyone truly took their own life in their hand. It was right around dinner time, and traffic was quite heavy. Rather than risk potential catastrophic injury, Alex bid his time, watching the cars and trucks pass by on their way to where they were eventually going. There had been a fair amount of through traffic lately, people using Main Street to cut off corners of their daily commute, especially when there was an accident on the

Turnpike. Even with the influx of out-of-state drivers, Alex was still able to pick out those from town. He had met many people around the quaint little village over the years and figured he could probably strike up a conversation with each passenger that he spotted.

With a break in the vehicles, Alex trotted quickly across the street to the other side. He continued on his way, with the next stop not far away. As he proceeded through a few more of the nondescript pieces of scenery of Old Town, he found himself at the intersection on Main and Church Lane, then hung a right. The currently non-denominational Church of Goodness still stood at the end of the road, bookended by two large black oaks that towered above the building. From the outside, it gave off the vibe of a medical facility more than that of a place of worship. The outdoor space that surrounded it was less inviting than the typical place for playing children or open areas to provide the congregation for discussion or reflection areas. Behind the church stood a dense wood, full of thick briars and ivies. But once a visitor entered its doors, the inviting atmosphere of a kind and accepting practice hung in the air and on the walls and ceilings.

Alex was well acquainted with the church. When he was a young boy, many moons ago, his parents would take him there every Sunday morning, Good Friday, Easter Sunday, and Christmas Eve night. Marianne and Alex even had their wedding ceremony in front of the cloth laden pews, also many moons ago. Many of his formidable times growing up took place in this location. Most of his memories of his religious life here were quite pleasant and enjoyable. There were a handful that were more nervous, anxious, or terrifying than pleasant, but Alex just always pegged them on the presence of God. Of course, his timeline of experiences and growth in this facility seemed like a lifetime ago and not just many moons. The truth was that the Catholic presence in this part of town had left decades ago, leaving most of the whole town devoid of Christian guidance. Not only Christian, but all sense of religion had vanished one day, and stayed that way until the nice older couple that fixed up this former Roman Catholic establishment from the years of decay. And they did an admirable job too. The few times that Alex had visited after the Church of Goodness laid their roots in Hex Point, the interior no longer emanated rot and mold born from endless times of neglect and wear, but came close to its former glory, minus the Catholic symbolism that draped all surfaces.

Alex approached the front of the Church and took a moment to give it a once over. While the building was in no means new construction, the upkeep seemingly erased the aging process. A new coat of paint on the shaker siding must have been completely recently applied, as the bright blue hue appeared to glow in the dinnertime slowly setting sun. The assorted shrubbery lining the outside was evenly trimmed, as well the lawn contained not one dandelion. Given the sheer age of the church and its plot of land, it looked like it reversed the aging process. Alex knew that was not true, it was all the handiwork of Mrs. Goodwell.

The front door cracked open ajar, and she poked her head out. Once she saw who was nearly at the church, a smile planted itself across her wrinkly, aged face.

"My dear Alex Peters. What a pleasure seeing you today," Mrs. Goodwell exclaimed. "To what do I have the honor of your presence?" As reliable as the sun rising in the east was the cordial and gracious manners of the nonagenarian.

Alex responded with a smile of his own, "Just taking a stroll, Missus Goodwell. I guess I was just walking down my memory lane."

Mrs. Goodwell stepped fully out of the doorway and into the light. For an active lady well into her twilight years, she has held up extremely well over the decades. "Well, it is always a good day when you come around. Did you want to come inside for a spell?"

"You must excuse me. The last thing I would want to do is to disturb the many tasks that a church requires of yourself to be in the most presentable of states."

Mrs. Goodwill chuckled a bit. She gave him a curious glance, and then tried to bring his attention to what he was previously examining. "Oh, Mister Peters, if you couldn't have already noticed, all such tasks are completed once and over again. Please take a small break from your arduous line of work."

Alex's mother had always stressed to him and his siblings to respect one's elders. A part of respecting was also listening and obeying, so Alex provided no resistance this time and started down the sidewalk. Mrs. Goodwell held one of the oversized foyer doors open with one arm to provide an easy entry for Alex. For a woman somewhere in her nineties, her spryness and energy were quite apparent.

"How is the venerable Mister Goodwell holding up?"

"Oh, George has his good days and George has his bad days. Of course, you would be hard pressed to see the difference. Thank you for asking, I will let him know," Mrs. Goodwell answered.

The two of them made their way through the narthex and into the sanctuary. That is how Alex remembered it in his mind, but those terms no longer applied in this iteration of worship. They both found spots to sit down in the last pews, close to where Alex sat next to his parents and two brothers each and every Sunday. Being back in the same spot brought back all sorts of memories and a strong sense of déjà vu. Alex, despite the interior modifications to the walls and windows, could see through his memories from long ago and visualize as it was when he was a young lad. There he saw the times when all the pews were filled with eager lay people, ready to receive the word and provide their tithes and offerings. He could imagine the events on the Christian calendar that brought only standing room to those that might have shown up a bit late. He could see old Mrs. McGinley sitting in the pew directly in front of his family and could even sense the waft of the fragrant perfume with tinges of flowery tones. His brother Ray would always whisper disparaging comments about how he felt his nose was going to melt off if he had to endure another minute sitting in her vicinity. That was always during the times that both parents couldn't make out exactly what he was saying, but the smile on Ray's face always gave it away. Alex never understood the jabs. He always felt it to be pleasing to the senses.

Mrs. Goodwell, seeing that her visitor was a few miles down a stroll on Memory Lane, settled back into the pew rather than rudely force

Alex back into reality. She mimicked his stance and where he was staring off. While the moments that passed might have seemed like minutes or even hours to Alex, it was only a matter of seconds.

"The mind is such a strange thing, isn't it?" Mrs. Goodwell politely snapped him back to the present.

"Excuse me?" Alex responded, mildly startled.

"I see the same from others your age that drop by occasionally. Their business that brings them here is never to stir up old feelings and memories buried by the endless years that stack up new and current experiences. It may have been a delivery or an inspection, but it always ends the same. Their eyes lead them from location to location, each shedding a ray or two of light upon something that had been long forgotten. While we have adapted this lovely building from what it was to what it is, George and I tried to keep as much as possible the same. We never had intentions of claiming to be things we are not, so change was inevitable. While it was George's idea to overhaul the atmosphere, I never budged my stance to leave some semblance of the past in place." Mrs. Goodwell turned towards Alex and inched closer. "Memories, to me, are extremely important. Memories help us measure the past. In a world without memories, we cannot truly know who we are. If we were to completely renovate this wonderful establishment when we first came to Hex Point, we would be giving the people with history here the reason for their memories to evaporate like the morning dew in the hot sun. I never wanted to be the cause of that. People need to remember who they are and how they got to where they are now."

"But what of those that are not pleasant?" Alex retorted.

"They are all the same," Mrs. Goodwell calmly answered.

"Do continue, please." Alex hadn't necessarily come to the Church with the intention of getting into a philosophical conversation with one of the older residents of town. He was here to see if he could find any clues, anything at all, to help him figure out what was rapidly approaching the horizon. Something was going to be happening, that Alex was convinced. He couldn't pinpoint the who, the what, the when, the where, the why, or the how. When times like this reared their ugly heads, the best course of action was to start with the usual suspects, which is why he left his Toyota Camry at the office and took to the street. In doing so, he found himself in a deep and thoughtful sermon from the church head's wife. He had experienced similar spots when he was working on seemingly unbreakable cases and had found that it was wise to not fight what the universe was spoon feeding you.

"You see, dear Alex, all our memories have a way to shape us one way or the other. Whether or not they are pleasant is beyond the point I am trying to express. You are who you are because of what you have done, for the decisions you have made, for the path you have chosen to follow. All of these things have made you what you are today, and the memories you hold are the connections between the Alex Peters that sits with me today and the Alex Peters of long ago. Our memories have helped to shape the person that we are, good or bad. If one was to lose one's memories, what would become of them? Are they born anew with a fresh slate, only years into their journey in this world? Or is it that a piece of their own being has been robbed from them? What do you think, Alex?"

Taking a moment to gather his thoughts together, Alex settled back into the pew. "It is hard to say. On one hand I have felt how we react in the few dark and pivotal times of our lives helps to shape the person we are, regardless of our memories. You are who you are, and how you react in those situations is more a reflection of your being, and not of your experiences. Who you are, the colors of your soul, come to the surface in times of stress."

"And on the other hand?"

"Well, I would say it is a blend of mine and yours. Everyone still has their color, but some of the events that come to be might bring another hue to the mix."

"So, the man who grows old, bears a beautiful successful family throughout the years, and happens upon an accident which leaves him without any recollection of his life up until that fateful event, will he continue on as he did? Without any recollection of his lovely family and the memories that solidified in his mind over the course of his life, will he continue on the same path as he had?" Mrs. Goodwell asked.

"Probably. Maybe. I guess it depends."

"Depends on what?"

"Depends on the circumstances that surrounded the accident. If he was reaching to grab a container in the back of the refrigerator and a glass falls from the top shelf, giving him a concussion, the innocuous accident will lead to a period of memory loss. Time passes, they come back, names of friends and family return, in the end no real harm and no real foul."

"What if said accident was something more malicious? An event of lasting and possibly devastating effects. I would think that you, in your line of business, had seen plenty of these examples. What would you have to say about that?" Mrs. Goodwill inquired.

"Colors will mix. I can say that for certainty. I have seen many people who had drifted along be rocked and their entire outlook flipped on its head. Some of them knew it was coming, and felt it was well deserved. Their colors might deepen, but definitely will not move along the spectrum. Others...well some have had their colors change over time, with the addition of varying hues. It might have been how they felt invincible because of their success, or they just were like that, but the reality finally showed through." Alex finished.

A slight smile had grown across Mrs. Goodwell as she found Alex's eyes. "In the end, we may never know. It seems we are debating the true reality of nature versus nurture. You say we are who we are because of how we start out and how we go about our days. I say we are who we are because of the things that go on while we go about our days. Using your vibrant picturization, our soul's color can change over time. I appreciate your input on this matter, Alex. There are some things that I am sure George can use in his preaching. That is if you do not mind."

"Of course not."

"But all this back and forth was not your true intention, Alex. Is there something you are searching for that brought you to our church?" she asked frankly.

Alex was expecting the change of topic at some point. Mrs. Goodwell could read anyone in town for their true intentions but tended to hold her hand close to the chest. "I just needed to clear my mind, I guess," Alex responded, not fully truthful.

"I understand. I have those times as well. While you might visit spots around town that may bring you inspiration, I opt to tend around this beautiful place, making sure it keeps its visuals for another generation." Alex couldn't tell if she was calling him out, but in the most polite way possible.

"And you do a great job as always, Mrs. Goodwell."

"Please, Alex. You were one of the first people in town to welcome us. Despite having grown up in this place when it was a different ideology, you were still warm to us, and helped us out many times over the years. I would prefer if you would just call me Nancy."

"I can try, but my mother had always taught me to show respect to my elders. I can try, but it will take time," Alex finished as he rose from the pew, and started to move towards the aisle.

"That is all I ask, Alex. By the way, your partner dropped by earlier today. He was bringing over donations for the food bank. He is such a great young man. Very respectful. I am sure he has been such an asset to you," Nancy added as she rose to her feet as well. She still had a fair amount of spring in her step.

"Rus is a great kid. And you are correct, he has been a tremendous help with my business. He has been such a help that I think his time with me is quickly coming to an end."

"An eaglet spreading its wings. I am sure you knew that day would come, Alex."

"Time has a way of slipping away sometimes, Mrs. Good…, I mean Nancy. I knew the day would come, but it still snuck up on me," Alex finished as he made his way through the narthex.

"Time is another funny thing. It has a way of changing things, making people reflect in different ways that they might have previously seen it. But I digress. Alex, you must be proud of him. Rus has turned out to be a wonderful young man. He must feel like a son to you in some ways, considering how things between Marianne and you transpired."

While he knew that it wasn't intended to be hurtful and was as close to the truth as it could possibly be, the reality still brought a twinge of pain from inside of Alex's body. While it was not a point of contention through their marriage, the lack of a child was an overarching downfall between the two. They had remained good friends since they went separate ways, but Alex would constantly go through what if scenarios in his mind in the middle of one of his many sleepless nights alone. Nancy Goodwell didn't mean to push the blade a little closer to his heart, and anyone looking in on their situation would have come to the same conclusion. The obvious pain was still pain in the end, and Alex turned back towards the Church with a grimace on his face.

"Oh bother, I am sorry Alex. I did not mean to cause any grief," Nancy apologized.

"Oh Mrs. Goodwell, it is fine. And you are right, time is a funny thing."

With that, Alex turned around again, and started down the sidewalk. The dinnertime air had given way to brisk nightfall during the time he was visiting. It was a quick walk back to Main Street and a few more side streets before he came to Bryant Street and his quaint and quiet abode. As he began to make his way home, Nancy called out one more time, and made Alex abruptly turn around.

"There hasn't been anything here," Nancy called. Once Alex backtracked a bit and was closer than earshot, she continued. "What you are looking for. Everything has been normal here. That is why you came. You are looking for that something. I can tell you that I haven't seen, heard or sensed anything."

Alex approached closer. "Are you sure?"

"Alex, I have seen somethings since we have been moved to town, things that we cannot explain, things that would scare a hardened criminal into nightmares, things that, well, just shouldn't be. Lately, everything around here has been just as the usual. My advice to you would be to just keep digging. Some lead will show up, I have faith in that."

"Nancy, I am sure of that as well," Alex agreed. "I just hope it is not too late."

OFELIA 1

The time was closing in, and it was getting quicker. The trees continued their dance through the thin air, shifting positions back and forth like the tides. They could sense it. There was still hope, but it was shrinking with each passing minute. Hope was in short supply, but in their conversations with her, hope was glimmering like an oasis in the desert distance.

They reached the edge of the water and peered out towards the town. The sweet little town had a small amount of hustle and bustle, as any good one did. The people scurried along to complete their odds and ends, without any real understanding of what was truly going on around them in their world. Ignorance, in any time period, was absolute bliss.

"What are we going to do?" the little girl asked.

"*We must believe. What else can we do?*" her companion answered.

"That is true."

The duo retreated from the lake bank and back into the woods, hand in hand. The trees pushed along in their strange dance around the ground. The significance was clear to both of them. Only a few more days around, and then they would return. If they could not do what they needed to by that point, there would be grave consequences.

As they strolled through the thickets and into the heart of the wood, they continued their conversation.

"Well, what should we do if the time is close, and we haven't finished what needs to be finished?" the little girl asked.

"*I really don't want to think about that.*"

"We have to. We must have a plan. If we leave this place and not have what we need with us…"

Both stopped abruptly. The answer to the unasked question was one that caused both to cringe. In the end, they both couldn't afford to leave this world empty handed. The outcome would be too grim to even think about. It could not happen. The Midnight Sable was awaiting them both on the other side…

"*Let us not talk about that, Ofelia.*"

"Yes, let us not," the girl agreed. "We must figure out a way."

"*What the Sable asks of us, do you think we can do it?*"

"Do we have a choice?"

"*No, we do not. But, Ofelia, please answer my question.*"

Ofelia, staring out towards the distance, looking through the forest as the oaks and maples slowly traversing aimlessly over the landscape. The way she peered made it seem the correct course of action could be read in the tree leaves. Involuntarily, she began slowly swaying back and forth.

The girl, turning her head up towards her oversized companion, stated firmly, "Yes, we can. I am not saying this because that is what we need to do. I believe we can. It goes against everything that we know. It is not in our nature. But we can."

It couldn't hide the doubt that covered its body, as every single one of its furry tendrils flopped downward. While Ofelia was confident that they could accomplish their goal, it was not completely convinced.

"Listen to me for a second. I understand you have your doubts. There is a part of me that is there too. What I am asking you to do is indeed something we have never done before. But the thing is that we have never tried. For so many years, we have helped, never hurt. There is nothing there to say that we cannot. It is clearly not in our nature, but there definitely must be a way."

"*What about the girl?*"

Once again, Ofelia took her attention away from the behemoth. "There is a reason why she was brought to us. I know you can feel it too. I am not sure how she fits into the scheme of our plans yet, but she surely is a key."

"*She will help. Indeed, I feel it. We must speak with her.*"

"We will. She is another confused and broken soul."

The blue monstrosity turned his attention to something else that was bothering it. "*Something else came through here. Right after I did.*"

Ofelia, while caught slightly off guard by the statement, did indeed feel something askew this time that they were together. It had been quite a long time since the last time the two were reunited, but she was confident that it was different. The entire vibe that hung delicately in the air was unlike anything she could remember. There was a tension and uneasiness felt around her, and it could be felt from her cohort.

"I am guessing that whatever came through, it is not benevolent?" Ofelia questioned timidly.

"*I wish I had a better answer. I am hesitant to say, but I think our task has become unduly complicated.*"

"Not benevolent. That does make this difficult. But, please believe me, it is not impossible." Ofelia was not holding anything back. What was previously a formidable task for the pair appeared to be now monumental. But even with the most extraordinary tasks, there always exists the slim possibility of a remarkable ending. "There is a reason that things have turned out the way they have. The stars had to align for us to be here together. And that means that we need to focus on the task at hand. We will succeed, no matter how difficult it is. Even though we both might not be truly living as others might see it, we can still show growth. This is a task of growth. Becoming better."

The monstrosity appeared to be slightly more content, given Ofelia's logical response. "*That makes sense, Ofelia. But it doesn't help completely. I think it was Erwin that was here with us.*"

While it was a bit calmer, what it said made Ofelia a bit more uneasy. She had come in contact, and in some cases blows, with many of the different entities from her companion's side. Some of them had been pleasant, some had been worrisome, some had been downright terrifying. The complete end of the one spectrum was the Sable, but its intentions had always been well known: pure evil. It was the one constant in this ever-changing world. Right below it in terms of intensity was the Devious Crimson. That being, coupled with Erwin, was not only pure evil, but enjoyed the mayhem it caused. The only other time that Ofelia had come by Erwin, lives were lost, and cackles were let loose.

"Then time is of the essence, my dear friend. Let us make haste. I feel that we will be seeing our visitor soon."

"*How do you know that?*"

"It is just a feeling."

With that, Ofelia turned back towards the direction of the lake. There was a change in the air, and not a change for the best. Erwin was lurking around, intentions unknown, but surely, he was not around for charity work. She felt inside of her that an end was close but couldn't tell what it ended. Pain was inevitable, and, for herself and Cobalt, they needed to do something they hadn't before. Pain could bring growth, and Ofelia believed that, as it really was the theme of her living life.

While peering through the thickets and over the water, she closed her eyes, and whispered, "Find me. You find a better place."

PERRY 3

With each step they took down to the lower level, dust and allergens shot up from the carpet. The stairway screamed dated movie theatre, with their feet slightly illuminated by the low set red strip lights leading the way down into the abyss. The walls were littered with upward angled candle lights, helping the visitors find their way down the steps, which felt unreasonably steep. Scents of popcorn and stale air filled their nostrils, but there was also a heaviness to the atmosphere as they descended. With each stair the duo could feel the palpable energy surrounding them. The stairs ended after a flight, led to a landing, and turned to the right.

Once they both got down the stairs, Perry and Lucy found themselves gazing upon the movie theatre converted basement. The room opened to reveal three full rows of seating, each fashioned with amenities not normally seen to the average joe going on a cheap matinee date with his steady girlfriend. Each seat was situated with drive-in style speakers on either side and built-in neck roll pillows that Mr. Doe Executive would take on his red eye flight. The kicker was that each had a small refrigeration spot located just slightly beyond where the viewer's feet would extend to when fully reclined. Compared to the rest of the house that they had seen, Perry and Lucy could tell that this part was the most attended to by its owners, and surely held most of the potential scarce visitors.

Perry scanned around the expanse that she had entered. One glaring spot that appeared to be completely out of place was situated in the middle seat of the middle row. She could see a heap of unkempt hair sitting upon a head, poking above the seat top. Small trails of smoke were rising from the head, slowly and steadily. Without a movement, whoever was sat and ready for the movie blurted out, "Holy shit, Tan. You really gotta get your shit in order. You are gonna end up in a fuckin' ditch somewhere face down with some horny piece of shit on top of your sorry ass."

Unfazed, Tania responded, "Thank you for your concern. I am perfectly fine."

"Ha! And I am the next comin' of the Christ!"

Perry didn't need to look at Lucy to know whose presence they were around. By the looks of the disheveled and neglected car in the driveway, what lied before them was what Lucy had warned her about before they entered the mansion. Both girls didn't realize they had stopped in their tracks and were blatantly staring at the head.

It turned with half smoked cigarette placed firmly in the side of its mouth and looked at the two of them. "A lil miss high school wanna be cool and her latest lesbo friend, lovely. Can we jus' get along with this goddamn movie now?" Missy spouted.

Perry couldn't help but stare. She had no idea how old Missy was, but if she were to cross paths on the street, she would figure her to be in her mid to late thirties. Perry knew it was a drastic overestimation, but it had appeared to her that life had been overly hard on this soul. Her skin was pockmarked with early onset acne, possibly brought on by genetics, possibly by a stressful upbringing. Perry figured it may have been mostly the ladder. Her clothes were completely non-discrete, completely disjointed to be settled into the basement theatre of an enormous mansion. Her feet were kicked up on the seat next to her, with her worn out tennis shoes showing stains of mud or worse. When she opened her mouth to spew insults, Perry noticed some distinct shadows amongst her tooth line.

"What the *fuck* are you looking at?" Missy shot at Perry. To Perry, through everything that she was forced to endure as a thirteen year old girl with a broken home, a deli counter number counter at the front door, and a delinquent mother figure, she had never experienced a person with so much venom so easily spewed.

Perry held back the urge to sling an insult back at her. Instead, she opted to be the bigger person. "I am sorry. Didn't realize I was staring."

"Well, the hell you were. Donever let it happen 'gain." Turning to Tania, Missy continued, "Who the hell are these two and what gutter didja pull'em out of? Your mother's ass?"

Tania, clearly not affected by her apparent friend considering how far out of this world her existence was currently at, responded, "This is Lucy. You have met her. And this is Perry, her friend that we talked about a few days ago."

That last part sent a shock through Perry's system. What could they have been talking about? Given her gut feeling, it couldn't have been good. Lucy had been quite reserved and held back when they were walking together on the streets. That wasn't a good sign. Now she was down in the bowels of the mansion with seemingly one way out, in the presence of three girls, which she thought of that term loosely when she thought of Missy, who had been talking about her without her around. If it wasn't for Perry running directly into Lucy before homeroom, would she have even been in this situation? She couldn't know for sure, but with every sign fiber of her being and her intuition telling her, flashing large neon letters telling her WARNING!, there was also something deep inside that she couldn't shake. Something pushed her to continue onward despite all of her nerves. Perry had to see this through.

Missy gave both of them a thorough look over through the smoke-filled theatre, up and down and sideways. Her bloodshot eyes inspected every detail of the two, sizing both up. Satisfied that they didn't pose a threat to her, Missy finally retorted, "If we did talk 'bout these two, didn't make much an impact. And I sure as hell don't remember this one." Her middle finger extended to point right at Lucy.

"Missy, you know that we did," Tania responded playfully. Turning to Lucy while using a lower tone that she had to this point, "Missy is really a nice person. She is very unique."

"Hah, I've been called many things before, but sure as hell not that!" Missy overheard. She shifted her body back towards the screen in front. "We waiting on any other assholes or are we gonna watch *College Slashers III?*"

"All present and accounted for, Missy." With that, Tania retreated to a small room directly adjacent that must have held the mechanics to the theatre. Perry and Lucy stood there momentarily before making their way to the back row, trying not to be in the near vicinity of their newest truck driver-mouthed companion. The seats settled down deep as they sat down, with lingering smoke pushed out of the cushions. Timidly, both tried not to bring any unnecessary attention to themselves.

"What the hell are you saying?" Missy mumbled to herself, slowly shaking her head as she did. The disheveled, and well overdue for a wash now that Perry was closer, locks rocked back and forth as she did. She brought her hands up to her ears, forcefully fighting her head from movement. "Yeah, yeah, I heard ya. I know what's goin' on."

The conversation between Missy and whatever demons were bouncing around in her head made the girls completely on edge. Perry's stomach was one solid knot, and whatever body part that could pucker had done so. Being a witness this close to a clearly troubled individual brought a deeper level of fear than both had ever seen in their brief and bumpy lives.

"grrrrrreerrreee…," came from the next row. The guttural growl appeared so out of place and unnerving. Missy dropped her head downward and out of sight. "eerrrGGGerrrrr." The sights and sounds, not to mention smells, that were coming out of this girl were closer to those of a wild animal. Hair began thrashing around over the seat back.

"Rrrrrrgggeee...okay, okay, OKAY!" with that Missy snapped back to reality, whipping her body back upright. The cigarette that was holding its place in the corner of her mouth flipped up momentarily into the middle of the air. Without even a glance, she put her hand in the air to snatch it. To Perry's surprise, Missy had almost perfect extra senses, save for the fact that her fingers closed on the lit end. Lucy saw this as well and cringed, but not even a flinch went through Missy. Calmly, she turned it around using the other fingers of her hand to right its position. "I understand," she smoothly whispered to herself while bringing her cigarette back up its home.

Perry found Lucy staring in abject horror at what was transpiring. Deep down inside, she felt the same way, but in her long thirteen years of existence, Perry found it best to do everything she could to hide any adverse emotions from the outside world. That uncanny skill, honed through years of dealing with and managing her inebriated, broken mother, allowed her to help make bad situations a bit less hurtful. Looking at Lucy, it was apparent that she hadn't attained the same skills in life, despite having a similar childhood.

Perry couldn't and could understand why Lucy was here. On the one hand, she had always desperately yearned to distance herself from her sordid broken home life, though she never had come out to say that directly. Lucy had always been there for her when the bad John Does had gotten their key to the house. Lucy was there for every birthday party that her aunt and uncle had in their backyard. For as long as her cousins were alive, they lived for the times that she would accompany her for weekends in the summer, so much so Tristan would often ask for her over Perry. Lucy had been as close as family, more so than actual family. On the other side, Perry could relate to wanting to change everything. Sometimes people get the short end of the stick in life while others get all the gold. It was not fair, and Perry did find herself often wondering what could have been if the smallest thing was different. In the end, there was nothing she could do to change who she was, and now it had brought her together with her recently distant best friend to the lowest level of a mansion that had oddly been rotting with what appeared to be a schizophrenic delinquent.

"Mmmmmm, yes it will be soon," Missy continued.

Lucy, partly out of panic, grabbed Perry's arm. Her mouth was completely agape, and the shock and fear were pasted over her face. It looked like she was trying to say something to her friend, but her insides were not letting it get out. She was mouthing words and sentences, but nothing was coming close to making any sense. Her mouth stopped, and she reached into her purse, fumbling through its contents. In the end, she stopped abruptly and pulled an object out.

She reached over, and dropped a bottle inside Perry's hand. No labels, no distinguishing features, and smaller than a normal water bottle. It was half filled with a thin, pink liquid. As soon as Perry laid her eyes on its contents, she looked up. Lucy nodded. Perry opened the lid, and, in one quick gulp, drank the whole amount.

Despite not making much of a commotion at all, Missy perked up, and slightly turned her head towards the two. Both brought their eyes back to their unwanted companion to find the knotty, frizzy hair now laying neatly down on the shoulders. Only seeing the side of her face, her cheek, now smooth and pristine, bunched up with a slight smile. An eerie calmness, completely in contrast with the disheveled and highly unhinged state just moments prior, held sway over Missy. Even the cigarette was absent from its locale. Nothing was as it was.

"Are we all settled in for the night's festivities?" Missy asked coyly. Her presence gave the chills run down both of their spines.

Fear and anxiety did not allow for any responses. Both, openmouthed and stunned, could not find the power to speak. Without fully turning to face them, Missy continued.

"Please excuse my prior appearance. Just know that that was not truly me. An optical illusion of sorts. And on top of everything, please know that my manners have been inexcusable. I have been under plenty of stress of late, and it has manifested in my reaction to others. I wish to apologize if I have caused any undue stress or concern. I am sincere in my feelings and wish for you to have a pleasant experience."

The complete dichotomy of Missy's presence shocked the lot of them. Short seconds and a complete one eighty later, the person that sat directly in front of Perry and Lucy was different in all senses of the word.

"Okay, Missy. We are good," Perry nervously replied.

Missy shifted her whole torso and placed her arm around the back of the neighboring seat to gain eye contact. Perry was not surprised that, when in sight of her entirely, the person in front her was a stunning individual. All the imperfections that were hard to avoid looking at were now simply clean lines that add to a full, picturesque face.

"I do appreciate that. But please, call me Melissa."

With that, Melissa, née Missy, shifted back towards the theatre screen. The entire vibe in the room had turned on its head. When they entered there was a palpable, tense feeling that lived through the air. Now, despite their companion being a polite and composed individual, fight or flight was in full effect for both Perry and Lucy. Everything was on edge.

The side door opened, and Tania returned, to the relief of the duo. She was still sporting a grin across her face when approached the three of them. "I am completely sorry. I had to shift things around in the machine room, and, by the time I got everything in order, I realized the movie was still upstairs. Silly me!"

Melissa, still sporting the creepy beam, responded, "Oh, Tania. It is completely fine and understandable. We all have those moments."

"Well, thank you for that, Melissa," Tania answered. Turning to Perry and Lucy as she walked past to the stairs, "See, didn't I tell you see is nice." Before she got to the doorway, she turned back with a thoughtful look on her face. "Do you know what would make this the best ever?"

With the absence of any possible answer from the girls, Melissa took the lead. "Tania, if you could make some popcorn for all of us, I think that would be just delightful."

Instead of a quick concurring response, Tania stood still at the base of the stairs. Now that Perry was no longer new to this environment, it was clear that she was having yet another episode. How this girl was not the victim of her own devices was beyond any comprehension.

Before she could make any stains on the carpet, Melissa recognized the situation, and spoke out loudly, "Tania, dear. I hope everything is okay." With that, Tania snapped back to reality.

"Oh dear. Where would I be without you, Melissa?" As she finished, Tania was already halfway up the flight of stairs. Melissa returned the nice words with a smile and shifted her body to get a head on look at Perry. If she hadn't just witnessed any of the venom and vileness this human being was spewing, the eye contact would be sincere and gentle. But the opposite was completely true. To Perry, it was intimidating and unnerving at the lowest level. What might have lasted only a few short seconds felt like a lifetime. The newfound beauty that had set up shop on Melissa's being was the icing on the proverbial cake of uneasiness.

"As you might have noticed, Tania has some...well...issues. Troubled past. Disjointed family life. On the outside, one would figure that, with such an expansive residence, top of the line vehicles and every new line of high fashion to choose from, life might be easy for her. But, in all confidence, I would tell you that not everything is as it seems. The ghosts that live in this house were exceptionally cruel at every step of Tania's youth. The torture, both seen and unseen, that had been brought upon her was not a result of her own doing, yet, in the end, it is all the same. For all intents, constructs, and purposes, she is well put together on the outside. The inside is completely hollow unfortunately. Book cover judgement if you will."

With Lucy still in shock of the unexplainable transfiguration, Perry saw an opportunity to try to get some answers, "And what about you?"

"Pardon?" Melissa responded, partly off guard.

"Where does Mis...I mean, does the book of Melissa match the story?"

Melissa's smile turned into more of a lemon puckered smirk. While slowly relaxing back into her seat, she responded, "Well, I guess all that may come out in time."

The reply did not give either any comfort. It was clear that something was truly amiss with the situation, and everything that was part of it. And it appeared that there was a possibility that things were going to go south quickly. All sat in silence, desperately waiting for Tania's return and for the uneasiness of the situation to pass.

As swiftly as she left, Tania returned to the theatre, her arms full of items from the kitchen. Every single item that a person could have robbed from the concession stand was hugged tightly within her slender arms. Popcorn, with kernels falling gently to the floor, was next to all sorts of multi-colored candies, a few cans of sodas, amongst other toppings and things that anyone could ever want while indulging in a guilty pleasure flick. Despite having a myriad of items clutched close to her body, Tania still sported her impeccable smile. She placed everything onto a small end table that was placed behind the final row of seats.

"Okay! Everything is all ready! Please, take what you wish, and I will get the movie all set so we can have a little fun!" As soon as she had arrived back downstairs, Tania was already in the supposed machine room, film in hand. A few assorted clinks and clanks, and the backlight illuminated the screen. The overhead lights slowly dimmed, and Tania returned into the theatre. She found her way into the front row, sitting petitely and attentively, and, if Perry could hazard a guess, it was with a smile pasted on her face. Melissa leaned forward and whispered something into Tania's ear. Without acknowledging her, she nodded her head politely, eyes still on the screen that was now showing the opening credits. Apparently satisfied with the response, Melissa settled back into her seat.

Perry felt she should be more worried. The uneasiness hung thickly through the air. She was sitting in a custom basement with her recently reunited former best friend, a highly self-medicated, potentially abused, and affluent teen and her once disarrayed now fully put together and all the time unnerving and mysterious friend. Nothing about the situation lent itself to be calming.

And that is when she felt it. Perry's eyelids began to feel as if they weighed thousands of times what they did. Slowly, it became a struggle to keep each one open. Involuntarily, Perry's eyelids alternated powering their way to stay open. She forcefully pushed her eyesight to the ceiling to help her floundering lids. It all seemed futile, something was bound to happen, and happen at any moment, and Perry was desperately fighting to not doze off.

Unaware of Perry's accelerating drowsiness, Melissa rose from her seat, and made her way out of the aisle. Perry couldn't keep her eyes on her, as Melissa approached the snack table that Tania had so neatly set up.

"Would anyone like anything while I am up?" Melissa asked her mostly nervous companions. "Popcorn, snickerdoodles, fruit snacks, an old-fashioned pee bee and jay?"

Before Perry could even react, a hand wrapped around her face and connected with her cheek with a force completely unexpected. The pain was instant and fierce, as her skin began to burn and tingle. While she could have expected something was bound to go awry in this unnerving situation, Perry could not have anticipated the ferocity and anger that had just struck her palm first. As the hand retreated away from her rosy right side, no doubt to proceed again with its violent intent, Perry felt some sticky substance making it slightly harder for the hand to remove from its point of impact.

"Le's make this lil bitch turn *blue*," growled the perpetrator hovering closely behind Perry, with her left hand holding firmly on Perry's shoulder, bracing her from movement. The fuzzy mop danced around above her head, as she reached back and brought the left hand down upon Perry's other cheek. A low cackle came from behind, completely removing any easiness that could be found.

"Missy, is this really all necessary?" Tania calmly probed, now sporting dual lines of red which came close to staining her perfectly white teeth while finding their way down off her chin.

"Who the hell knows, and shore as hell I don't care!" Missy screamed, while bringing both hands upon Perry's face. She rubbed her hands around her face with a firmness and force that felt that she might break a bone. Perry tried to keep her eyes wide open, so that she could fight through it, but she realized the power upon her made her stand no chance. With all her effort, Perry tried to pull Missy's overly large and aggressive hands from her being. But it was to no avail.

Lucy, watching in horror as things were transpiring, sat frozen in shock. She could not believe her eyes. She had brought her best friend to this house and now she was being assaulted by a deranged assailant. But worst of all, Lucy had left them at an earlier time with the ammunition to bring this from a petty crime to a felony.

Missy, sensing she had a moment to push forward her plan, reached behind her and grabbed the half empty jar of creamy peanut butter. Fully intent on finishing her business, she shifted her body to place an elbow on her victim to smear the rest of the allergen over the rest of the exposed flesh.

Perry felt her opportunity. She wiggled her body and was able to break free of her hold, falling onto the carpeted floor. In an instant, Perry was army crawling down the aisle, operating purely out of survival instinct. As potentially disgusting as it might have been, she let her face rub against the carpet with each lunge. Desperately wishing to escape this situation with her life intact, Perry frantically picked up the pace and exited the aisle. Once free of the seating, she rose to her feet and started sprinting towards the exit. She only managed a few strides before Missy grabbed hold of both shoulders and swung all of her weight onto her frame. The surprisingly muscular build of her assault easily placed Perry back to the floor, holding out her hands to brace the impact.

"Jesus Christ, *GET OFF HER!*" Lucy screamed. She finally was able to break out of the shock that had previously held her paralyzed in her seat. She rose to her feet and frantically began her way to her friend. Before she could make it halfway out of the seating, a hand grasped her ankle. Lucy dropped to the floor, narrowly missing catching her face on the back of the seat in front of her. The moment she hit the ground, Lucy yanked her leg towards her body to free herself, but to no avail. Tania, despite her petite and unassuming figure, was exerting a grip upon her ankle that would leave severe bruising later. She jerked her leg another time, but the only thing that was dislodged was her cell phone from her pocket, which somehow rolled forward a few seats away. She peered back and her look was met by a calm and perky, yet not fully blood stained, smile looking back. Lucy mustered all her strength, reared back and planted her heel right in the middle of Tania's perfect face, forcing the streams of the nosebleed to speed to a squirt. The smile never left.

While Lucy was trying to break free, Missy had placed her knee in the small of Perry's back. Completely immobilized, Perry closed her eyes tightly. Slow deep breath. The intense pain that was no longer in her cheeks, but now spread throughout her body. All that she could feel was a sense of impending doom. Perry felt her eyes beginning to fail her, with her eyelids' weight increasing exponentially. The knee, that was threatening to separate rib from spine, increased the pressure. The physical pain didn't bother her anymore. Perry felt her nose begin to drip on the carpet. It seemed like just a matter of moments.

"*STOP!!*" Perry heard Lucy scream from the theatre. It was too late. Missy forced three of her fingers on both hands into Perry's mouth. They searched around, depositing any of the remaining peanut butter deep towards her throat. Left eye closed and wouldn't open up. Perry felt a digit make its way over her molars. It was her last chance. She clenched her teeth, and the taste in her mouth changed instantly. Right eye started closing, without any possibility of reversing.

The moment before her eyes succumbed, a voice came out from an unknown corner in the theatre, appearing both distant and near. The moment the voice touched her ears, Perry relented and let her eyes close.

"*You find a better place …*"

MARTIN 2

June started out just as every month so far that year had for Martin. On this ordinary Wednesday, the alarm went off, pulling him out of the dream world. To accommodate all of the gearing up, warming up and starting up with enough time afterwards for a cool down before starting the day with the rest of the family, the alarm went off at four thirty. He reluctantly switched off the alarm on his phone rather than opting for a snooze or two. Drowsy eyes slowly fluttered open and closed before any legs swung over the bedside.

Martin crept out of the master bedroom and did his best ninja impersonation to avoid the squeaky floor landmines that have appeared over the years. Caution was paramount when the twins were sleeping, because, as a parent, some of the most energy spent was getting the little ones to recharge their own. Tristan was never the problem, considering he had slept through multiple natural disasters. Maddox was the lightest of all the sleepers in the family, even though he typically talked all throughout the night.

After successfully maneuvering down to the basement, it wasn't long before he was out of the house. The sun was still far off from its awakening. A dry coolness hung in the pre-dawn air. Martin's inner gauge guesstimated outside was in the upper fifties. It was the perfect condition to drop time off any personal best and to boost any waning motivation. Mentally, he plotted out his route; straight down Main Street, through the business district to Old Town, throw in a few assorted loops and directly back to home base. Lucky number seven miles, easy-peasy. That would allow him to be back home with time to spare.

The first mile ended in the middle of the business district, the heart of Hex Point commerce. This labeling was kind of loose, as the section of town consisted of twin rows of assorted shops and stores, serving as a natural divider between Old and New Town. In true small-town fashion, all of the businesses offered up their handmade wares or specialized services, no chains or names. As he made his way through the district, a quick glance at his watch revealed a shade over seven minutes for the first leg. It was a great start and a great something to build upon.

After pushing through the remainder of darkened businesses, the next mile pushed towards the antiquated section of Hex Point. While there weren't many houses located on Main Street, those that followed were the same shape and size as if there was only one contractor commissioned to build the town. It did bring a sense of identity to the town despite the uniformity. These sporadic houses were limited to the east side of Main, as all Old Town was as well. To the west side, dense brush held together like a barrier wall, only to give way to enormous oaks and maples further from the road line. The contrast between civilization on one and wilderness on the other was often not appreciated by the locals, Martin included, yet rather they were taken for granted as normal.

As the second mile came to a close, so did the spareness of homes. Martin hung a right, directly into the heart of Old Town, Hex Point. A vibration from his wrist furiously indicated one more leg bit the dust. Another quick glance showed the last split a shade over seven and a half. Whether it had been the slight incline that was naturally built into the current course, or the distraction caused by the details of the town, either way he felt in danger of wasting the perfect conditions of the morning. Times like these don't happen that often, and the last thing Martin sorely didn't want was to end on a low note.

He did everything in his power to pick up the pace, most importantly tried not to get distracted with the sights in the early dawn. This wasn't the hardest task, as this section of town resembled an early settlement of the state, containing no real luxury nor eye-catching sights. All the houses were linked in their uniform consistency. The only commercial buildings of the area were long converted into residential sites, and the only non-dwellings were owned by the municipality. Even those seemed to lack individuality, hastily created out of necessity. The oldest structure that still stood was the town church, and that had a distinctive void of any defining characteristics. To an outsider, the main purpose of the building was near indiscernible. The uniformity of Old Town had helped his running in the past months, but this Wednesday it had an almost hypnotic effect. Block after block, the houses blurred together. Trees in near perfect symmetry some decades after being placed in the soil only compounded the dizzy consistency. Martin tried his best to focus on running form. Heal strike. Roll to ball. Push off. Repeat. The pattern continued its unending repetition. The uniform streets of Old Town seemingly drew into a numbing vortex, if it wasn't for his watch.

A slight vibration that emanated from his wrist pulled Martin right back to reality. The backlight projected the update upwards. It read 'Mile 5 - 7:14". He couldn't hold back the shock from crossing over his face.

"When the holy hell did I pass three? Or even four? You gotta be shittin' me. Watch must be busted," Martin openly questioned himself between breaths.

It appeared to be true, as he noticed that Main Street was rapidly approaching. The hastily planned route was now bringing Martin towards the home stretch, as the last two miles would put him directly back to his mailbox.

As Martin made his way back to the town's main drag, he always found it easier to cross over to the opposite side sooner rather than waiting until closer to home. It was a different morning in the not too distant past that he had to scoot across Main Street to get to the development when his legs saw the true volume of traffic up close and personal even at that predawn hour. The sun was slowly making its way towards the tree line, and whatever commuters on the road at that time erred on caution's side by leaving on their headlights. After scanning up and down the street, it was safe, and Martin crossed over to the west side. Each stride put distance between him and the monotony that seemingly stole the middle section of the morning run.

"I truly do not even remember miles three and four," Martin contemplated to himself. With one swipe down, the watch provided an accurate time and distance.

:5.21 miles --- 42:35 minutes:

A quick mental computation confirmed what Martin was feeling: His average split was over eight minutes per mile, way off the pace he was striving for. The two miles that were seemingly missing from memory banks, or more accurately blurred together to create one long livid daydream, had pushed time up to the point that the motivational tank was in danger of being under empty by time the course winds its final bend.

Martin was doing everything in his power to traverse the sidewalk while pushing pace, futilely trying to catch any personal records. This side of Main Street, the one lined with a thick wall of nature, tended to be more treacherous than the other. Most of the flora was left unkempt, usually growing wildly as if to be reaching out towards the road. Years of the sturdy oaks laying root in the soil had drastically shifted the tops of the concrete. Wild thickets held themselves out, causing minor pain if a person strode through. Denizens of the forest seemed to scamper and scurry as an outsider approached. A gentle breeze made its way through the thickest of brush, setting off a symphony of wooded noises and an undulating wave of leaves and branches. It was difficult to tell if the commotion existed behind, but, glancing forward at the tree line, it appeared Mother Nature was keeping the same pace.

As Martin was trotting along at a pace that very well may have made this specific uneventful morning not a complete motivation black hole, something caught the corner of his eye. The sun had managed to forcefully burst through the forest, cascading beautiful rays of color down on the forest floor up towards parts of the tree line. Vibrant hues danced amongst the leaves. At first glance, all members of the rainbow made appearances throughout the landscape, with even a deep, nearly pulsating, indigo maneuvering between the trees. Of what could be seen of the mighty trees, the rays of light made their appearance contain more life than the stoic arbols already had.

With each stride, Martin managed to turn and look further to the right. The beams of light swung through his line of sight. More details shone and faded within the dense brush. The gentle breeze that had raced along had dissipated. Stillness had forced its way in, holding the nature scene frozen while the sun's light explored the area. The diverse palate of colors started to fade taking the wind's lead. A burning, intense orange had coalesced from the wood, no longing peeking from behind trees like a curious child. In the center of it all remained the bewitching and barely discernible indigo. The color twitched and pulsated, just as one's heart after running six miles. The orange rays danced around the outside, as if taking orders from the controlling interior. The intensity grew brighter with each stride. Other details of the forest became fully engulfed by the expanding light phenomenon.

Martin found himself fully entranced by what he was witnessing. He could not determine what was truly happening, rather seemed completely absorbed by the occurrence. *"Could the sun really be doing this? Was there someone or something hidden deep within the trees, doing only God knows what, causing what I am seeing? Am I having some kind of medical thing?"* The head asked too many questions with too few answers.

As quickly as the light poked through the trees, so too did it retreat. Martin's eyes readjusted to the lower levels of brightness of the dawn. The gentle breeze returned as if on command, bringing the symphony of nature throughout the woods once again. Scurrying of the woodland creatures commenced across the forest floor. Everything returned to how it was mere seconds prior.

Martin took his eyes away from the thick forest lying to his right. He was left thoughtless and flummoxed by what he had just witnessed. His mind raced faster than his feet as Martin tried to rationalize some type of answer to the unanswerable. His feet desperately were trying to keep up with the wheels in his mind, but to no avail. He glanced down and found himself barely making any type of contact with the concrete.

As he returned his line of sight back to the remaining two miles that stood before him, Martin spotted an opening a few strides in front. There stood a hole in the thickets, wide enough for a person to make their way into the heart of the foliage. The pathway looked more like a fork in the road than anything else. The branches of the surrounding trees seemed to avoid the open space like a feline on the shore. With the sun's help, Martin could see far enough to determine the trail of sorts peeled away from the street the further it continued. The sheer existence of a pathway through the dense forest was quite intriguing to Martin. With his personal bests seemingly off the table, he couldn't resist.

As the fork approached, Martin took it and penetrated the forest. He kept alert to avoid any type of footfall in front. In all reality, he was a roadrunner, through and through. The closest he was ever to trail running was when he hopped off the sidewalk and onto gravel to demonstrate his best evasive maneuvers from a rogue distracted driver. Martin pulled his pace back a fair amount to navigate the myriad of roots and rocks jutting out of the ground, making even a normal stroll treacherous. The mighty oaks and other flora denizens that had laid root many decades ago provided a venerable obstacle course.

The challenge ahead of him raised Martin's spirits. He found it entertaining to make sure his toes didn't catch any obstruction in their way. With each half stride, Martin meticulously landed each step in an opportune location. The occasional leaf laden branch brushed against his side each time he strayed from the center, which itself was slowly but noticeably curving towards the right, furthering the distance from Martin and Main Street. The breeze that infiltrated the deep wood gently shook the bushes and shrubbery surrounding the path as he continued his trek off the beaten path. Neighborhood animals traveled all around, scurrying over the forest floor. Each and every one of the new sights and sounds pushed Martin along, and he found himself less striding over the terrain and more bounding like a frolicking fawn. He felt the smile come onto his face while his breathing, often struggling at this distance of a run, was not laboring at all.

Martin felt that he was now running completely perpendicular from the road, and into the forest. As he made his way further, the trees slowly began to be sparser yet more gigantic. The thick shrubs that lined the street and paved the way from the fork onward were now nonexistent. The floor became less of a minefield with the trees naturally separated. Martin was able to bring his stride back to normal, into the wide expanse under the forest canopy. The pathway gave way to this broad field, littered with the occasional hulking tree that dotted the landscape. The shrubbery was nonexistent this far into the wood, yet some of the massive oaks laid roots that ridged out of the ground like waves in the ocean. Martin didn't pay them much attention. This area was completely new and exciting. Every sight, sound and smell seemed fresh, and completely different from the senses he experienced on Main Street and the rest of Hex Point, even though they were not too distant.

As Martin penetrated deeper into the forest, something caught his sight. Sticking out of the ground, running parallel with Main Street was a monstrosity of a barrier. At first glance, which was more of a squint as the sun's rays were in full force at that point in the early morning, it looked to Martin so much like a castle wall that part of him was expecting to come upon a swampy moat brimming with ravenous alligators patrolling their guard. At the distance he was away, the structure was intimidating and ominous in appearance and mysterious in location. With each stride it came more into focus, and the details began to emerge. Sunlight could be seen through the wall, and it became brighter as he approached. A tinge of dark orange blanketed the holey structure as far as Martin could see. The foreboding aspect was laid securely on the top. At the apex of the wall was a twisted spiral of danger, clearly reinforcing the purpose of keeping the curious onlooker or busybody in their lane and not snooping around. Anyone brave enough to attempt transferring over would not have been successful, only if the purpose was to inflict severe harm on themselves.

With all the distractions and sights abound, Martin had forgotten exactly where he was currently running. At that point, while he was less concerned about his current mile time and more intrigued with this hidden world, his focus was no longer on where each foot would land. The toe of his right foot had caught a wave of protruding root and caused his upper body to shift dramatically forward. Martin awkwardly forced his feet forward, trying to regain some semblance of balance while avoiding any further trip. Stride after stride, balance slowly shifted back, and he progressively resembled less like a baby deer. Just as Martin was about to regain perfect running form, that is when he felt it. A quick, sharp pain emanated from his left knee. It spread immediately through the left leg and into all other extremities. Before he could react, all strength was zapped from Martin's lower leg, and he dropped in a heap onto the forest floor. By a heap, it was really a tumble. Like a child is taught growing up, Martin stopped, Martin dropped, and Martin rolled. The stopping was less like a stop and more like a soar. Limbs flailed forever as his line of sight rotated from leafy bottom to cloudy skies and back again. While most flesh felt the varied texture of the ground, his right knee found its way into another protrusion. Instead of a root, Martin's knee caught a jagged rock, easily piercing the flesh. The impact slowed the spinning, but also brought a sense of intense burning to both lower extremities. With one last quarter turn, Martin found himself squarely on his back, eyes glazed up towards the treetops and the occasional spot of sky between. Fully knowing that this was the abrupt end to the pre-day festivities, he took a moment to slowly catch his breath and reached towards his timekeeper to mercifully end its recording of the day. After halting the run for good, the watch inquired whether or not to view the event's details or throw it in the trash. Rather than ignore what had happened, he opted to save and move on from this incident. A few minutes passed on the ground before he found the strength to pull himself up and attempt to make the way home.

"If a runner falls in the wood and no one sees, do they really fall?" Martin chuckled nervously, not truly knowing the extent of his injuries. Just still in a state of shock.

As Martin collected himself, he took some time to review all the damage that had been done. What stood out first and most prominently was the gash that traveled from top to bottom of his right knee. Both hands felt warm from the impact of desperately trying to stop his roll. There was not any other major bleeding, save for the right knee which was now sporting a thick crimson line that was destined to reach a sock. A few nicks and scrapes around the ankles and elbows, but they had felt very minor compared to the knee. The intense burning sensation emitting out of his beat-up joints slowly and mercifully subsided. Also catching a large amount of collateral damage were his shoes. Both sported new scrapes, resulting in parts of stitching unwound or even cut. The right one had the lion's share of damage, with the sole of the shoe slightly detached at the toe. Definitely worn in, but still had some life left, and, considering they were being counted on for another fifty miles or so, they still had some utility remaining.

Rising back onto two feet, Martin began to flex and shake his lower half, testing to see if there was any additional unseen damage dealt. All the bumps and soon-to-be bruises seemed superficial, nothing to worry about. After a moment or so, most pain had dissipated, only that remained radiated from his bloodied right knee, as well as the left. The left was more concerning considering the fall was an indirect result of the feeling coming from inside it and not the other way around. For a quick little test, he shifted all weight to the left side and pushed off.

Nothing seems to be hindered structurally but taking it easy was probably the best course of action. Probably was the key word, considering as a runner, Martin was always eager to get out and keep pushing hard. But the even thought of a longer-term injury gave him pause.

The pain and distress experienced in the last few minutes temporarily subsided as Martin was now within a few quick steps from the mysterious wall laid straight through the forest. It became clear that it was indeed a fence, rather than a wall. Chain links intertwined with chain links, reaching upwards of over ten feet. Rust coated nearly all exposed spots, giving the whole structure less of a dated feel and more of an ancient feel. The patterns of metal reinforced the sight considering it looked like nothing Martin had ever seen before. At this distance, the guard perched on top of the fence came into full view. The spiral of twisted and rusted metal gave Martin literal shivers. It appeared like something straight out of a torture chamber only worse. Whether it was the wear of time or the assorted forest debris over time, the jagged spikes had unusual clumps attached, hanging off and slowly rocking with the breeze.

"Whatever is in there is definitely not supposed to get out…," Martin uttered to himself. With a second of reflection, he continued, "…or nothing should get in."

Martin scanned in both directions, curiously looking to see if there was a break in the fence. He couldn't make out any variance in the structure. That wasn't overly shocking to Martin, an inauspicious barrier like the one that laid in front of him didn't seem to be built to allow visitors. A gate or even a slight door would negate the entire purpose of the tonnage of aged metal. But the strangest aspect of the sight was not just the missing entry point, but it was the missing flora. One would assume if a metal fence was erected decades ago, if not even more, Mother Nature would have wound her everlasting fingers over and through her domain. In this instance, Martin could not find a single vine that ventured up or around the rusted metal.

Getting his bearings straight in his head, Martin turned left and started making his way along the fence with the intention of heading to Point Lake. He guesstimated it should be only a few hundred feet from his current location, given the path that brought him this far. With his curiosity piqued, Martin wanted to investigate this new discovery while he could. He wasn't sure that he should be back this way, in fact he was pretty sure that this was trespassing of some sort. By making his way back towards Point Lake, he was still working his way in the general direction back home.

With each step alongside the fence, Martin felt a sense of panic rise through his being. He couldn't pinpoint exactly why his stomach started churning up like an ocean with a category five hurricane ripping over it. Maybe it was the impending doom feeling of what was beside him. Maybe it was the uneasy feeling that he was probably breaking a few lower-level local or federal laws or statutes. Maybe it was the pulsating feeling that was slowly returning to his right knee which had now soaked half of his sock and was staining his shoe. Martin couldn't put his finger on it, but everything mixed inside of his being told him to pick up the pace and get the hell out of Dodge.

Martin tried his damnedest to get back to running. At first it felt like a trot coming out of the gates. His newly creaking joints fought him with each step, causing shots of pain to emanate throughout his body. Stiffness had been setting in, and now had to be pushed away forcefully. While it was not full-blown panic mode, Martin felt the lump start creeping up through his throat. Each step brought him closer to the lake as he traversed through the forest. The pattern of his steps continued to increase, as Martin desperately pushed through the pain, desperately trying to run away from the panic, desperately trying to get his mind back to running.

Martin could hear his steps as they pounded along the dry forest ground. The pace reverberated through his ears, allowing him to gain his pace easier. With each step Martin came closer towards Point Lake. In the distance, the thickness of the low-level forest began to appear, signaling the outskirts of the forest innards. He found himself closer to exiting the despair that his mind found alarming. Martin tried to keep his focus on the sound of his feet contacting the dry leaves and other assorted flotsam on the ground. Heal strike. Roll to ball. Push off. Heal strike. Roll to ball. Push off. Heal strike. Roll to ball. Push off. The recurring sound of his strides began to take Martin's thoughts off the sense of impending doom and back to running. He progressively extended each stride, settling back into running mode. With his typical stride length on his best day, he hit the road two and a half times a second. Working as an analyst, numbers just came naturally to him, so he constantly ran calculations through his head, which helped him maintain the pace he wished to achieve. So, he started counting. Six steps, two seconds. Eleven steps, three seconds. Five steps, two seconds. Back in business.

Five steps, two seconds. Five steps, two seconds. Six steps, two seconds. Eleven steps, three seconds. Eight steps, two seconds. Something was wrong. Martin heard too many steps for the length of the strides he was currently pushing. At the pace he was hearing in his ears, Martin might have been breaking all sorts of land speed records. But the irrational fear that had recently spawned inside his insides seemed to be crystallizing around him. With each step, Martin heard two others, coming from the right. He desperately tried to extend his already elongated gait, but to no avail. Something was rapidly approaching with a manic fervor, and there wasn't a thing he could do about it.

Before he could even turn, a light unlike he had ever experienced overtook his entire line of sight. A myriad of colors rushed over his eyes, completely engulfing everything that Martin was able to see only a moment ago. He instantly stopped running, partly out of fear and partly to avoid the same outcome that had befallen his poor right knee. He desperately turned his head, hoping to find relief or answers from this optical distortion. As soon as the light had hit him, Martin came to a potentially frightening conclusion. What was blinding him was the same thing that was beckoning him from the street. And now he is here, moth drawn to the light in the end.

The steps started up again, this time pacing back and forth near

Martin. He couldn't ascertain what lay before him, where its intentions laid, or why it took a liking to him. The steps continued, but with less frequency than before. Despite not being able to see a single thing outside of the cavalcade of colors parading in front of his eyes, Martin could determine one thing. Whatever was observing him, didn't appear that it was getting any closer to him. Which was a good thing, considering each time it moved along, Martin could feel slight tremors through the soil. There was a definite reason for the massive fence that had tracks through these woods.

And with that, everything was still. Not a single sound came from any corner of the wood. The stillness brought on yet another sense of depravity to Martin. Nothing that could be seen or heard. He dared not get closer to where he thought the fence was. He stood as still as he could humanly stand, which might have been tough given he was on the back end of a seven-mile run. But at this point, Martin felt the adrenaline coursing through his veins, helping to keep him statuesque.

It hit him all at once. An overwhelming aroma of cinnamon filled Martin's nose. The scent was so out of place in the middle of a forest in New Jersey, at first it struck him with a sense of complete confusion. At the same time, the smell ignited a curiously calming reaction from inside. The subtle notes of the spice that wafted around his body brought a sense of relief to his being, and, with that, Martin completely relaxed. His breathing suddenly returned to its normal cadence, and all the pain seemingly melted away. It was a feeling that Martin had never experienced before and couldn't at all explain. The multitude of light colors that had engulfed his sight was now slowly wavering back and forth. The soothing warmth of the lights sent Martin into a further state of calmness.

When he seemed to be at the utmost point of serenity, a voice came from in front of him.

"*Be still. Be well,*" it whispered. What sounded like a young child speaking softly filled the entire expanse of the forest and echoed off every single tree, making the whisper rock Martin with a strength that he could not have expected.

The moment the last echo stopped reflecting around Martin, the light disappeared. The fence, in its terrifying appearance, was once again staring him straight in the face. The noises, smells, and sights of the mysterious forest were back to where they were only a short time prior. Nothing at all seemed out of place. Nothing seemed out of the norm. The abrupt end to the phenomenon left Martin truly debating whether anything really happened.

"I must've cracked my head on the ground with that fall," Martin uttered to himself. "I thought I heard somewhere that head trauma can cause all sorts of hallucinations. Lights and sounds, all that is possible. Brings back to those college days." Martin tried to rationalize the irrational in his mind. He was trying to fit some possible logical reason to explain what just happened, like children in the grass coming up with their best visions of what the clouds showed.

Martin reluctantly took a few steps forward, and grabbed hold of the fence, bringing his forehead to press against it. Peering back and forth, nothing appeared out of the ordinary. The feeling of the aged metal on his hands was quite sobering and shocking at the same time. Martin could almost feel reverberations of the past coursing through his hands as he tensely gripped the fence. The oxidized metal gave off an ancient smell. What was most striking at that time was that after all the searching and inspecting that Martin had done, he still could not find a touch of ivy at any spot.

Instead of staying there and looking for any answers, Martin backtracked, and easily found his way out, back to Main Street. There he hung a right and headed back towards home. Once he got to the bridge that spanned the narrowest portion of Point Lake, which also was the beginning of the Clarks Run River by all that Martin could gather, it was roughly a shade over a mile and a quarter from home. Looking down at his wrist and found it was a quarter after six. Even at a ginger pace, he would be lucky to be back by seven. Everyone would be up and ant'em, possibly worried senseless, but definitely at least wondering. And by the time he could manage to get home, when Sasha saw his current state, she would know. The two had been together for over a decade, and she, having grown accustomed to his varied nuances, would immediately ascertain that a fall had befallen him. The only other option would have been a run-in with a vehicle or some sort, but it would be doubtful he could manage the walk back in that type of injured state.

As Martin crossed over the bridge, he took a moment to stop and rest, draping his arms atop the railing. He peered out at the lake, as if searching for answers to what he honestly believed to be unbelievable and unanswerable. His eyes got lost in the serenity of the view. The vast expanse of the lake nearly put the other side out of view. The banks on each side were littered with foliage and wildlife. Breaks in the tree and brush lines dotted the south side of the lake, showing spots popular with locals for fishing and swimming access. The northern side followed the same growing pattern as that section of wood did on Main Street, mainly dense, thick brush followed by a trove of mighty trees. No real access spot could be found nor any sandy slow inclines spanning wet to dry. The plant life extended into the reaches of the lakesides. It appeared as if the forest was growing out, and absorbing part of the lake. The gentle breeze seemingly brought the forest to life, causing the green wave to force its way down the banks. Tree branches resembled a multitude of arms, flailing back and forth, reaching for the unknown.

Martin forcefully pulled his attention from the picturesque serenity and willed his body back to the task at hand, namely returning to the warm abode with his tail placed firmly between his legs. Traffic had begun to pick up on Main Street, with the occasional commuter stopping to refuel at the Stop 'N' Fuel, which was a popular place as it was the only station in town where most of the passersby were fighting to board the Turnpike. The stores of Main Street remained without their Open signs as he continued the slow trek homeward. Commercial gave way to residential, and after a few developments, Martin managed to reach the oldest one of the lots, as well as his own, Washington Crossing. Once off Main, a left onto Jefferson Terrace, then a quick right onto Johnson Way, and the Shiner abode was five houses on the right.

As Martin slowly approached home base, he could see the front door was open, leaving the storm door shut. He was still three houses away, but Martin could sense the worry on her face. The closer that he had approached, the little panic on Sasha's face gave way to concern. By this point it was evident to her that she wouldn't have to call the police on this calm June morning, let alone bring out the life insurance policy. It wasn't a scene that was new to her, as her husband has always been a good bit clumsy and uncoordinated at times, and, most likely, it wouldn't be the last. Her concern fully melted away as Martin came up to the stoop, and she held open the door.

"Are you okay?" she lovingly inquired. Sasha was never much for words, and typically kept conversations to the necessary.

"I have seen better days, that's for sure," Martin responded, looking towards her feet.

"Come in and wash up. I will drop the boys off at school," she replied, as flexible as ever.

Martin climbed upstairs while Tristan and Maddox were finishing off the hot breakfast laid in front of them in the dining room. Grabbing a new pair of underwear, he disrobed in the bathroom, while keeping the sweaty, partly bloodstained and fully beat up clothes in a pile in the corner. He stepped into the shower, getting the temperature just hot enough while not burning any flesh, and let the morning's events wash from his body. The mixture of blood and sweat caused the shower floor below him to look like a red pool with his feet squarely inside. As the layers of the morning's experience had found their way down the drain, the full extent of his injuries started to come clear. As he rinsed off the remaining debris, Martin could not believe what he was seeing. With the remaining line of dried blood removed from his right leg, his knee was completely unscathed. The gash that traveled the entire length of his kneecap was nonexistent. It took Martin a few moments to let it truly set in.

"I swear that knee was banged up. I didn't hallucinate that. I felt the pain. There was blood. What the hell is going on?" At that moment, he was brought right back to the woods and what he heard. He couldn't let it set it, as his reflection was cut short.

With a quick rap on the bathroom door, both boys' heads popped in.

"Buh-bye, DAH-*DEEEE*! Love you," Maddox shouted from the doorway.

"Be careful, Daddy. Don't get any more boo-boos rest of the day," Tristan advised.

With that a smile crept over Martin's face, pulling him temporarily out of the morning's events. "Thank you both! I needed that!"

As quickly as they burst into the bathroom, the boys were gone. Whether or not they got the idea of checking in directly or not from their mother, it didn't matter as everything was genuine.

Sasha proceeded to enter and provide further words of encouragement. "Well, you would be hard pressed to find another day that starts like yours and doesn't end with anything but a rainbow."

The smile returned in full force. With a brief sigh as the water completely removed the last remnants of blood and sweat, Martin had no doubt that every word she spoke couldn't be closer to the truth.

Sasha could have chastised Martin for a number of different things; for not bringing his phone on the run, for not wearing the reflective gear she had gotten him for Christmas or for a myriad of other reasons. She was always concerned for any and everyone else's well-being. Martin never liked carrying all the protective gear on his body in the morning, especially considering his phone always felt like it could and would find a way out of its pocket and be lost forever. Even though that is the most unlikely of situations, Martin had always stuck to his rigid routine. His mind would derive the most asinine and improbable scenarios when she brought it up. The dourest being "If I get hit by a car in the morning, not sure if I can use it to call the morgue". She never seemed to like that one, for fairly obvious reasons. But this morning, maybe a camera may have come in handy.

"Thanks, honey," Martin replied.

Sasha remained in the doorway, when she should have been off and getting the busy day underway even if the morning proceedings hadn't brought much more to take care of. Martin could sense she was standing still, stoic as usual, but different.

He poked his head out of the shower curtains to get a good look at her. While Sasha typically didn't let any emotions bleed through her facial expressions, this morning, not being the typical one, was different. A slight look of concern was worn across her facial features. Something was amiss, and it wasn't Martin's bloodied and late return to the house.

"What's wrong, babe?"

"We received a call this morning from the hospital," Sasha replied, her voice a bit uneasy.

Martin's heart dropped instantly, and his stomach balled up just as quickly. For a moment, everything that had transpired seemed like light years away.

"Martha?"

Sasha shook her head.

"Perry…" Martin said as he dropped his head. It wouldn't be a very big surprise if it was his sister. She had led a rocky path since their parents, and that story. Perry was the sweetheart. She was the innocent one. Adored by all of them, twins included, and not just because of her personality, but of her situation. "Shit. Is she okay? What the hell happened? Is she still there? Can I…"

Sasha interrupted Martin's rambling questioning, "She will be fine. All questions will be answered in time…I hope." She paused to reflect before continuing onward. "The hospital needs one of us to pick her up this morning, she is being discharged. It was only one night, and she will be fine. I have already called the high school to call her out for the day."

"Jesus. Not Perry."

"I will pick her up after dropping the kids off. Don't worry yourself. I will bring her here to let her rest. Please call your sister and let her know."

"Okay."

With that Sasha was rounding up the twins and keeping the day moving along. For it being still quite early in the morning, so much had transpired, it was hard for Martin to really get a grasp around everything. He couldn't help but worry for his niece. She was closer to a daughter than a niece. He had banked a fair amount of vacation days at his work, and today seemed like the most opportune time to cash one in.

"Perry. Be still. Be well."

MARTHA 1

The light had been flashing nonstop from the kitchen counter. She couldn't tell when it arrived. She was never a technical person, even to the level that an answering machine purchased years ago from Radio Shack completely bewildered her. She might have heard it if she hadn't turned the ringer off before making her way to bed. That was routine for a long time. The night before the rare day off from work at the restaurant was one where she could let all of her worries melt away, and leave all of the bad feelings behind and memories be released as well. Never mind that it was a Wednesday.

Martha Shiner swung her two legs over the side of the bed, head pounding incessantly from between her temples and to the back of her skull. Both eyes unwillingly cracked open to fully see the impact of the night prior. Nothing was truly out of place. She could have sworn she escorted a cute face home from The Hole last night, but she could not find any signs. He might have left in the middle of the night.

"It isn't the first and it sure as shit won't be the last," Martha thought to herself.

The Hole was a place where mostly locals dropped in to wet their whistle, so if she did have company recently, Martha would surely hear about it soon. Must not be the case. This time of the year was normally the time when she shied away from any company. This year would be the twentieth year since her parents…

Her foot, while dangling down towards the floor, caught something cold and hard. Poking her head over the bedside, she found her answer. A fully empty bottle of whiskey laid next to her bed. There was no going out for ol' Miss Shiner last night. There were times in life where a person buried themselves into their underground catacombs, and this was the case for Martha.

She found the strength to bring herself to her feet, and, while wobbling mildly, neatly folded the blankets on her bed. The meticulous compulsivity that flowed through Martha's veins did not allow her to have anything out of place, even a few hours from tying a whole bottle on. The venom crept up her throat, and singed parts of her esophagus. After she attended to the answering machine, she definitely had to make her way to the medicine cabinet for some much needed antacids.

With a couple unsure steps, she was at the desk in her room. The one thing that Martha Shiner was honestly proud of in this life, and one of the only pieces of advice she heeded that came from her brother, was using some, if not most, of the life insurance money she received to buy a quaint little house. It was big enough for her and Winky, but not much more. But it was something they could call home. At least that is what Martha called it, Perrywinkle would always use a different H word: house. In the end, it was something that she could afford, albeit on the smaller of the small size. While being a town away from where her brother and his family resided, it was under a mile from them. Being close to family could often be a gift and a burden, but she didn't mind. Her home was the size which a person getting from one spot to the other didn't take much effort.

Standing at her desk, Martha took a moment to blankly stare at the blinking light. There weren't many people or places that kept the house line. With a life closer to an emotional nomad than a rock of dependability, Martha was never anyone's emergency contact. Part of her liked to keep it that way. The less responsibility, the better in her mind.

"Must be the baby brother. Good, old checking in call," she convinced herself. Using her best baby brother voice, *"Hey Marth, it is your brother. Just callin' to see how you are doing. We are here if you wanna talk. Sasha's making meatballs tonight if you and Perry want to drop by. Or we can just skip that and meet up at Morey's. Anyway, give me a call, 'kay?"* Martha's impression of her brother brought a smile to her face.

Pressing the PLAY button, the voice on the recording left her with a pause. "Miss Shiner, this is Janet from St. Joseph's Memorial Hospital. Your daughter Perrywinkle was admitted last night. She...eh...you can call us if you have any questions. Miss Shiner, I... dammit, Martha just please be there. Perry'll be fine, just make sure you pick her up in the morning. She asked for you, and it'd mean a lot if you can make it." An abrupt click ended the message.

In an instant Martha was simultaneously embarrassed and distraught. While she was trying to drown the demons in her head, Martha had opened a potential disaster. With things still hazy and a churning inside her, Martha couldn't comprehend what she heard. She could have sworn that she heard Perry come in last night.

The answering machine continued.

NEXT MESSAGE

"Martha, it is Sasha. Perry is fine. She is with us." The message ended. Martha cringed. She still didn't know what Mart had seen in that woman, let alone procreate. Her brother is one thing, their offspring was another, but she was a completely different beast. The two of them had always got along like oil and water. The wife's voice had always reminded Martha of nails on a chalkboard. Now, she was in possession of her daughter. Aside from the fact that she would never hear the end of this, Martha also worried about having Perry. This kind of happening may give her brother and her succubus of a wife the ammunition to steal her away. To Martha, that sure as hell wasn't happening.

While the pounding rocked the inside of her skull, Martha stumbled out of her room and into the bathroom. With a quick purge into the toilet, luckily the seat was completely erect and no need for added clean up, she centered herself with both hands on each side of the bowl. Everything was going from bad to worse. She never admitted to anyone how much her parents' disappearance had continued to affect her. Mart would always say that it was nothing of the sort, that they were hiking up in the Catskills and fell into one of the many mountain creeks. He still tells Martha every single, goddamn year that they will show up or that their bodies will be found. But she isn't that stupid. Maybe that wife of his, but sure as shit wasn't this one.

Another wrench in the midsection, and Martha felt well enough to stand on her two feet. Fumbling through the cabinet, she pulled out the antacid bottle. But to her wonderful luck, not even one remained.

"When worse goes to shit."

Splashing a handful of water over her face, Martha stared into the mirror. There she found someone staring back at her. Someone with deep bags drooping under her eyes. That someone looking back at her looked like the weight of the world had been crushing her for years. That someone looked like it wasn't just the world's fault, but it must have been some of hers. That someone looked like she wouldn't let anyone know that she admitted she should take some responsibility. That someone felt it was easier to just live up to what everyone thought of her. That someone that looked like she yearned for some semblance of a normal life. That someone looked like everything that she ever had wished for might have been slipping away.

Martha couldn't continue to stare into the mirror. As much as she wanted and desired, she knew she was her worst enemy, and, after the long twenty years since her world was flipped up on its end, she wasn't sure that she could make it right.

Rather than dwell upon everything, Martha got up, and knew what she needed to do. She had to go to her brother's house and try to bring back her daughter. The pain of dealing with her sister-in-law gave her even more anxiety than explaining to her only offspring why she wasn't there for her when she needed it. Then again, Perry would understand. Not that she was a bright individual as intelligence is something that she had in spades, but it was Perry who was conditioned for this. That thought made Martha's spirit drop from the floor into the basement.

She must have been standing in front of the mirror for minutes, thinking about the past and debating the future. Her body kept slowly rocking back and forth as the sorrow drowning of the late night and early morning was still pulsing through her veins. Without grabbing a hold of the sink, who knows how far the rocking would have pushed her. With that, she tensed up, and poked through the medicine cabinet one last time, but this time with success. She slapped some deodorant under her shirt, which was the exact shirt, and shorts for that matter, that had adorned her the day prior. Martha felt presentable enough to deal with the inevitable daggers sent her way.

Martha stumbled out of the bathroom and towards the kitchen. She grabbed her car keys. After a moment of debating whether or not she should truly be an operator of a multiple thousand-pound weapon, Martha figured it would be just fine.

"It isn't the first and it sure as shit won't be the last," Martha repeated in her mind.

Completely disregarding her purse and, as a result, her driver's license, Martha left the house, leaving the front door unlocked as she continued. In her mind, she had insurance so anything of value, which there really wasn't, that might grow legs and find their way out of the house would just be another claim with an inflated value. Martha often debated what upgrade she could make if another burglar made their way into the house, uninvited of course. That would be a decision for a later time if she was lucky enough, so she focused back on the goals at hand.

On the drive over to her brother's, Martha tried to get the story straight in her mind. The moment that she pulled into the driveway Martha would be under attack to provide some sort of defense for why she was unavailable at such a crucial moment of need for her daughter. Martha could come up with dozens of less questionable alibis and much more of the reasonable sort. The drive was not long at all, so if she was to produce an excuse it would need to come soon and be airtight. Her head was the antagonist in this situation, as with each thought that popped into her head, there was an increase of the velocity and intensity of the pounding. She couldn't really come to a definitive choice, and she had already arrived at her destination.

Before Martha could put the car into park, she already spotted Sasha behind the storm door, arms crossed her body. At least Martha knew what kind of bee nest she was entering. As soon as she stopped the vehicle and opened the door, Sasha was gone, replaced by her brother. Worry draped his person, which had a way of weighing on her. Growing up as an older sibling, there were certain mores that a person was to attend to. For the most part, Martha was the ideal older sister, not being jealous of her parent doting sibling, rather a caring and protecting big sis. When she felt she had let her brother down, a small part of her sank further.

Martha got out of the car and closed the door behind her. She tried desperately to look the part of a normal, sober person as she approached her brother, but she failed miserably. As she moved from driveway to sidewalk, her flip flop caught the median and she fell in a heap. As strained as their relationship had been through the latter part of their lives, Mart was still her brother, and he came to her side to help brace her fall.

"Jesus, Marth. You need to be more careful," he playfully chided. Animosity aside, Martin, too, always appeared to move forward.

"Yeah, yeah. You know your sister. Class-A klutz." It was at this moment Martha realized that she hadn't brushed her teeth or the ghosts of the night away before she left. Mart's face expressed it was obvious and disappointing. Rather than take the opportunity to further push Martha into the ground, he took the fork in the trail and went the high road, fully knowing how they both had gotten there.

"Good to see you, Martha."

"Same," she returned the familial fuzziness. As she gathered her things, as well as herself, off the concrete, Martha noticed Sasha looked out from one of the front windows. Involuntarily, she shot a quick sneer her way with which Sasha once again retreated.

"She sent me out here to talk to you first. You know, have a little sibling talk?" Mart put out there, noticing the look on his sister's face. "I figured it would be easier if I met you first. Definitely wouldn't want a full-blown cat fight on the front lawn."

"You an' me both know it wouldn't get to that. I would have taken her ass down the first chance I got."

"Martha. I am just trying to help. Whether you like it or not. End of the day, we always got each other."

"But she sure as hell ain't going anywhere. You met her and you changed, Mart. There is no denying that."

"I am not sure how that is. The thing is that we met right around when the parents passed…"

"Abducted, Mart. If you are gonna bring up the parents, you gotta get it right."

"…and she helped me deal with the emotions that came with that. I faced up to that. I got through that. I was able to move on."

"She fuckin' brainwashed you, plain and goddamn simple."

Mart paused. He had a ton of patience with his sister, but there was always a line in the sand that, when crossed, he made her know. It didn't always have to be verbal, as a stern facial response was just as effective.

"Okay, okay, brother. I give. I will leave the sleeping dog die."

"It is 'lie'."

"I know what I said." Martha paused. Still a bit inebriated, she realized her venom was misguided and relented. "What the hell am I to do, Mart?"

"Million-dollar question, sis. You know our doors, phones, and, hell, mailbox are always open."

"You say that, but what if something came up and she is the only one available?"

"Well, that is exactly what happened. I was out for a run, and Sasha was home with the boys, getting ready for the day. That is when she got the call. As soon as I got home, she dropped them off at school and picked up Perry."

With that Martha went silent. As much as the two never got along, she knew that Sasha would always have Perry's best interests in the forefront. Martha could rest easy for a moment on that given. The problem arose from the fact that Sasha had on multiple occasions inferred, or in some cases overtly accused, Martha of being a delinquent and unfit mother with the end potential result of having custody of Winky. Martha knew she hadn't been there as much as she should have been for her one and only child but never outwardly admitted. Nothing like this had ever happened that she was aware of, but she really didn't know any of the details of the situation. The churning stomach wasn't just a result of the alcohol.

"Well for that, I shall send a fruit basket."

"Please Martha, be serious. This is not something that can be laughed off. She has been through a lot in her life, and this is up there. As a parent, half the job is being there for your kids. You and I both know that she is a really, really special girl. For everything that has happened around her, she is still a very grounded person. And don't get me started on her smarts. You and me both combined don't add up to what she has going on upstairs. No clue at all with that one. But, in all seriousness Marth, she is just a kid at such a pivotal age that is longing for family. Longing for stability. The one thing that she wants in this life is to have a happy and normal family. She is just a thirteen-year-old darling of a girl. That should be above and beyond the one thing that your life revolves around."

Mart stopped his monologue. The mission he was sent when he came out to meet his sister before her getting any further was a success. While he didn't mean for Martha to be a snort dripping, teary eyed mess, Mart really just wanted to get through. Over the years, they had gone through some semblance of the same conversation on dozens of occasions. As much hopefulness as he had afterwards, each one had always ended in disappointment as time marched onward. The hopefulness this time seemed different.

Martha couldn't help but let the water flow. Her eyes poured down streams over her rosy cheeks. All of the emotions that she had been holding back were out in the open now. There was no way to piece back together the dam after the flood had breached. Everything was too much for her, and Martha sat back down onto the sidewalk. Her loving brother sat right down next to her. He not only cared for his niece, but he was afraid for his sister. In the back of his mind, he always braced for the call letting him know that Martha Elizabeth Shiner had finally succumbed to her devices. He never had to tell her that is how he felt, Martha could sense it.

"Martha, this is the time you have to change things. This is when you can make your and *her* future different. It can all be if you want it to be. You just need to want it."

Martha continued to sob. She hadn't ever cried like that since the funeral. All the pain that had been bottled up finally had the cork popped. There was no use fighting it. Her brother, who might have been the only one under the age of ninety to have one handy, pulled a handkerchief from his pocket and handed it to her. Noisily, Martha cleared out the flowing mucous from her nose with an echoing honk. She stopped, took a deep breath, held it for a few seconds, and exhaled. Everything started to calm down.

A few sniffles later, Martha turned to face her younger brother. "Where is she?"

"Backyard. She felt good enough to pull a shift on twin duty. Brave soul."

"Thanks. What the hell happened?"

"Run in with a bully. That is the short version. If you want the long version, think you need to talk to her directly."

"Got it." With one more swipe at her nose, Martha rose to her feet. The emotional letting helped her mind focus. The fuzziness at the edges subsided, and everything appeared clearer. She understood the task at hand, not completely fully up to it, but nonetheless Martha made her way around the house to the back.

Once she turned the corner, Martha found her daughter alternating turns pushing her cousins on the swing set, making sure both kept their feet high into the air. She always had a way with the boys, and now was not an exception. Each of them took turns cackling as they reached their toes high up into the air, kicking their feet uncontrollably.

After a few steps, Perry noticed the new addition to the play yard. Her appearance turned from joyful to somber in an instant. The twins picked up on it as well and dragged their feet to slow their flight paths. When it was safe enough, both Tristan and Maddox hopped off, rolled in tandem across the grass and beelined for their aunt. Martha was not ready as both leapt into her arms.

"AUNTIE, AUNTIE, AUNTIE!" Maddox exclaimed, squeezing with all of his five year old might.

"Auntie Em, we looooove you," Tristan added.

The feelings were mutual, as Martha hugged both tightly back.

"Oh boys, I love the hellos."

They both snuggled closer to her body, fighting for positioning. Maddox lost the battle and hopped off. He cocked his head at Martha and added, "Auntie, you smell baaad. Are you ookay?"

That one hit home again to Martha. Eyes slowly watered, but she was able to hold them back.

"Oh baby, I have just had a bad day."

"Oooh, you should tawk to Paaee, she had a bad day too," added Tristan.

The tear dropped to the ground this time.

"I will. Thanks, boys. Could you go inside now? I think I heard your mom calling you."

"I din't heaa anyting," Tristan replied.

Martha pulled his face close, gave him a kiss on his forehead and gave him a wink. Maddox was the over the top sibling, but Tristan was the one to pick up on things that others might not. With that both boys bolted for the back door.

Martha turned her attention back to her daughter. She was seated in one of the swing seats, slowly rocking back and forth with her head down. While she clearly didn't want to have any conversation, she also didn't flee with the boys. That deterred Martha slightly, but she gained the courage to make her way over. There she stood. Not making a noise, not knowing what she could say to make things right, not completely understanding what type of mess had just befallen her daughter. Everything whirled around inside her, as Martha took one last step forward.

"I...I am truly sorry," Martha offered.

Perry stopped rocking. Without making any sort of eye contact, she questioned, "For what?"

"For not being there," Martha answered sheepishly.

Perry started rocking once more, keeping her head down towards the grass. She was visibly worn and shaken. Whatever had befallen her just hours before had taken a toll on the poor girl.

"I needed you. I needed my mom."

Martha, knowing that the reason why she wasn't there wasn't enough of an answer to the situation and that, despite spending the night in the hospital, her daughter knew exactly why she was absent, had no rational answer.

"Listen, I have fucked up. I have no excuse." Martha, in all her issues, had strived to be as prim and proper around her daughter. She could count the times that she let an expletive slip on one hand. It was not something that Martha thought would help most situations.

Perry once again stopped rocking. This time she looked up at her mother. The worn look that she showed was unlike any girl her age should have worn on their face. Her under eyes were swollen and red. The whites of her eyes were redder than anything. Both of her cheeks had the same hue. For the first time in a long time, the two had met eyes. Martha couldn't even remember the last time they had anything near a passing conversation, let alone a heart-to-heart moment. Part of her had yearned to connect to her only child. Most of her was completely embarrassed and hurt by her actions that she had inflicted upon her own blood. For the times that Martha had raised enough courage to apologize for not being there, for not providing for her, for putting her in all types of unenviable situations for a child to be in, for everything that made Martha Martha and not Mother.

She slowly approached Perry, not realizing that both had their heads down as the eye contact was just a fleeting moment in time. All sorts of emotions drove through her head. She desperately searched for the right words that would make everything better. But Martha knew differently.

"*Words are just that, actions are what matters*," went through Martha's spine. The voice that spoke had been gone for years, but the advice that her father laid down on the rare occasions where she had stepped out of line from her parent's wants still echoed somewhere inside her.

"What would he say if he was here…," Martha whispered to herself as she made her way to the empty swing. She slowly sat down. The churning was back, but it wasn't from the alcohol, but from the magnitude of the moment.

Both sat silently for a minute or two, rocking back and forth nervously. Neither wanted to make the first move, something that a seasoned parent would have seized upon. Instead, it was Perry to break the silence.

"I would want to ask, 'Why?' But I know what the answer will be. So, I won't," Perry utterly lowly. "Instead, I just want to know one thing."

"Ye..yeah?"

"When?"

Martha was taken aback by the question. She truly didn't get its purpose and replied accordingly, "When what?"

"When will all of this be over?"

There wasn't a good answer to the question. Martha couldn't reply to how she truly felt. The answer would not be the easiest nor the least painful. Instead, she stayed silent, inspecting the ground below with her flip flops.

Perry, seemingly not dissuaded by the nonverbal answer, continued. "I mean, you are my mom. But I never felt like that. You have never been there for me. You never disciplined me. How could I ever have called you mother. I can't. I won't." Perry's voice increasingly cracked as she forced the words out, words that had been set aside and simmered for years. "The funny part is, there was a part of me last night, while I was being beat up, that was calling out for you. To be there to save me, to protect me. I... I, and that made me angry. Angry because I had fooled myself." Tears started to roll down her puffy cheeks. "When I needed you most, when I wanted you there, you weren't. And I had hoped upon hope that I would have you, and that I could be your daughter." Tears turned into full blown sobbing. "But I can't..."

Perry trailed off and put her head down into her hands. Martha forced her hand to her back, and gave her a few pats. It didn't help the situation, and it left her with even less to say. So, Martha didn't.

As she tried to catch her breath and stop the snot from flowing out of her nostrils, Perry managed, "Aunt Sasha said I can stay here for the night if I want."

"Of course, she did," was the reply that Martha could muster. Anger rose from her insides, seeing exactly what was happening. It was another moment in their history that her adversary was trying to drive a stake between her and her daughter. Not even the sight of Perry's marked face could subside the rage. While she had slowly approached the situation, this time Martha abruptly made her way out of the backyard. Her animosity held her from turning back and seeing the broken sight of her daughter. Instead, she beelined around the house and towards her car. As she fumbled for her keys, the rolling returned, and it couldn't be held back. Martha doubled over and threw up a puddle upon the sidewalk. With a quick smear against her hand to haphazardly clean up, Martha righted herself to find Sasha staring through one of the front windows. With an instinctive flick of her middle finger, Martha swung into the front seat and retreated back to her safety zone.

SASHA 1

The moment the car was out of sight, Sasha turned from the window. The anxiety that always accompanied a visit from her sister-in-law seemed to ebb with her leaving. While the tension was no longer present, the aftermath of the storm still remained.

She made her way through the house and out the back door. Before exiting, Sasha made sure that the twins were with their father, so that she could have a moment with her niece. She never saw herself as a surrogate mother to Perrywinkle, but just simply felt that this young, impressionable, brilliant teenager that was currently weeping into her lap needed some type of actual guidance through this world. Was Sasha the one to provide that? In her mind, anything was better than what the girl had received so far.

Seeing that she was approaching, Perry did her best to clean herself up, rubbing the remaining snot from the tip of her nose. One final sniffle, and she sat up right. Sasha took the seat next to her, leaning towards to dry the tear soaked cheeks of her niece. For a thirteen-year-old in the beginning stages of puberty, Sasha couldn't find any signs of skin blemishes. To her, Perry, in a different situation, could truly blossom into a person with all the glowing potential.

Settling down together, Sasha opened their conversation. "Your mother loves you," she stated bluntly. "You might not see it, but that is the truth."

"If that is the case, she's got a strange way of showing it," Perry replied.

"Well, it is because she doesn't show it. Your mother is a deeply broken person."

"That's harsh."

"Do you believe me?" Sasha asked her niece. The silence that responded confirmed the answer. "Being broken doesn't mean a person is bad. It just means that they haven't healed."

"Can she be healed?" Perry inquired curiously, feeling tiny droplets starting to fall from above.

"That is not for me to know. That is truly up to that person. If they truly want to be healed, to be better, then they will need to find it in themselves to make that happen. Sure, their circle of people around them can help, but only if that person is ready to accept the help."

"Kind of like those shows on the artsy channels?"

This brought a chuckle to Sasha. "You mean an intervention?"

"Yeah, that is what I was thinking."

"I guess you can consider it a form of an intervention. Usually, an intervention deals with some type of addiction that is having adverse effects on various aspects of one's life. As crazy as it may seem, your mother doesn't have that."

The end of that last sentence brought a glare from Perry. "Tell me you aren't serious?"

"Unfortunately, I am. Your mother holds it together just enough. She is able to provide just enough. She has enough wherewithal to make sure she has a dependable job. These things are because of you. Because she loves you."

Sasha shifted around in the swing seat, trying to get a bit closer. The slow tears had started again, and her maternal instincts engaged. The tears mixed with the calming drizzle that had started to pick up.

"The truth is, Perry, that I know she loves you as a fact. Before you came along, she was really not in a good place. We all worried for her. Nothing that we could say would help. Every time the phone rang, your uncle tensed up, expecting the worst. It just seemed like something big was going to happen, good or bad, that would end that phase of her life. In all honesty, while we didn't say it, we all thought it would be bad. No one could keep going with how she was. Each day was touch and go with her. That is when she really needed an intervention. We all thought it was a matter of time before we got the call. But when the phone rang one day, I held my breath. The look on your uncle's face went through the gamut of emotions. In the end, he had a smile from ear to ear. Your mother was ecstatic. It was as if she had won the lottery. She had a meaning in life. That day…, well, Perry, you were her intervention."

Perry sat still. She moved her feet over the top of the ground, pushing the wet dirt around, looking to find the answers to be revealed. She was clearly letting things settle. While what was revealed to her was all new, it wasn't as if Perry couldn't have assumed the whole thing to begin with. Sasha could see the new perspective sinking into her.

"So, if you are right, and I was what turned her around, then why still be like, well, her? I mean, if it was like an intervention, then why does she still do what she does?"

"Well, that was a turning point, in my opinion. She made the necessary adjustments in her mind in order to provide for a family."

"I don't really feel like a family."

"Well, you are. We are part of your family."

"Yeah, I know that. I feel that. I love that. What I feel with her is kinda empty."

"Perry, she is still broken. The trauma that she and Martin went through was a lot to swallow. Martin was able to find his way to the other end of the tunnel. It is not to say that he is the same as when he went in. No one would be. He accepted help, she did not. Your mother is the one that is stuck in that tunnel."

"Is there any way to get her out?"

Pausing slightly to contemplate the answer, Sasha stopped her seat rocking. Slightly shrugging gave Perry most of the answer that she was not really looking for.

"Listen, dear. Do I believe people can change? Absolutely. Both of them had changed. There are times in this life where events occur, and the severity of it causes a person to adapt in a way. That is life. If a person does not change, the problems haven't gone away. They are just placing whatever baggage, trauma, issues, whatever you may call it, onto the mantle, then neatly covered over it with some ornamental doily." Sensing that she was losing Perry, Sasha finished, "My point is that it is up to your mother to finish fixing herself. We can put out our hands to support her in whatever way we can, which is what we always have, but it must be a two-way street."

Feeling that whatever she wished to convey had gotten across, not necessarily fully understood or accepted, Sasha reached out and held Perry in a loving embrace. She felt that, at least for the time being, that her niece would make it out okay. Sasha didn't realize that it was that tender moment, seeds were planted deep in Perry's mind that would finally pull Martha out of the tunnel that her head had been trapped inside.

The hug ended abruptly when Martin called from the back door. "Perry...Lucy's on the phone." While it might seem odd to some for a young girl to have the phone numbers of their friend's family members, Lucy had spent more time growing up at Martin and Sasha's house than at Perry's house. She was close enough to be a part of the family.

"Must be worried about you," Sasha added, as Perry rose to go get the phone, which might have been one of the last corded telephones in the state. As she made her way back inside, the sky began to open up, and a deluge came down. Both hurried into the house to get out of the coming storm. When she had checked in the morning, the weatherman said nothing of precipitation in the forecast, let alone the rolling thunder that could be heard in the distance.

After gaining shelter from the storm, Perry picked up the phone.

Martin was still attending to Tristan and Maddox, who were fully cranked up since they had their favorite person over the house to play, which was a full-time job in itself. Sasha had found her way to a wall on the other side of the dining room and lent against it, a perfect location for eavesdropping.

"Oh hey, Loose," Perry greeted once she put the phone up to her ear. "Yeah, I am doing okay…. Yeah, I will be fine…. How about you?... Yeah… What about your mom?... Oh, gotcha… Well, you know her. It wasn't the first time. I hope it will be the last. I think it will be the last… Lucy, please don't. It is okay… Listen, I get it, I really do… Of course we can, as long as you get yourself together!"

Sasha could surmise it was two best friends hashing things out. That brought a smile to her face. Lucy had always been good to the family, and especially to Perry. For all that she could tell, the two were more than kindred spirits. Sasha couldn't understand why she stopped coming around recently, but she just pegged it at the social pressures of a growing teen. That tended to explain most odd behavior.

"Uh huh…," Perry continued. "Of course, I know your birthday is coming up… This Saturday?... I will have to check, but I am sure that I can make it… Oh yeah, I didn't know that was where the place was… Okay, I got it, thanks!... Yeah, I will probably be in tomorrow. I can't really take another day off this week… Both were excused, so I am in the clear… Okay, we can catch up tomorrow… Oh, hell no, I will take the bus, I am not walking through that part again... Oh, geez. Yeah, I hope I never see those again… Okay, see ya!"

Perry hung up the phone and turned to find her aunt watching her intently.

"Everything okay?" asked Sasha.

"Yeah, I think it will be. Lucy was just worried about me. She was just checking in."

"She has always been a good friend. I haven't seen her or heard from her lately. Are the two of you getting along?"

"We are now," Perry answered shortly, and found a seat at the dining room table. The rain was now pelting against the siding and the windows, making the reverberating sound like thousands of tiny pistons echoing through the house. Rather than further indulge her uncle's wife, Perry literally sat down and twiddled her thumbs. Even as a younger kid, she was quite adamant to not answer any questions when she felt she was being interrogated. Perry had been quite quiet when she was picked up at the hospital, not letting any details of the previous night's events loose.

Sensing that she would get no more answers to the questions she wanted, Sasha relented, and opted to take over playing with the boys. She didn't go far with them. Pulling out the assorted puzzles and cars from various baskets in the living room, Sasha made herself planted in the middle of the floor. As she settled into play mode, Sasha made a point to wave Martin towards the dining room, while keeping an ear in the same direction. Martin, being the obedient husband that he was, followed the nonverbal instructions and took a seat across from Perry.

MARTIN 3

Looking at Perry's body language, the same tactics would have the same results. Instead of directly engaging with his dearest niece, Martin found a different way to let himself in. He took a few seconds to look over her a time or two, then sat back, imitating her to the best of his ability. Martin matched Perry's slight slouch with a little lowering of his shoulders. He twisted his stiff lips into a scowl, along with furiously twiddling his own thumbs. Perry realized what he was trying to do, as it was one of the many ways that her uncle had found to break the ice and lighten the mood. Determined not to crack, Perry lowered her head and scrunched up her eyebrows to provide a glare of warning. Not deterred, Martin matched the glare with one of his own, but added a guttural growl. And that was the key as Perry broke her angry face and giggled.

"Really, Uncle Em?"

"Oh, you know it!"

And she cracked. The smile that Sasha was so used to seeing plastered on her face was in full force on Perry's face. Despite the hard knock life, Martin always had the key to her heart.

"From what I heard from the good ol' grapevine, you hadn't had much to say so far about what happened. Classic stone face. I know, I get it. I am a Shiner, too. We try to keep everything close to the vest." Martin took a moment to grab a glass of water that was on the table. Half choking on a swallow that went down the wrong pipe, he pushed through, "But honestly, kiddo, you know we are here for you. We don't judge. We've been through shit just like you. Truly and honestly, we know. I mean, I know. It ain't been easy for you. I get it. But you don't need to hold it all in. Can I help? Dunno. Can I try? Only if you talk and open up."

Begrudgingly, Perry took a deep breath and let it out. "Well, what do you wanna know?"

Martin responded softly, "Take it from the top."

"I figured you'd say that. I guess it started with running into Lucy in the halls at school. She invited me over to a house after school. Supposed to be with some rich kids. I figured it was something nice that she threw my way, considering our past. It was just some new movie someone pirated. Yeah, before you read me the riot act, I didn't do it, just there to watch."

"What about you and Lucy? I mean, I haven't seen or heard from her in, I don't know, a year. You guys were more inseparable than flies on shit."

"Yeah, well time is a funny thing, I guess. Only thing I could come up with is that she was tired of being…"

"The outcast?" Martin interrupted.

"Yeah, the outcast. I had accepted that a long time ago. I am good with that."

"Are you?" Martin interrupted once again.

Taken aback slightly, Perry responded, "As much as I can."

"Fair enough. Continue onward, I swear I will try not to jump in anymore."

"Annnywho. I meet her up after school, and we head over. It was a dead-end place. Over in the Fifth Ave development. You know that area?"

"I have driven by it. Feel like a fish out of water in my used sedan with two car seats in the back."

"Yeah, big time money. The place we head to is this huge mansion. Not the new age McMansions, but a legit big ass house," Perry explained. Not being one to put out an expletive even as mellow as that drew an eyebrow raise from her uncle and aunt alike. Sasha had been creeping across the room as the conversation had been going on.

"So, you get to this pristine place, then what?"

"That's the thing. The place. It looks amazing in the distance. But once you get close, well it is a different story. It was kind of like those pictures you see with all of the tiles."

"A mosaic."

"Exactly, it was like a mosaic. Or a Monet. One of those paintings that look great from a distance. The moment I got inside the fence, everything was just wrong. You would think that everything would be all put together, but this place, for a bookoo bucks house, was just out of sorts. Plants were dead, paint was peeling. The inside could have been straight from a low budget horror movie. The girl that lives there goes in and out. Not really here or there. That wasn't the problem. The other girl. She was the problem. She was all out of sorts, crazy as a nutjob one moment, the next she was all put together, cool and collected."

"Like bipolar?"

"Not at all. She seemed like she was someone else at one point. Her frazzled self seemed bad, but then the calm side came out and it was downright terrifying."

"Got it."

"Then, the movie starts. That is when everything went south. The crazy one is back and she is smacking me around. Not really trying to beat my teeth out, but it was something different. That is when I realized what it was about. She was trying to smear peanut butter all over me."

Martin cringed when he heard the last part. Perry always had a peanut allergy. It hadn't been fatal, but it really could make a lasting impression. A detail that intimate was something Perry had always been careful with whom she shared.

"I tried to fight back. Couldn't get out of there. I guess someone must have called some help."

"Lucy?"

"I guess. She must have had a change of heart."

"What do you mean?" Martin asked, perplexed.

"Well, before all this happened, she slipped me some allergy drink. She knew it was coming."

"Oh, Perry…"

"Well, it sucks. But she must have saved my life. Not sure what would have happened if that hadn't happened."

"What do you think? About Lucy."

"I don't know. I wonder what I would do in her shoes. The more I think about it, I get it."

"Well, who else would have known about your secrets? What do you think about that?"

Martin was clearly alluding to Perry's allergies. That made her a bit sour and looked down. "Yeah, I get that too. But in the end, she was there for me. I think she wants to go back to where we were. She is having her birthday party this weekend. She invited me to come. No presents needed."

"Do you think it was out of pity?" Uncle Martin was not one to mince words sometimes. Occasionally, Perry thought she was talking to his significant other when she was really talking to him.

"Not really. It was pretty real. And it is at a place in town. You know Best Position Dance?"

"The dance place on Main Street, across from the Diner?" Martin asked.

"Exactly. It is on the other side. Right before the bridge."

"I got it. I have been by that place so many times, hard to say I remember the name. Then again, there isn't much in town that goes unnoticed."

"Anyway, she invited me. I am sure I can go. It is on Saturday.

Pretty sure nothing is going on at home. Even if it is, you promise you can give me a ride?"

"Perry, if it's something that your mother cannot help with, then we will be there." Perry was not too keen on that statement, but at least she found support in her family.

"Okay. Thank you, Uncle Em."

Nervously, Perry shifted around in her seat. Something was simmering below the surface, which Martin could sense, that was close to the top. Also closely looking was Sasha, who had shimmied almost over to the dining room, while keeping the boys at bay throwing assorted toys their way.

"Perry, is there anything else bothering you?" Martin asked bluntly.

"Well, yeah kind of," Perry responded. "I just don't know how to say it."

Martin appeared flabbergasted when he replied, "Perry, I am your uncle. There is not a goddamn thing that you can say that would bother me."

"Well on that note, there is this thing…"

"What thing?"

"When I have an episode. You know... when I have a reaction. I can't explain it. It is one of those things that if you don't live it, then you don't believe it."

"Okay…"

"Uncle Em, when I went into that state, that allergic state, I guess you can call it. I am not in my body. I guess how people who have a near death incident say they were not in their body. You know what I am talking about?"

Martin, not truly knowing where the conversation was leading but fully wanting to push it forward, continued, "Yeah. I think I heard about that in a TV show."

"I used to have horrible nightmares when I had reactions. Night sweats, constant dream running. You know, crazy stuff. But now it is completely different. Lately I have been having the same kind of dream. Same place. Same thing. Just a different conversation."

"What do you mean by different conversation?"

"I mean that each time I have been experiencing these things, I have been going to the same place and talking to the same person. Well, that...I am just not sure."

"Please continue, dearest niece."

"Easiest way to say this is the quickest. I have been talking to a big bluish, furry thing that sounds like a little girl."

With that. Martin halted the jovial back and forth. His demeanor turned to stone. "Not sure I am following."

"Didn't think you would. I was in some strange forest. This thing was there, and we actually talked. Not only talked, but we also had a conversation. It was the craziest. The first time I just put it on a weird dream, you know? Anyone would. But the next time, well it was the same thing, kind of like a continuation of the last time I was there. And you know what? That made it one hundred percent real. That wasn't a dream."

"Oh, okay," Martin added cautiously. "What did you talk about?"

That question stopped Perry. The answer was not so easy. Even if Uncle Martin, and the overhearing Sasha, who was obvious to Perry from the beginning, could really understand, she truly doubted it would really set it.

"It was just real. I just wanted to be still. Just to be well."

MISSY 1

The whole ordeal only took a matter of minutes. It all worked out as good as it could. When Missy had rolled towards the house, she had turned off the beater's headlights and crept slowly to park it on the street. His truck was right where she was hoping, parked cockeyed in the middle of the driveway. It was the telltale sign that the old bastard took off to belly up to the bar after work. He was a man of habits, and habits turned into predictability. The one thing that Missy had always made sure of was that she would never grow up to be like him. If a person becomes predictable, the game is over.

There was a time that Missy truly believed that everything was fine. That the two of them could manage to the point they could develop as a family. There was nothing more that she wanted or yearned for. But all that was when she was young, dumb, and frigging naive. Whenever she was reminded of back then, anger boiled up from her insides. Even as a child, how could she have been so stupid. It all went downhill from there, and Missy swore that would never happen again.

Missy had quietly cracked the door open to exit, and closed it softly, just enough to have the latch click. Something about keeping to the shadows and being the aggressor was extremely arousing to her. Something about not being taken advantage of, something about being the one wielding the power, something about being the inflictor not the acceptor. All of it was intoxicating, and, when that bottle was open, Missy was not taking that from her lips.

Slipping from the ebony shadows that the large oak in the front provided had kept Missy like a ghost avoiding the moonlight. If anyone had looked out of a window and was lucky enough to spot her, the only thing that was visible were the stained teeth that she bared out to the world. Each step brought her to salivate more and more. The anticipation was building and every sign that Missy found as she approached the house was glowing with good signs.

Rather than walk right in through the front door, which was surely locked because good ol' Reggie was as predictable as the sun rising in the east, Missy hugged the outside of the house while spinning around to ensure there were no unlucky spectators. No one in sight, Missy calmly made her way to the backyard. The chain linked gate was rusted shut, with the lock broken amongst the debris at the base of the fence. But the roadblock was just a mere pause in her mission. With a quick jab up on the rusted mechanism, the latch popped up, and she was on her way.

The yard was even more disheveled than it was since the last time Missy had seen it. Assorted car parts were strewn across the place, with tall grass popping through empty spaces. The decay of the area was palpable in the moonlit night. A newer addition to the backyard was what appeared to be a newly wrecked sedan. Clearly another fixer upper, as Reggie had always claimed. Each time was another project that would end up being discarded like everything else. Worst yet, when he finally conceded defeat, then the rage would build up. Once the rage built up, the rage was taken out. Missy was the only one around…

As she was scanning the grassy enclosure that faintly resembled the location of her youth, Missy caught sight of something in the back. Hidden behind the various debris was a structure still standing. It was leaning quite a bit and the overhang door was well beyond the point of opening. Moss and ivy had crept up its sides, and the lone window was missing parts of its glass. Despite its broken down look, the place was still the same structure. It was the shed in the backyard. It was the first place that…

"*Never a-fuckin-gain*," went through Missy's mind. Her teeth clenched up to the point that she didn't think she would be able to move her jaw again. Instinctively, both hands became balled up tightly. Every fiber of her being went from excitable to unhinged rage. She began huffing like an infuriated bull ready to gore. Harnessing that pure and unadulterated fury, Missy stormed towards the porch. She grabbed the knob of the back door firmly. The lock was not engaged. Just as she had expected. This cat never changed its stripes.

As she was about to rip the door open and unleash holy hell upon the only familial link to this world, Missy hesitated. The opportunity that was in front of her right now seemed too good to pass up. Unless something had drastically changed, Reggie hadn't had any friends in the area to care if he didn't make it out of the house anytime soon. There was that ugly bitch O'Grady down the street, but Missy was sure he fucked that up. He always fucked it up. If things were still the same, whatever job he was at was something that he just started. Probably under the table. No insurance to speak of. He never had insurance. What a provider. At this point in the night, he wasn't feeling anything much more than regret and his crotch. Easy fucking pickin's.

The more pressing need was the house. Missy could use some cover for the time being. She needed to figure out what her next moves were. The end goal was the two of them. What they did to her was inexcusable and they needed to be punished. They needed to feel the pain.

"Two birds with one stone," Melissa whispered to herself. Everything was back under control. The sloppy other one could have left something to chance. There wasn't much room for error. "No mistakes. We will get this done."

Still gripping the knob, Melissa turned it and entered without making a sound. Once she was inside the dining room, her steps were all calculated, and not one of them landed on a squeaky board. Nary a heel touched the floor, but by the time she made her way to the kitchen Melissa was walking on the fronts of her toes. The anticipation was back. Feeling the closing of a chapter made everything exhilarating. The noises from the cluttered living room sounded like it was either a late-night low budget horror movie or a high budget tug job flick. Either way, good times for all involved.

Once she made it to the kitchen, Melissa slowly pulled a knife out of the butcher block. Each one of them was of a different set, and half of them didn't fit into the slots they were clumsily shoved to their place. In the end it didn't matter. Melissa meticulously removed each one at a time to inspect their worthiness. The flay knife seemed too flimsy. The steak knife was a lot better, but it didn't seem enough. The paring knife was nice, but too small. The chef's knife...that would be it. Large enough to do major damage. Not too big to be unwieldy. The coup de grace was found at the end. The tip had been broken off. Whether it was purchased like that at the local flea market or good ol' Reggie had troubles opening a can of baked beans. It didn't matter. It'd be just fine.

With the knife in tow and a smile touching one ear to the other, Melissa tiptoed from the kitchen towards the living room. The glow from the television illuminated the details of the room. The amount of junk and waste that was covering the floor made it difficult for the average person to maneuver without alerting the slouch on the recliner. But that was the average person. Melissa confidently stepped over all the obstacles that laid between her and moving on.

In no time, Melissa was directly behind the used Lay-Z-Boy. She noticed that her instincts on the night's entertainment were spot on, as Reggie's pants were undone and halfway down his thighs. That made her job even easier.

As Melissa placed her palm on the old man's forehead, he was caught off guard to the point where his hands, which were diligently working on their previous duties down south, had no time to spring up to defend. Melissa figured it was the overpowering smell of booze that saturated the entire house. Reaction times were completely deadened, all playing to her advantage. As Reggie tried to bring his hands up towards his head, they got caught in the folds of his pants. When it rained it should as hell poured.

Melissa put the point of the knife up against the side of Reggie's neck. Panic ran completely through Reggie's body. Being caught with his pants down in more than one way was too much for him to take. The hardness subsided, and the fear and flaccidness set in. Everything was just going her way.

Melissa leaned in, knife tip pressed securely against the side of Reggie's neck, and started whispering in his ear, "It has been a long time. Did you miss me? I am sure you have. All of those late nights. After each and every beer. Thinking about what you had done to me. Just getting back from school. Having to clean the house and make some dinner. Oh, but you loved your dessert. It didn't matter if there wasn't enough more for booze and food for us, it was always beer for dinner and then dessert. Do you remember those nights?"

Shivering for his life, Reggie could not respond. The number of empties on the floor showed he was too far gone to respond.

"Well, I do. I relive each and every one of those encounters each and every night. When I close my eyes. It is just like one of those old tapes you put in the VCR. The tracking wasn't all too good, but you got the idea. Every single detail is placed in my head, just as it happened. The sights. The smells. The feel of your touch. It is all so fresh and so real. For you? Just another hazy dream, I guess."

Tears were now rolling down Reggie's face. The end was near, and, whether he was sober enough to understand it, a world of pain faced him.

"I could keep going. I could keep telling you how much you messed up my life. How much you took from me. How much you destroyed my future. I could, but I won't. See the thing is the day of reckoning is here. For the first time in your life, you have something I need. And

I am going to take it."

Melissa exerted a small amount of force onto the knife handle. The jagged end popped through the skin and punctured a jugular vein. Feeling that she had passed the moment of no return, Melissa held the handle just where it was. Hoping to keep the neighborhood oblivious to the situation, she didn't want to provide any opportunity for a fight back. But she did wish to savor all that she could.

A few low whimpers from the decrepit old man were all that Melissa needed to shut the door on the previous sections of her life. In one swift motion, she forced the remainder of the blade into his neck, and, with the strength of many men, twisted it a full ninety degrees. As the knife spun, sprays of blood coated Melissa's smile along with the side of her face. She could taste the iron flavored emancipation throughout her mouth. With one more push, the remainder of the blade made its way through the rest of Reggie's neck like room temperature butter, and the jagged tip poked out the other side. Any possible squirming or push back came to an abrupt end. What he thought of his life was gone for sure.

With the job completed, Missy let go of the handle, leaving the chef knife remaining in its victim like a carving knife in a roast. Satisfied with herself and how everything went, she rose back upright and let the moment sink in. The man who had damaged her youth, who broke her innocence was gone. In her mind, it was glorious and could not have gone any better.

Life had been an endless pile of shit for Missy, but ever since she made that simple agreement with the drifter, everything seemed to be pointing up. He was very strange to say the least, even to her, but the promises he made were too good to pass up. Missy had heard plenty of promises in her time, but the only ones that had been followed through had been from law enforcement. The goddamn cops were the worst and had always pissed on her parade. But she could rely on them always following through.

Missy remembered that chance encounter and had played it back in her mind each time she closed her eyes. Seeing how far she had come in such a short amount of time, she took a moment, closed her eyes, and took a deep breath. The replay started immediately.

***

The previous days had been blurring into one. Each day worse than the last. There was a streak of a solid week that Missy thought her maker was around the corner, waiting for her to trip. Her short life seemed destined to come to an abrupt end. Then she did trip, but a hand was there to help brace her fall.

It was a Tuesday a few weeks back. Missy was days away from making her way back to Hex Point. Every other little shitty town had run her out, but not before she became well acquainted with the local cops and cheating husbands. Sometimes they were one in the same. But at each little hell hole, Missy made sure not to kick up too much dust and land herself in county. The line was fine, and she was good at it. A spare wallet here or there, enough to get by. But the life of a vagrant grew tiring. She had been on the run, running from the past. It was enough, so she pulled one last job, but once she was done with old man Joe Executive, he caught her swiping his wallet on the way out. He swung and connected with her jaw. Who knows if it was broken or not, but she took his nose and put it up into his cranium. The kicker was Missy used the only thing that wasn't nailed down in the rundown roach motel, the goddamn Bible.

She had to get out. With the old man's keys in tow, Missy hopped in the beat-up Benz that he was driving. She figured it was less flashy in that seedy part of town to ride the used and abused one, probably a kid's or the unloving spouse. Either way, she had wheels. The whole situation gave her massive flashbacks to her childhood. The similarities were too eerie not to think there was some divine intervention. In that position, Missy took control. Payback time, and to do that she had to head home.

Before Missy could get reacquainted with the town, she had been spotted by the local force. Even though they could have been of great help with things, the cops always liked Reggie. They went way back, chummy pals, some of them. Her nerves hit high, and she did the only thing she could think of and pulled off Main Street to a dirt road and dropped off her lights. For the first time in a long time, Missy's heart dropped down through her stomach. She was being followed through the trees, but the cruiser behind her didn't engage their flashers or siren. They were slow playing it too.

Missy killed the engine and slunk down deep into the driver's seat. She positioned her head so that she could peek over to see anything. A blinding light illuminated the inside. Most likely one of the damn strong flashlight clubs they carried. Wishing to live to see another day, Missy slunk lower, out of sight if anyone should approach.

The light continued to get brighter. One of the officers sure as hell was getting closer. A knot formed in Missy throat. She had been teetering on the precipice of legal trouble for a long stretch, but she never thought it would come to this. First degree murder, she knew the jury wouldn't buy her self-defense defense with her suspect past, along with a litany of peripheral charges. That would be hard time for sure. But that didn't stop the officer from rounding the corner. No favors could be asked in exchange for freedom with what was looming over her head.

Before she knew it, the officer was standing outside the driver's door, light held slightly above his shoulder. As blinding as it was, and damn painful to boot, Missy could make out some of his features as he leaned in for a closer look. She recognized him instantly. The gash across his right cheek gave it away. It was Officer Harris of the HP Police Department. While he wasn't always on the up and up in town, it always seemed like he had a conscience. Now things were real.

Officer Harris leaned in further towards the glass. His face nearly touched it, as it began to fog up from his breath. His eyes searched around and came to rest directly on Missy's. Game over.

Officer Harris reached to his shoulder and engaged his radio.

"This is Harris. I found an abandoned vehicle off Main Street. Looks like it has been here for a while… Hard to tell, must have been here for ages. I would say it is a Mercedes… I already said that. Off of Main. There is a small dirt road… Are you serious?" Officer Harris stood up straight and shone his light throughout the empty forest. "I don't see anything. But I am not taking any chances. Can someone call for a tow of this thing in the morning? It ain't going anywhere… Okay, I am leaving now."

With that, Officer Harris made his way back to his patrol car, all the while looking over his shoulders to scan the area with his flashlight. Satisfied that he was alone, he got into the vehicle and backed it out towards Main Street. In an instant, he was back on the street and long gone, and Missy was alone, narrowly missing the end of her road. She was as relieved as she was curious. She had seen the man's pupils, that is how close they had come to each other. A moment later, he genuinely believed that the stolen car was abandoned. Nothing about it made any sense.

Before she could make any sense of the bullet she just dodged, a voice came from the passenger seat.

"Close call, huh?" whispered the froggy, low voice next to her.

Her heart dropped, the knot in her throat seized up, and Missy partly soiled herself. The car door did not open, but there was someone clearly inside of the vehicle with her. Her eyes were still adjusting from being partly blinded by the flashlight, so she couldn't make out who or what was now occupying the car. All that she could make out after blinking and rubbing like a mad woman was a very indistinct shadow figure sitting upright in the passenger seat.

"That cop almost had you, didn't he?"

Absolutely confused and equally astonished, all Missy could manage was a few incoherent mutters.

"I gotcha. Cat got the ole' tongue. It happens. Happens all the time."

Still nothing came out of Missy's agape mouth.

"Well, I figure that we could make a great team."

"W-what are you… who are… what the hell…" Missy replied. Her eyes were slowly adjusting back to the dim ambient lightning of the night sky. Her vision was playing games with her, as the shape of her new companion was fading in and out. Nothing made any sense.

"Oh, you can talk. That is just dandy. That will work for both of us. Thought for a second you were a mute. One of those strange fellas," the low voice continued. "Now that we figured out you can talk, then let us chat, shall we?"

"O-okay."

"Wonderful," the shadowy figure responded, crossing its legs while holding his raised knee. "I do not think we were properly introduced. You can call me Red. Not my birth name, but what you may call my given name. Not too clever to those who gave it," he leaned forward towards Missy, and his body caught a few of the strong moonlight beams that had gotten through the trees and into the car. The light illuminated his upper half, and what could be seen was terrifying. His hair slowly floated around his head with streaks of deep crimson weaved through his curly locks. It didn't appear natural, but nothing about him did. One of his eyes glowed with a bright green pupil. The other was completely black, devoid of any color. The smile that he wore across his face accentuated the maze of scars that made their way from what appeared to be the inside of his mouth outward. Worst of all, every outline of his features and frame were indeed slowly changing shape the way a one celled amoeba would. His whole appearance was quite shocking to Missy, but there was something intriguing that nearly put her at ease. She was in deep, and there must have been a reason this man, or whatever it may be, was in the vehicle with her.

"And you might be?" Red inquired curiously.

"Missy," she answered obediently.

"Missy, pleased to meet you. Your name is no doubt short for Melissa. I can see that you are not the kind of person who likes their real name. Maybe from a bully growing up, or an abusive family member using it during the dark recesses of your memories."

"What the hell are you?" Missy asked curtly.

"Well, I am the one that just saved your skin from a long sentence in prison. I think you would be more appreciative."

"What are you talkin' about? That cop just couldn't see his asshole from a hole in the ground," Missy retorted, back to her usual self.

"Oh, well, he had some persuasion on him, that is for sure. You see, I can provide some help with your situation. Like I just did as an example. People can see what I want them to see. It is a very enjoyable ability. And it looks to me that you would need the help of someone like me."

"I can manage just fine."

"How long before someone finds the body of that poor middle-aged bastard you left sniffing his brains? Or find some evidence of his car driving around a quaint little town like this? It is just a matter of time before you are found, my dearest."

Shocked, Missy stammered on, "W-who the he-hell told you? W-w-who the fuck are *YOU*?"

Sensing the palpable fear hung within the car, Red retreated from the moonlight just enough to leave his mouth visible, the rest of his body melded with the shadows. "Me? I am just someone with a proposition. See, I have something that you need. I can help you. You started to take control of your life. I can help you finish that job."

"What do you want from me?"

"Well, I just need a little help too. There are only some things that I can do. Many I cannot, unfortunately. I just need to take something from someone. Nothing much. Based on your experience, it should be a problem."

"Why me?"

"That is a wonderful question. See, you have potential that I can help unlock. A force is running through your veins, and I can bring it to the surface."

No more words were spoken. Red, just as he appeared in the car, was gone. Missy couldn't help but smile.

***

Leaving the body to go through its final shakes and convulsions as the blood had already started to coagulate throughout the scene, Missy headed to the kitchen again. This time not to arm herself, but instead she picked up the phone and plugged away at the numbers. The voice on the other end picked up on the second ring.

"It's Missy… We got some work to do."

MARTIN 4

The alarm rang out through the room, beckoning him out of his slumber. The events that transpired yesterday completely drained Martin's internal batteries. Sasha had seen it before retreating to bed and took the liberty of pushing the time on the alarm back a few hours. Rather than rising before he gave the sun a chance to, the roles were reversed, and Martin was rising second this Thursday.

After waking up and slowly making his way downstairs, Martin was still trying to digest his conversation with his niece. Nothing really made sense, but everything did make sense. He could not point his finger on it. For everything that he could tell, Perry was being completely sincere in what she believed. That much was completely obvious. She was never a child to make up stories and lead her family on wild goose chases, or in this case wild blue monster chases. She was genuine in what she experienced, but the story was so far-fetched, Martin questioned whether something else was at play. Maybe a chemical reaction or a hallucination. But on the other hand, would he also question his own strange experience?

Martin went to the kitchen to find it devoid of his family. The remnants of breakfast were still laying across the table. Cereal boxes left open on the countertop stood next to used dishes. Luckily, the jug of milk was tucked away in the refrigerator. It was a scene that he rarely saw, but it was usually when Martin was in charge of the twin's hurricane. Then again, as focused and controlled as Sasha could be, sometimes the boys could overpower even the greatest of challengers.

After glancing around at the scene, Martin happened upon a post-it next to the home phone. What it said cleared every question.

Took Perry home
Dropping kids off at school
Was running late, sorry for the mess

Having been in that boat many times before, Martin took a moment to put everything back as best he could. It was the least he could do, considering the mayhem that he must have slept through. With everything put away in their respective cabinets, Martin took a moment to review his work calendar. For a change of pace, there were no meetings or conference calls in the morning.

"Well, after working over the weekend, I think I am due for a short break," Martin spoke out loud to himself. He didn't need much convincing, the new boss in the office was a complete idiot. Just roll those extra hours over to today, and suddenly the morning was clear.

With a quick peek outside, the weather looked optimal. Overcast, a slight breeze, no precipitation. Good time to get a quick run in. The time was not ideal. With rush hour rapidly approaching, there would be more and more obstacles out and about. In the end, Martin couldn't be dissuaded. Before switching from pajamas to running gear, he jotted a quick addition to Sasha's note.

Went for a run. Be back later.

For the first time in a while, Martin made no mental plans before leaving the house on his running excursion. He kept his mind from any time or distance goals. There were a few times that he had done it in the past, and it usually turned out quite refreshing. While he had no course to map out, he did know exactly where he intended to end up. He had to go back. Answers were paramount.

Martin headed out, and, before long, he was headed down Main Street. He was quite unaccustomed to the amount of cars and trucks steaming by him only a few short feet away. It gave him an uneasy feeling. There existed the off chance that one of the vehicle operators might be distracted or tired or inebriated. He could easily be wrapped up in a bloody wreck of twisted metal, limbs scattered. Of course, the odds of this happening were slim to none, but that damn slim was always problematic.

The sights and sounds, and even smells, were very different a mere few hours later than Martin had usually hit the streets. The world had appeared to be nearly fully awake, with commuters scurrying around through town, making their way to whatever destination awaits them. The amount of traffic moving along seemed to be greater than the average Thursday in the mildly sleepy part of New Jersey. Even the number of patrolmen appeared to be double the norm. Martin couldn't think of anything in the area and time proximity that would necessitate a large police force nor the added number of commuters.

As Martin passed through the heart of downtown, he saw customers in and out of the Diner. When he passed the front of the plaza, patrons were entering and exiting at the same time, allowing the wonderful aromas to waft out and flood the humble little town. The scents of a myriad of freshly baked goods and tantalizing breakfast meats made Martin's mouth water subconsciously. If it wasn't for his wallet sitting on the kitchen countertop, which Sasha tended to remind him to keep his personal effects while out of the house, he might have broken his morning run off early and indulged himself. He even thought he might be able to get a meal on credit and pay after he got home. Martin had frequented Morey's a fair amount, with and without the family. He was friendly with some of the wait staff, it could be possible.

As soon as that thought crept into his mind, Martin pushed it out. This wasn't just a typical jog. He had a purpose, and it wasn't just to break his times. He fully intended to go back to the forest, where he had come to the fence and to the hypnotic light show. And where he, and his running shoes, had been somehow mysteriously healed of his wounds.

Martin pushed onward. Once past the plaza containing Morey's as well as various other little shops and offices and subsequently the bridge, the forest rapidly approached on his left. For all the runs in the wee hours of the early morning, the location looked amazingly different during a later early morning jog. The trees danced in the sunlight, the bushes swayed with the gentle breeze rolling off the lake, and the branches twisted and turned. Everything moved in lockstep, creating a mental matrix of a siren drawing a sailor towards a rocky death. The enticing environment even felt alive.

With each step, the wilderness drew closer. Once past the bridge, a path appeared, that cut through the overgrown thickets and ran like a fork in the road. His synapse fired all over his skull. The forest was inviting him back in again. His first experience was the same, just backwards. These entries into wood were not natural, they did not resemble animal crossings or teenager trails into nowhere. As Martin's father had once told him 'When an opportunity arises, take it'. He was never too sure how applicable the motto of life was and what tight spot Martin had got himself into, but he always felt it was a smart thing to do or say for that matter.

Once he got to the opening of the path, Martin veered to his left. He was not concerned with the potential snoopers that lurked along Main Street, on the sidewalk or behind the wheel. It was not unusual in this day and age to see someone alongside a main road out for a morning run and opting to take the road less traveled.

The moment Martin pulled from Main Street, he realized that the forest had the same vibes as the other morning, only much more excitable. It appeared to Martin that the mighty oaks were actually moving across the forest. When he approached a root system, spanning many feet and treacherously jutting upwards in the air, his foot, surprisingly and not surprisingly at the same moment, caught the upper edge of a root causing him to stumble slightly. After his last deflating tumble in this area, Martin slowed himself and regained his balance.

"Fool me once, shame on me," Martin muttered under his breath.

Continuing on, the ominous fence broke into Martin's line of sight. All the confusing emotions bubbled back up to the surface. The aged metal stood looming not far away. The details that remained unseen in the predawn hours were brought forth into the light. The stoic, mangled appearance of the structure made Martin feel even more uneasy and intimidated. The fact that nothing natural had laid its hands onto the fence reinforced his feelings of this place.

Once he was closer, there was one discernable feature that Martin was taken aback by. It was illuminated by the rays of light that made their way to the forest floor. Completely obvious and exposed in a clearing of trees laid a gaping hole within the fence. From afar it appeared relatively minor, but as he approached it became clearer. The missing portion was not very small in stature. It was a large missing section. Martin stopped to a halt as it set in. The metal was torn and bent outward. The angles of the prongs did not feel a result of some type of machinery. Whatever or whomever was responsible for this impressive, yet horrifying feat must have been massive.

As Martin was surveilling the opening, his eyes began playing tricks on his brain. One of the wide white oak trees that was set a stone's throw behind the fence was not the steady anchor piercing the veil of the upper crust. Without moving himself the mighty arbol slowly peeked past the twisted metal, inched through the open area it now inhabited, and tucked behind the other side of the fence. In his entire life, Martin hadn't seen anything close to what his eyes were seeing, albeit without anything recreational. It would have made more sense if its roots had pulled out of the ground and walked around like a wooden octopus. Then again, the experiences that he had experienced during his last excursion made it much more plausible.

Trees shifting around the landscape aside, the place exuded the strange and creepy aura just as much in the daylight. Every nerve in Martin's body was firing on all cylinders, making him a combination of queasy and uneasy.

"I shouldn't be here…," Martin whispered under his elevated breath.

"*Be still,*" came from inside the barricade.

In the blink of an eye or between a worried heartbeat, Martin froze. The voice was faded and hoarse. It was in no way similar to the voice he heard speak those same words. That only made the entire situation even more unstable.

"Martin," the little girl's voice spoke this time, and he was sure that it was the same one from yesterday. "Martin, I need you to help."

Surprisingly, instead of losing the ability, Martin was able to respond. "Who are you? How do you know my name?" He found himself involuntarily creeping towards the opening in the fence. Across the scene, there was no strange light phenomenon. No footsteps. All that Martin could hear was his own heartbeat pumping through his skull. As much as he wanted to turn around, vomit and run as hard as he could back home to wash the memory of this place away, something pushed him forward. Whatever was hidden in the ether had called out his name, and he was pretty sure it was not a hallucination or audio matrixing. And above that, the voices that had called out to him sounded benevolent. While attempting to move his feet from their firmly planted stance, the smell surrounded him. Cinnamon.

Martin slowly traversed through the gaping hole in the fence and into the other side. Once he was fully through, everything seemed to gain an extra level of detail. The trees throughout the enclosure were indeed drifting left and right and back and forth, aimlessly moving about. A thick mist hung low deeper into the forest, keeping him from truly inspecting the area to its fullest. The most astounding part lay behind him. The wrought metal fence behind him was not at all the same on this side. When Martin twisted his torso to get a look at where he came from, he found he was inside an ornate rock wall with intricate details and carvings from base to top. Odd animal looking creatures made of marble stood fastened to the top as if overlooking the inside. The opening which Martin had entered was now a section of this masonry that was carefully removed, with blocks and stones placed in organized piles on either side. What had previously appeared to be a result of a forceful exit was now showing evidence of an orderly removal.

Steps crunching dry leaves on the ground brought Martin back to reality and turned his attention to his forward. As the trees meandered around, one of them moved to reveal someone or something standing in the distance. Once again, Martin could not believe what images his eyes were bringing to his mind. Then again, nothing made much sense at this time.

What stood afar was a massive, stout-looking blue being. From that distance, the only details that Martin could make out was not much. He could not make out any head or limbs or anything that might give him a hint at what lay before him. A haziness blended its outer edges with the woods around it.

"*Martin…,*" it called out to him. In any other instance, Martin would have hopped on his horse and got the hell out of there. This time was different. He noticed an arm extending from its left side, as if beckoning him to approach. Martin obliged.

As he began to walk towards it, Martin slowly took his time, and placed each foot carefully. The trees, and in turn their sprawling roots, were moving around randomly in lockstep. He paused occasionally so as not to get it any one of their ways. A human going up against an enormous, uncompromising tree would turn out bad anyway possible. It was smart to be cautious.

Martin grew closer and closer, and with that so did the details of the being. What he perceived as haziness was actually hair. But it was not hair in the normal sense. More like thick tendrils that floated in a nonexistent breeze. Enormous, solid, black eyes were placed deep in an oversized head. A mouth, devoid of fangs or sharpened teeth, stretched from one side to the other, and hung agape showing wide, flat teeth and a curling, red tongue set back inside. While it appeared striking in the fact that it shouldn't exist, it was not the thing that nightmares are made of, rather a cozy, confidant of a little child.

Once Martin had gotten within ten feet, his feelings seemed to be justified. Despite standing over twice his own height, the deep blue thing provided no intimidating sense. It was, on the other hand, more inviting than anything as if one of the largest rewards that one can win at the boardwalk had come alive and inhabited a haunted wood.

They stood there still, face to fuzzy face. Martin thought that they were staring into each other's eyes, but he could not tell because what he was looking at appeared closer to buttons than eyes.

"We did not mean to scare you," a little girl's voice came from inside the body. "We just needed to make ourselves known."

"Goal accomplished," Martin quickly answered.

"*You are Martin, uncle of Perry. Is that correct?*" the gruff, booming voice coming from the being's top.

"You didn't answer my question. How do you know my name?"

"If it is your name, then you must already know your answer."

"*Perry,*" Martin thought to himself. She had opened up about her dreams, and now he was smack dab in the middle of them.

"*That is correct,*" the strong voice answered his thought out loud. "*We have spoken with Perry. She has told us about you. Now seeing who you are, we are glad that our paths have already crossed.*"

"Why Perry?" Martin honestly questioned.

"We are like souls. Perry and myself."

That answer brought up many more questions. Seeing Martin quite perplexed, and now worried about his niece, the being continued.

"My name is Ofelia. You may call this body Cobalt. We are one. It truly cannot be explained at this time. Time is our problem. Perry had come to us and agreed to help us. Now we fear she is in danger,"

Ofelia explained.

"Danger? What kind of danger?"

"A vicious and unrelenting danger," she answered.

"Holy shit… Are you serious?" Martin worriedly asked.

"*Yes, we are.*"

Anxiety filled up Martin's facial features. Life had not been going well for Perry lately, and in general, but he had always felt like a father figure in her life. And he cared for her dearly. Any threat to herself, even the most mundane, brought the protective ire out of him. That was always the reason Martin tried to pull his sister through into the light, anything to help make things easier for his beloved niece.

"From you?" Martin accused.

"No, please. It is not in our nature to harm. In fact, we are the opposite. Please remember your wounds."

Martin looked down at his knee, and, below that, his shoe. It was hard to argue with the evidence. He should have felt more skeptical, but, even with everything askew, deep inside he felt the little girl was being truthful.

After a deep inhale, Martin let it go and pushed the conversation forward, "So what do you need from me?"

"Protect Perry. Keep her safe. There is something else that has come through the waypoint. It is not just us here. What came through, well it is just our opposite. This thing thrives on chaos and manipulation. It is just evil. And it has eyes on her," Ofelia explained.

"Jesus, that is heavy." Martin took a moment to let everything settle in. "Yeah, I will protect her. Of course, she is like a daughter to me. What is this thing, what does it look like? How can it be beat?"

"*You cannot beat it,*" Cobalt replied bluntly.

"Martin, you will not be able to see it. It is cunning and slinks in the shadows. You can only see it if it wants you to see it."

Getting a bit exasperated at the task unfolding, Martin dropped his shoulders down. "What the hell. What can I do to something that can't be seen."

"It does nothing itself. It seeks out vulnerable, like-minded people to carry out its tasks. It makes them stronger, more confident. It provides them with what they were lacking, which makes them listen and obey without fail. That is what makes it dangerous," Ofelia explained.

"So, what, I need to find its zealots and stop them? What am I supposed to do? Tell the friggin' police that some big blue hallucination told me to stop a couple of crackpots that are supercharged by some unseen force that wishes to do harm to my niece? Do you know how quickly my ass will be thrown in the loony bin? This is insane. Why the hell..."

"*One,*" Cobalt interjected.

Caught off guard by the one word forced into his rant, Martin sat back on his heels.

"It will only be one person. It is not powerful enough for more than that. Even if it was, it thrives on the ability to make things drawn out and painful. It torments. It inflicts. It tortures. It must be stopped. To do that, you must find that one person, endowed with its deviousness."

"Okay, okay, that is a bit better. Not by much, but beggars can't be choosers my old man would always say. So if this thing can pass along powers to others, and it came from where you all did, then you can just give me some of that healing power. You know, as a backup plan. I ain't letting my niece get hurt."

"We cannot do that. Its power is different. The positivity that flows through us must stay with us."

"Great. Well, any other groundbreaking tips or special cheat codes that I can put in my back pocket? Like, if I swing a black cat by its tail thirteen times over my head during a full moon, will I grow wings?"

"*Be serious. This is serious.*"

"Just trying to process it, you know? Deflection issues or some shit like that. But this is me being serious. Anything else?"

"Time is not on your side," Ofelia pleaded. "There are only a few more days. Once that time has passed, the waypoint will be gone, this place will go back to what it was. We fear there is an urgency to its plan. It will try to strike and stop Perry."

"Stop Perry? What the hell does that mean?"

Both Ofelia and Cobalt sighed concurrently. Clearly there was a part of the story that was to be kept behind the wizard's curtain.

"Answer me, what is Perry doing?"

"She is helping us."

"How? What is she doing? C'mon you big blue hairball. This is my *NIECE* we are talking about. What have you done? Answer me!" Martin shouted firmly.

"We are also in danger. She agreed to help us. If she can, then everything will be as it should. Every part of this was her idea, she volunteered. It is her sacrifice."

The last sentence struck Martin in the heart. It was never a good word to use in a conversation, let alone one of this content and magnitude. But Martin could understand why Perry might agree. She has had a rough time, and no one would blame her. But all of that didn't mean that Martin couldn't try to intervene.

"Geez."

"She is a very powerful and strong person. We have no doubt she can do what she needs. We just need you to be there, to protect her. Everything will work out as it should as long as everyone tries their hardest."

Martin, dejected and overwhelmed, started to turn toward the entrance, or exit depending on who was looking. The severity of what was just explained to him hung heavy around his neck. In the end, he was sure he would do whatever he could for Perry, but he just didn't know what the whatever would be.

As he made his way back the way he came, Ofelia called out to him, "Whomever is out there, looking for her, is going to try to hurt her. Try to exploit her fears and weaknesses. That is what it flourishes on, makes it go stronger. Just look for someone that is targeting her."

His stomach balled up at once. Every part of Martin's body tensed up. It had already begun.

"*Shit…,*" Martin murmured under his breath. This entire level of craziness was set before him, and others that Martin had not met as of this point, appeared like a thousand-piece puzzle of a polar bear in a blizzard. It had just dropped on Martin's kitchen table, and he figured out the outside. The inside needed to be figured and fast.

The distance home, while being around two miles, went by like mere seconds with Martin sprinting all the way home.

PERRY 4

Trauma can make the average person shrink and erect walls for a long time. Once the damage is done, some people might throw in the white towel, call it a day, and lock themselves in their emotional house, never letting anyone else ever in. Given the events that led up to that Thursday morning, no one would blame Perry if she simply turned her back on the world. She had consistently been given a reason, not an excuse, to slam doors on friends and family. And, in the end, no one would have blamed her for following in the same, wobbly footsteps of her mother. In spite of all of the things against her, Perry kept her head held high, in desperate hopes that things would change, that the dues that she had paid growing up would grant her some type of amnesty later in life. And most of all, she wished that her home life would be even remotely normal, and that the relationship with her mother would become more strong than nonexistent. Even though Perry could have made the trek back on foot, she had asked to be dropped back off at home in the morning.

Sasha gave no pushback when Perry asked her first thing in the morning to drive her home. If she hadn't done so, her aunt would have tried to convince her that it would be okay if, given her grades and attentiveness to classwork, no one would give her harm nor pass any judgment. But it did not come to that, so Perry packed her things up and left.

"Will Uncle Em be okay?" Perry asked sincerely.

"He will manage. It is only picking up after the boys. I think a little daddy duty will do him good."

That brought a slight chuckle out of Perry and the twins parked in the back seat. Sasha was normally one of the most serious and compassionate people in her life. When she had ever made something close to a joke, it always gave Perry a pause followed directly by a smile.

"But on a serious note, Perry, you know you are always welcome at our house," Sasha offered. The switch back to stoicism sent Perry back deep into the passenger seat.

"Uh huh."

"Even if you just need to talk…"

"Yup…"

As Sasha started to drive off, she finally let loose a bit, as much as her personality could. She intentionally raised the volume of the radio and spoke a bit lower than her norm, keeping the boys out of the conversation. "Honestly, Perry, your mother is not going to change. Over all of these years that I have seen her waste, I have seen nothing that tells me that there will be any day in your lifetime that she will make that turn and get out of that tunnel she is stuck in. I am sorry if this hurts your feelings, but it is what I firmly believe."

Perry was completely flabbergasted. Never in her life had she heard her aunt speak like that, let alone about her sister-in-law. The content of her words, while shocking to hear, was not at all surprising. She had seen on many different occasions the two of them send daggers through the air at each other. The verbal animosity, from her mother, and the nonverbal, from Sasha, were present and accounted for every time the two were in each other's perimeter. With all the close calls and near altercations in the books, Aunt Sasha had always taken the high road and never spoke badly of Martha.

"Aunt Sasha, I was pretty sure that is how you had felt. I just always thought you were being nice, keeping the peace. Seeing the way she speaks to you…"

"And about me behind my back, I am sure."

"…Yes, that too. I am sorry for all of that. No one deserves that."

"Perry, please do not apologize for her actions. Nothing of that is your fault. There is absolutely no reason for you to feel like that."

"I just think that there is something that I can do. Something that will make her change. Just so she can be a mother. I just want that. I crave that, to be cared for unconditionally. I mean, I have never been grounded. She doesn't even care enough to ground me. Can you imagine that? It is just so disappointing." Perry paused a bit to think. "Please don't tell my mother."

"Do not worry about that," Sasha assured her, as she turned into the other Shiner's driveway. "It is safe with me."

"Thanks. I really hadn't told anyone that before. It kinda feels good."

"I understand." Sasha put the car into park and leaned over towards her niece. "In the end, you are responsible for yourself. You have turned out to be an amazing, intelligent, and mentally strong young woman. Don't stop growing. Don't stop reaching for your dreams. You can make all of that happen. You have the power, you got this far given all of that has been stacked against you."

Perry instinctively reached out and hugged her. She had never been a kid that showed much emotion, but in that instant someone for the first time had been very honest to her when it came to her home life. She could tell others wanted to say things like that, if not worse, but always held back. She was a thirteen-year-old girl, and what Aunt Sasha had opened up to tell her was something that she really needed.

The two held together in a warm embrace for a moment or two. Slowly, it was broken off when Sasha could feel the eyes on the two of them. Without turning to see if her feeling was correct, she simply let Perry go, looked her in the eyes, and said, "And please know, we are not trying to steal you from your mother. I don't know where your mother gets that from, but it is not true. We just care for you. You are family, and you will always be family."

The last part made Perry's eyes well up. It was at more than one moment that she heard her mother outright accuse Aunt Sasha, and implicitly accuse her own brother, that they were trying to take her only daughter from her. That always bothered Perry, she thought it was due to her mother knowing that she was such an absent, and overall shitty, mother.

Perry let go, grabbed her things, and exited the vehicle. With a quick wave back, Sasha was back on her way to her next drop off. Keeping her head down, Perry headed into the house, trying not to make eye contact as she passed through the door. Her mother left yesterday with no further resolutions or plans for going forward. On one hand, Perry desperately wished to get into some new clothes, grab her bookbag, and head out to school, avoiding any more uncomfortable or awkward conversations. They had always felt forced and reactive. But she dreaded the walk to school. The quickest way was through the Fifth Ave development for completely obvious reasons. Throw in an even more awkward car ride with her mother, and everything just screamed get to school as quickly as possible.

When Perry made her way into her house, she headed directly to her bedroom. Her mother was camped out in the living room by the window, keeping a keen eye on Perry's aunt. The moment she saw Perry inside, Martha approached her.

"Hey, I missed you," Martha blurted out. It was completely out of character. She was never one to say anything like that, and Perry found it more untrue than anything.

Perry tried to ignore it the best she could and went right into her room. She wasn't ready to talk like her mother was. Just a few moments, one to get her mind straight, one to get clean, one to pack up all her school things. She had to bum a ride from her mother to school, and there would be the inevitable conversation rather than silence.

Once she was done getting set in her room, Perry hopped out of her room, slinked past her mother, and darted to the bathroom. Martha gave her no resistance. At least she was cognizant of a high schooler's need to try to look and smell your best each day to avoid the heckling and comments she would have received if she didn't spend a few minutes.

Perry closed her eyes tightly, took a deep breath and held it. With her exhale, she whispered to herself, "Give me a chance to be your guiding light…" Once she opened her eyes, she turned the knob and left the bathroom, with Martha standing a few feet away in the hallway.

"I didn't mean to make you upset. I did, I really did miss you."

"Mom, can you drive me to school," Perry interjected, ignoring her mother's out of character comments.

"Oh, of course. I am glad you came home. Let's go to make sure you are on time."

The Shiner girls left the house with their things in tow, schoolbooks packed away in their bag for one and the other containing an apron and uniform for the latest waitressing job. Sitting back and buckled up, the two of them were off.

The drive to school was not very long, but, to Perry, it felt like forever. While she desperately wished to avoid the awkward conversations, it appeared her mother was on the other end of the spectrum.

"You know, Winky…"

"Please, you know I hate that name."

Seemingly not hearing a word her daughter had spoken, Martha didn't miss a beat, "I will always be your mother. I have my faults. I am not the greatest cook. I could afford to spend more time around the house. There are plenty of things that I could do. The problem is…," Martha paused as she pulled up to a red light. She turned towards Perry, trying to avoid eye contact. "You really can't teach an old cat any more new stripes."

Not caring where the conversation was meandering, Perry broke her mother out of her little preconceived diatribe by interrupting with, "I would like to go to Uncle Martin's house after school."

Taken slightly aback by the statement, this time Martha didn't invoke any venom towards her perceived enemy of a sister-in-law. Instead, Martha gave no resistance. "Oh okay. If that is what you need. Any reason?"

"Big exam tomorrow," Perry shot out without thinking. It was the first thing that came to her mind. In retrospect, going over to a house with a pair of rowdy and energetic twin boys might not be the greatest place to study, Perry continued her ruse. "Don't really know why, but I do my best review in their study."

"Okay, I guess that makes sense. How are you getting there? You aren't walking, are you?"

The question made Perry shiver down her spine. The sheer thought of coming across Missy again brought goosebumps over her arms. That was surely not going to happen again.

"Lucy's mom. She can drive me over."

And with that, the agreement was made. Martha was fine with Perry going over her brother's after school, and Perry didn't lie much to get to that point. And it wasn't much of a lie because each day had brought more tests at this time of year. She wasn't too sure why she wanted to go over, but she felt drawn. It did seem like a perfect time to have a sit down with her mother, spill out all her feelings and emotions, and try to heal. But deep down inside, that wasn't possible. Not at this time. Perry's time and effort was better spent with her loving uncle.

Martha pulled up in front of East Stone High School and put the car in park. "Take care, honey." That leaving comment took Perry by surprise. But it wasn't to the fact it was yet another out of character comment from her mostly missing mother. It was the sincerity at which it was said. Part of Perry felt like reversing course and grabbing her mother by the shoulders to hold her tight. She fought off that feeling, and left the car, not even realizing she didn't return the touching favor.

Perry navigated the crowds of kids either loitering or scattering towards the main hall, with the first warning bells ringing out through the halls. Through the mess of teenage chaos, she spotted a set of eyes locked on her.

"PEEEE!" yelled out Lucy from the front of the building. With everything that had transpired recently, it was nice to see a friendly face. Perry did have lingering anxieties that had to be worked out with her friend, but there always had been an inviting nature with Lucy, and genuine to boot. Those times always had come to pass between the two of them.

Perry smiled and forced her small stature through the throng of teens. They wouldn't have much time to talk before the homeroom bells beckoned them, but any time would be a good thing.

"Hey Loose!"

Once they were close together, Lucy grabbed Perry by the arm, and led her into the halls. They only had a few short minutes before both would have to scurry away to opposite sides of the school.

"Pee, I really, really, really can't say sorry enough. I didn't tell them about the peanut thing meaning to hurt you. We were talkin' one day, and Tania was having some kind of reaction, and it just came up. I just let it out. I didn't mean to, but I did. If I can take it back, I would…"

"Loose, don't worry."

"I just feel so bad about it. I couldn't sleep a bit until I talked to you, and then I still couldn't until I finally saw you…"

"Lucrecia Avendale, quiet you!" Perry shot her way, jokingly.

Lucy chuckled and obeyed. Not much time went by, but not much left.

Perry continued, "Lucy, I get it. If I were in your shoes, I cannot not say I would have done the same thing. If my English makes any sense."

"Clear as mud. How are you feeling? You don't look half bad for what happened."

"Foggy. And confused," Perry answered as the duo zigzagged through the traffic. "How on God's green earth did I get out of that scene? The last thing I remember was that she-beast going to town on my back."

"Tania's father had just pulled in and was upstairs. Heard my screams, and called the cops on Missy and or Melissa, but she booked it before they arrived. That is a whole nother thing."

"Yeah, talk about someone off her meds. Looked like she was a prize fight loser with that busted jaw. What about you? How are you doing?"

"Not even a flesh wound. That drugged out Tania did leave me with some bruises, ones you can see and ones you can't. With that one, the kicker was the cops just took our stories, didn't write much down, and straight up left. I guess just another perk that money can buy. What a mess, Pee."

"You can say that again."

"What a mess, Pee," Lucy grinned. They were in the center of the school, each needed to depart in opposite directions to push along the school day. Both stopped for a second, to give short parting words.

"Seriously, Pee. My mom doesn't want me walking around before and after school with this. She is picking me up. I don't blame her, I don't feel safe thinking those two are out there. Dunno what I would do if I came across them in a dark alley."

"I would kick that she-beast in her balls as hard as I could, then exit stage right." Both let out a hardy laugh. "Seriously, Loose. Do you mind if I bum a ride from your mom?"

"Duh, of course she would do that. I am guessing your mother is going to be not able to do her motherly duties at that time of the day?"

"Actually, nothing like that for once. Well, the day is long, so you never know. I want to go to my uncle's house after school."

"No worries, sure it'll be fine." With that, the last homeroom bell began to blare through the halls, and the two darted towards their respective rooms.

***

Once the final bell rang out, Perry waited for Lucy at the front of the school. The entire time while she was out there feeling exposed,

164

she made sure to keep her head on a swivel. She felt like a wounded gazelle alone on the savanna during the dry season. Paranoia made her feel like all sets of eyes were on her, watching her every movement. Luckily for her, those few short minutes, while feeling like hours, came and went once Lucy exited the entrance. There were further pleasantries exchanged, but neither felt ready to continue their earlier conversation. Instead, the two gossiped in the back seat of Mrs. Avendale's sedan while their impromptu chauffeur escorted them around town. Once they pulled into Uncle Em's driveway, the chit chatting slowed into goodbye's and thank you's.

"Are you still coming on Saturday?" Lucy asked as Perry was getting out of the back door.

"Of course, I am. I am not that much a dancer, but it should be fun," Perry replied.

"Yeah, you will have fun. It is mostly family friends that will be there. I didn't really invite anyone else. You know how it is."

Mrs. Avendale peeked through the rear-view mirror, "Do you need a ride home, honey?"

"No, thank you. I am sure I can bum a ride from my uncle."

"Well, if anything changes, just let Lucy know. We will figure it out."

Perry shut the door and made her way towards the house. As she approached, distant voices could be heard coming from the backyard. Instead of making her way into the house, Perry followed the outside around the back. There she found Uncle Martin playing a rumpus game of hide-and-go-seek with Tristan and Maddox, both of which didn't fully understand the being quiet or the hide part of the game. Even from afar, Perry could see the never-ending smiles that all three had pasted on their faces.

Perry couldn't help herself, so she crouched down and creeped closer to the lot of them. She found that Tristan was able to spend more than three seconds quiet and still in his hiding spot behind the slide. Perry got to his back and put her hand over his mouth. Instantly, Tristan shot his head around to see who was behind, and the smile, that only faded for a millisecond when it was taken over by the depths of fear, came back in full force. To him, Perry was the big sister he always wanted.

"Shhh. Let us get your Daddy instead," Perry suggested, to which he completely agreed with.

Both got low and stared at Uncle Martin, who was playfully peeking around the side of the shed, giving Maddox time to escape and get a head start. As soon as the five-year-old was out of his hiding space, he headed into the open, desperately trying to avoid his father in between involuntary cackling. Perry and her partner in crime seized the opportunity and shot out from the darkness. They both pounced on their unsuspecting victim once they were within distance. Martin went down in a heap under the weight of the three, as once Maddox realized what was happening, he nearly threw his body across the lawn.

The giggling and tickle attacks, the all-powerful secret move from a youngin's bag of tricks, caused tears of joy to run down both Uncle Martin and Perry's eyes. For a moment there in the backyard, with all the events that had transpired and all the ones that have yet come to pass, things were perfect. Cares were nonexistent. Stress was unheard of. The future was a worry for another time. But like everything in this world, nothing lasts forever. The perfection waned as it always does. Uncle Martin went from elated to confused as he processed what was going on.

"Perry. Is everything okay? Any reason you decided to crash our game of Kids-try-to-hide-but-Daddy-always-finds-them?"

"DAAH-deee!" Maddox clearly understood enough to take offense. "You got luckee dis time."

"Okay, okay, okay. You mighta made it out this time, kiddo, but I would have shirley got you next time!"

"His name is Maddex!" Tristan shot at his father.

"I know, I know, I know." Martin turned his attention to his niece once again, "But seriously, what's up, Perry?"

Perry's smile subsided. "Just didn't want to be home, that's all."

"Is that what you told your mother?"

Feeling caught, Perry grinned slightly and could feel a little redness in her cheeks.   Uncle Martin surely knew his favorite niece. "Something like that."

"Oh, Perry. I will let that slide."

The Shiners all made their way back from the grass and onto their feet, except for Maddox who was too busy making lawn angels while staring aimlessly into the clear sky.

Perry was the first to spot Aunt Sasha coming out of the house, into the backyard. For the first time that she could ever remember, Aunt Sasha had a look of worry on her face. She was never one to let her emotions show on her face, rather she was the absolute best at keeping things close to the vest. As she had stepped out completely onto the deck, Perry saw what the cause of such concern was. Two of Hex Point's finest in blue followed her closely behind.

The rest of the playmates saw those that were approaching, with the youngest not fully understanding what was going on. In all honesty, it appeared neither did Uncle Em. All of them, even Perry, had been quite upstanding citizens, and there really should be no reason why they were here.

"Oh shit, they are here for me," Perry thought to herself. It could have been anywhere from needing her side of the story from the other night, to alerting her to the deranged she-beast that was on the loose, to her mother…

The last thought stopped her thoughts. She could see on Uncle Martin's face that he had come to the same conclusion. While her mother seemed to be entering a small patch in life when things are no longer dark and gloomy but rather partly cloudy with a slight chance of rain. But her state was always in a constant state of flux.

Aunt Sasha stopped and let the two officers pass her. One of the two appeared quite fresh on the force, with a face that might need to be shaved every third day and still be clean. The other was the opposite, with time having worn all over his features. The lines in his face were pronounced and deep. He carried himself with the confidence that comes with years on the job.

"Martin Shiner?" the younger officer asked.

"Yessir," Uncle Martin answered immediately, bracing for the worst.

"I am Detective O'Bryan. This is Chief Williams. We are just stopping by to ask a few questions."

"Okay," Uncle Martin replied, shooting a glance to his wife, showing a deeper look of concern.

"Do you mind if we step aside, and everyone else can go inside?" politely requested Detective O'Bryan.

"Questions for Uncle Em? Can't be about my mom."

Without answering, Aunt Sasha gathered the boys, and motioned Perry to retreat inside their home. As they had grouped together and exited the backyard, the police chief stopped them.

"Perrywinkle Shiner?" Chief Williams asked.

"Yeah," Perry responded, caught quite off guard.

"Do you mind having a little chat?"

"What… the… hell…," went through Perry's mind. "Oh, okay."

The rest of the Shiner family promptly made their way back to the deck and through the sliding glass back door. Perry watched as they stopped once they got inside to look back upon them, concern and confusion now paramount. With a moment passed, Aunt Sasha shooed the boys away from the door and to whatever game or toy might keep their attention.

Chief Williams took Perry gently by the shoulder and led her across the yard. He exuded a patient, paternal vibe which helped to relax Perry a bit. As they walked through the grass, she tried desperately to hear whatever line of questioning had befallen her dear uncle.

"Mr. Shiner, what were you doing Wednesday morning and as well as this morning, particularly around town?"

That was the last thing that Perry could make out, but what she observed was redness almost immediately surfacing across both of Uncle Martin's cheeks.

"Okay, not mother. At least I don't think so. Sure he will fill me in later."

Once Perry found that the Chief had stopped walking, content with the distance between themselves and the line of questioning that had already begun, she stopped and got a good look at him. The more details that she could discern only reinforced her first impression of the man. His calm demeanor matched his inviting half smile that he wore on his face. His eyes wore a soft blue aura. Perry was sure that, over the years, that Chief Williams had used his outward appearance to his advantage. Probably not for any sordid desires, as Perry had seen plenty of times befalling her mother, yet for the sake of justice.

"Perrywinkle. I must say that is a very original name. Pretty neat, too," the Chief started. "Do you know what it means?"

"It was for the flower," Perry responded. She didn't realize it until later, but, with the Chief's presence, she almost instantly opened up. Something that almost never had happened before. "Except the spelling is different. I guess my mother thought it would be cool that way, or just didn't know how to spell. Either way, it didn't stop kids from teasing and just being downright cruel." She paused for a moment, then continued, "Call me Perry."

"Perry, your name also can mean the color from the same flower. It is part of the blue family. But it also can be considered a bit on the violet side. Violet has been a color of royalty throughout history."

"Funny, I never felt that way," Perry retorted.

"I can completely understand. A child like you, with your upbringing. It is truly astonishing how you have made it this far."

Taken slightly aback, Perry felt slightly confused and slightly slighted, "How would you know?"

"In no easy way to put this easily, but Martha Shiner is not an unknown to us, and has her own file."

"Figures."

"Perrywinkle...I mean, Perry. I am sorry for what happened to you the other night. We are on top of everything and have some leads. It is an ongoing thing, so nothing is closed yet..."

"You mean she is still out there?"

"Yes, and that is why I am glad we have crossed paths. I cannot stress this enough. You need to keep yourself safe."

"Understatement of the year."

"It cannot be understated. She is dangerous, unhinged and probably has her sights on you."

"Jesus, that kinda means a lot coming from the Chief of Police."

"With that, if you ever are in trouble, don't hesitate to call." Chief Williams pulled out a folded piece of paper from his front pocket and handed it to Perry. "That's my cell phone. Whenever you feel the need, you do not hesitate."

Perry tried to grasp the gravity of what just happened. She had originally thought she got roughed up by some off kilter nutjob wanting to delve into her strange and perverse desires. But something like that didn't necessitate the freaking Chief of Police handing over his personal cell phone number. And, with all that she could tell, it wasn't some type of perverted pass at an early teen. This man that stood in front of her, that she had just gained acquaintance with, has shown genuine concern to the point that he believed even calling 911 was not good enough.

"Perry, I don't wish to worry you, but this case is more complicated than you know."

"Holy shit...What am I supposed to do?"

"You should definitely stay low. Maybe stay here. Your uncle and his family seem like a very comforting and protective group."

"Can't argue with that."

"Just lay low. Be still."

"Be well," Perry answered without thinking.

Chief Williams paused for a second. A brief grin crept across his face, and he turned, motioned for Detective O'Bryan, and both were on their way.

RUS 1

"That's what you came up with?" Alex asked bluntly.

"You think I throw in a smoking cauldron with a warty witch hunkered over, black tattered clothes head to toe will make it better?" Rus shot back.

"It would make for a livelier story."

"Har-de-har-har-har. If you ever do ride off into the sunset from this detective work, you got a sure shot at comedy primetime in your twilight years, Mr. Peters. You asked if I could poke around, see what I can find out. And I did my best at following the warm leads of the going-ons."

"Rus, I didn't ask you to put in some overtime…"

"Nah, it was homework. Overtime you get paid for," Rus interjected.

"Okay, homework. And this…story is what you came up with?"

Rus sat back in the chair directly in front of Alex's desk. He had clearly put much thought to develop his thesis, connecting the dots by using various spiderwebs travelling through various wormholes. He had stretched his train of thought so far down the track, he wasn't truly confident about anything he was saying. Part of Alex could sense this, and, while not enjoying putting his protege through the painful process without much help or leads, he was more than excited to see the measurable growth radiating from within Rus.

"Listen, Alex," Rus let out calmly, letting his thoughts settle down from the ether into the positions he was grabbing for. "It sounds crazy. It sounds out of this world. It sounds...insane. But you gotta admit, there is some part that is legit."

It was Alex's turn to sit back, deep in his well-used executive chair. "So, you believe that the woods alongside of Point Lake are harboring a Cold War era nuclear base that may or may not have been decommissioned but is currently covertly being used by a secret Russian quasi-government organization to develop cloaking technologies and operate all testing underground using cavernous tunnels that traverse beneath the entire town. Did I miss anything?"

"You know when you say it with a little attitude, it makes it sound a bit less believable," Rus answered.

"My apologies. What I really would like to know is how you came to this conclusion?"

"A little bit of this and a little bit of that. I always had my thoughts about that place, you know from growing up here. What the hell is a section of prime real estate smack dab in the booming New Jersey 'burbs sitting around labeled Restricted for the past five decades?"

"Is that how long it has been?" Alex softly inquired.

"That is how far the microfiche goes back on that place at the library. No history before then, as if the place didn't exist. No ownership history. No data on the lot. Then, whammo, the world sees this black hole posted as Off Limits sometime in the sixties. Out of thin air. *Thin* air."

Alex gave Rus a cursory nod to acknowledge the reference.

"That is just the history part of that place," Rus continued. "You ever been through there? It definitely isn't a place you might go for a stroll when you need to clear your mind. I have been there a few times growing up. Doing kid stuff. You know the drill. The place messes with your brain…" He paused to reconsider his thoughts, but by doing so he didn't hear the office door open and close. "Nah, it doesn't mess with your brain, it messes with your eyes. Things just aren't what they should be there. The last time I was there, I could have sworn the ground was moving under my feet. Just strange."

"Okay, so that explains the bulk of your thesis. Time it appeared on the map coincides with the Soviet tensions, restrictions to access implies government related, and vibrations felt show an underground anomaly…"

"Movement, not vibrations. Big difference," Rus clarified.

"Understood and agreed. But what is this about cloaking?"

"Well, here is where we get into current events," Rus responded eagerly. He was so caught up in impressing his mentor, boss, and father figure, that he didn't even realize that Chief Williams was standing at the top of the stairs. He must have heard enough on his way up the stairs to be curious where Rus was exactly going, so he kept silent.

"So, I was poking around town yesterday, making small talk with the local folk. You know, being me. Everyone seems to be oh so comfortable with me. Must be my intoxicating charm or my dashing good looks. Either way, I ended up over at good ole Church o' Goodness, talking with the good ole Missus Goodwell. She is a doll, and quite informed. I was there the day before, doin' some of my good deeds for the day. A little muscle here and there, a little chore inside and out. Good deeds don't go unreturned, my father always says. So when I showed up yesterday, I let her know that I was just trying to help out my boss with some side project. So then she lets me in on something weird that happened in the not too distant past. Turns out, there was a stolen car rolling through town. An old beat up Benz, which is strange to me because if I were a car thief I would want to steal something pretty pristine."

"Brand new Benz stolen would garner more attention than an old beater. It is good to see that you would make a horrible criminal," Alex added.

"Exactly. But someone in town tips off the police to it crawling through town, and they start following close behind on Main Street. The car hooks a turn into those woods, cruiser still follows. Officer hops out, finds the car that he was following, couldn't hear a sound. He couldn't find a person or anything in or around the Benz. Not a god damn thing. Pardon my language, but it didn't add up at all. Kicker was the officer knew turning off the road he was tailing this stolen car, but when he calls it in, he swears this was some kind of lost car, left to rot."

"So, how do you get to a cloaking device?" Chief Williams asked curiously from the top of the stairs.

Rus jumped up a bit in his seat, quite startled by the voice. He didn't have to turn around to know who it was. Rus had his fair share of interactions with the Chief, all of which were cordial and business related. If Rus had decided upon entering the Academy earlier in life, Hex Point's top cop would have been someone to aspire to.

"Excuse me?" Rus managed.

"I am trying to find the connection to your story and cloaking."

"Well, I mean, how else would someone escape out of a car in the middle of the woods, with all sorts of leaves and branches around, without making a single sound?"

Chief Williams brought his hands up to his face, making a certain contemplating look. It was clearly not to embarrass the young man as it wasn't in his person to do such a thing. Instead, he was debating the connections that Rus had laid out.

"I guess it could be possible. It seems to be quite a stretch, I must admit, Mr. Brown."

"Please, you know it is Rus. And, possible doesn't mean impossible."

Inside, part of Alex couldn't have been happier. His protege was catching on and piecing together some bits of the puzzle. There was far to go as far as Alex knew, but if Rus could expand his mind to a deeper level problem solving.

"Rus, would it be okay if I take you out to lunch, and allow me to discuss all of the positives that a career in law enforcement can make a satisfying and fulfilling life?" Chief offered, half smiling.

"I appreciate the offer, but I must regretfully decline. You see, I am already accounted for. Life as the world's greatest dick. I am learning from the best."

With a slight chuckle, Chief relaxed his demeanor and made his way across the office to Alex's desk. "You know that I always have to try. All you need to do is give me the word and I can make a few calls." Turning his attention to the original detective sitting behind the old oaken desk, Chief Williams continued, "I heard you turned off your calls. I figured something was going on. You are the expert in this one, Alex. Got a lead for you."

Alex's eyebrows perked up, quite surprised at the potential news that may be dropped into his lap. "Oh really? To what would I owe for such a valuable assist?"

"You are one of the only people that I know that could figure something like this out. I am too old to get involved in all of this...this stuff. Whatever you may call it, it is above even my pay grade. I know that you are the one that will see this through. You always do."

Alex slightly bowed his head to acknowledge the compliment from his old friend. There always had been a mutual respect between the two. It was even to the point where certain points of the law may have been skipped over when the two of them were working together.

Before Alex could say anything, the Chief continued, "And I can rest even more assured knowing that you have a protege that is not just following in your footsteps but has passed you by leaps and bounds."

"Scuse me, Chief, but I must object," Rus interjected.

"Rus, when your boss was your age, he was happy to work on missing pet cases if there was a reward. And he barely got by with that!"

"Okay, okay, okay. I appreciate the niceties, not as much on the little glimpse into the past, but I can own that," Alex clarified.

The Chief smiled and tucked behind Rus once again, taking a seat in the other chair sat in front of the desk. "I am glad that both of you are here. I only want to tell you once," Chief started solemnly, the smile now nonexistent. "I have never been a fan of telling things like this to begin with. But considering that one of you has been knee deep in this stuff for a long time and the other destined to be just the same, I have full confidence that our conversation will stay here, in this office. The steps you take because of what you hear, just choose them wisely. I would like to not be involved in this going forward."

Rus was taken a bit aback. He had been around so many various types of scenarios within the detective world. Many of them might not have been to the lengths a typical person would go to get information, but nothing compared to what he was in the middle of right now. He was sitting in the middle of his private detective extraordinaire's humble office with the Chief of Police parked next to him, swearing the two of them to near secrecy as he was clearly about to provide information that should not be passed along.

"I will start by saying you did not hear anything from me. You came up with this by your own amazing reconnaissance. It is not that far a stretch. Two upstanding private detectives of your ilk surely have found Jimmy Hoffa, found the magic bullet, and have E.T. hiding out in the doghouse. My point is that find some kind of excuse, make up your backstory. My name, nor any of my officers, will not be brought up in this." Chief paused momentarily, and shifted his attention squarely on Rus. "I have gone through this same conversation with Alex before, but it is the first time for you. And I am sure it is the first of many, seeing that you will be taking the keys to the Camaro sooner rather than later."

If Rus hadn't been fully out of his element before, the last comment pushed him into complete confusion. "Not sure I am really following, sir," Rus questioned honestly.

"You know I am not going to work forever, Rus," Alex interrupted. "Depends on how this whole case goes, I might just ride out into the sunset like you suggest."

Rus shot a glance at his boss. It was not exactly how he thought the day would have unfolded when he strapped on his sneakers before he left the house. Rus was nervous to attempt to explain his quite convoluted, albeit admittedly possible, story detailing what has been going on around town. And in a mere few minutes, the man that he has been following around, absorbing up all the tricks and minutiae of the work, has come out and revealed he is thinking about stopping, handing over the keys to the kitchen, and calling it a career. Nothing made any type of sense in Rus's mind. He knew that Alex couldn't work forever. On one hand, Alex could reasonably work for a solid decade or two with his cunning and intelligence, or at least until his body gives him troubles. On the other hand, Alex had been slowly decreasing his workload, and taking increasingly more time between cases than he needed. Rus knew for a fact that Alex was in far better shape than others his age. It must not be the body, but something going on between his ears.

"You must excuse me for being a little bit lacking in the right words," Rus explained. "First the head of force comes in swearing us to secrecy about whatever tip he is about to bestow on us, and now the venerable Mister Peters is saying that he might just hang up his notepad when all of this shakes out? Anything else?"

"That I will be coming to you for things like this going forward," Chief Williams plainly answered.

Rus knew in his heart that he was good at what he did. It wasn't something that he would admit to anyone nor admit to himself. He was always of the mind that if he were to come to that conclusion, he may become complacent. There is always something that a person can improve about themselves, and Rus was no exception to that rule in his mind. It was a trait that had worn off Alex and onto him over the years.

"Yeah, and that little tidbit."

"You see, Rus, while all this sounds earth shattering and potentially unnerving, the thing is that you groomed for this moment. Every little nuance that Alex has prepared you while on cases, the mental structure needed to think and comprehend things that others might not connect, everything inside you is ready. You just are not accepting it yet," Chief paused to let it all settle in for Rus before he continued. The gravity of the conversation, with everything that had been said and things that had yet to be said, hung in the air making everyone involved take notice of what was transpiring.

Rather than Alex or Chief Williams breaking the ice, Rus found the opportunity to start anew, breaking free towards the person he was destined to become. "So, what was it that you wished to let us know, Chief?" he asked, with a serious tone not known to be a thread within the fabric of his being.

Chief Williams smiled, "Rus, this all doesn't mean that you have to be Alex. One of him is enough, I am sure he will tell you."

A slight nod and small ends of a grin from Alex expressed his agreement. "Just be yourself Rus. That is what makes you so infectious," Alex added.

"Oh, okay. Let me rephrase that. What lead could be so important that the Chief of the Five Oh would risk his career pushing it our way? Is it the Russians? It is the Russians, I knew it. Makes too much sense."

Chief chuckled and put his arm around the back of Rus's chair. "Oh, it isn't the Russians, but you are onto something. Definitely closer than you think. But, no, not the Russians. I just got back from a little investigation. It was simple trespassing. In the end we took the notes and moved on. It was nothing more than a simple misunderstanding."

"Who went with you? Harris?" Alex inquired, curiously.

"Nah, it was O'Bryan. He is new. And he is still quite impressionable. He might end up being my Rus, so to speak. But that is neither here nor there."

"I am guessing that the suspect was prancing down through the woods, looking for any clues of a long-lost civilization?" Rus theorized.

"Yes and no. He had actually stumbled through the area on one of his early morning jogs. He found a trail off the sidewalk, traversing past the thickest of the brush and into the heart of the forest…"

"Wait, what do you mean a trail?" Rus interrupted. "I have lived in this area for my whole life and there hasn't been any type of opening in that forest. And trust me, off the record, I have looked."

"Since it is off the record, I will let that one pass. The thing you probably would sense if you have lived here for long is that the Point Lake Woods are not right. There are things about the place that just shouldn't be, and I am sure, if you haven't already, you will see in the future what I am referring to. A long time ago, things started happening there, things that couldn't be explained. Eventually it got worse, and the decision was made to deter intruders by whatever means were necessary. It was deemed a Restricted Area, and then everyone in town let the memories surrounding it fade to black."

"How is that possible? If some shady shit went down, how does everyone just let it go?" a perplexed Rus queried.

"If you were close to believing that the area was led by Russians performing underground experiments, developing things like cloaking devices, this is not much of a stretch of the imagination."

"Touché, Chief. Continue, and I will hold all my questions until the Q & A portion."

"What happened when this suspect made his way in?" Alex requested.

"O'Bryan took his story. Long and short of it, this guy made his way there a couple times. His claim is that something lured him there, something big and deep blue. This thing spoke to him. He made some other claims, but you know how that goes." Alex nodded in agreement. "He stated that this thing that spoke to him also knew his family member's name. But here is the kicker. This guy took a nasty spill and got a huge gash across his knee while he was trying to run through the trees. The next thing he knows he is back on the sidewalk, dried blood down his leg and nothing else. Not even a scab of anything."

"Gotcha," Alex added. Clearly it was a piece of information that helped their case considering he perked up in his seat and was leaning intently towards the two of them.

"The name is Shiner. He lives with his family in Washington

Crossing, but I don't think I need to go into details. I am sure the two of you can take it from there."

"Anything else worth letting us in on?" Rus chimed in.

Chief Williams rose from his seat, stretched out the small of his back and started to move back to the stairs. He kept his hands pressed firmly on an obvious sore spot.

"Yessir, there was one more thing. It was another person. Shiner's niece."

"Are you referring to Martha's daughter?" Alex asked. Rus raised a perplexed eyebrow at Alex's understanding of the family tree. It must have been a former acquaintance or even a client. Either way, it predated Rus's time.

"Yes, that is correct."

"I am assuming that she is the family member that this big, blue body addressed by name?" Rus added.

"Yup. As it turns out, she has also been talking *to* that thing. I really don't know how, nor do I want to. That is for you two to figure out."

"Understood," Alex confirmed.

With that, the Chief started his way down the stairs, tender back and all. He was down to the fourth step, when he stopped in his tracks. Turning fully around, Chief Williams looked them both in the eyes. His tone was completely different than it was a mere minute ago. The tone was about to take a turn for the worse.

"Rus, that story you heard from Nancy Goodwell. Crazy as it sounds, but that is what apparently happened. I haven't known Officer Harris to make up anything as outlandish as that. Parts of the story, I really don't know how they fit in. Again, I am leaving that up to you guys. But that car that you hear about? It was reported stolen. The poor sucker that had his name on the title was found at a seedy pay-as-you-go motel close to the airport. One quick jab with the good Lord's book pushed his nose up to his deathbed. I thought it might be the poor wife he left at home, but she called in the report to try to get back at him. I don't think it was her for sure. Whoever did that is now lurking around Hex Point as far as I can tell."

The level of seriousness went up and off the charts for the young detective and put his boss on high alert.

"All I am saying, guys, is stay safe out there." With that, the Chief descended the stairs and left the two of them a bit on edge, contemplating their next move. The one thing that was evident was that they had to figure things out and quickly. Time was no longer a luxury in this case.

MARTIN 5

Five of the six remaining Shiners to still make New Jersey home were out back, finishing up what was left of the oversized dinner that Martin graciously sweated over the grill to cook. The early summer Thursday evening air hung hazier and more humid than it normally had been for that time of year. Sweat beaded above everyone's brow, especially for the times that the wind had taken rest from swaying the trees. Bits and pieces of leftovers from the twins were strewn around and below the patio table. Maddox, having barely finished half of the hotdog and bun on his plate with the other half smeared with ketchup and mustard, could barely contain himself. The backyard was alight with the flashing of lightning bugs. Even the usually reserved Tristan was nearly shaking in his seat. Seeing the last few shreds of restraint bursting at their seams, Sasha smiled at both of them, and with a simple nod, the boys darted off the patio, serpentining across the grass.

Perry, having neatly finished her plate, cleaned up her face and sat back. The overall scene appeared to help let her emotions and stress ebb a bit. It was the overwhelming feeling of family that settled into her heart, and, in the times when that actually happened, she tried her hardest not to let other thoughts creep in. To her right was Martin, sloppily eating the rest of the baked beans, getting drips and drabs around him like a piece of abstract artwork. Across the table, with her napkin neatly folded next to her plate was Sasha, exuding her usual calming presence.

"So, Perry, do you have any exams tomorrow?" Sasha inquired, making conversation.

"Meh, just Spanish with Señora Rivera," answered Perry, trying her best to over accentuate each of the rolling. "So, yeah, not really."

"Spanish is a subject in the end. It does count to your overall grade point average, do not forget," Sasha politely implored her niece.

"I gotcha. And you don't need to worry, I am pretty good with the stuff. Plus, it seems like I might be in the remedial class. I am like a shining star when you look at the mouth breathers in my class."

Martin, taking a quick break from his beans so he didn't choke, chuckled a bit without picking his head up. HIs counterbalance shot him a quick scowl back his way, as Sasha continued, "Perry, you more than anyone else I know can see value in every single person."

"Okay, okay, okay. I gotcha Auntie Ess. Thank you for the concern, but if I don't ace that I should really have my head checked."

"Don't we all," Martin muttered under his breath.

"Oh Martin. Don't sell yourself short, my dear," Sasha assuaged her other half from the self-deprecation. "Your head is the least of your worries."

"Touché," admitted Martin. "Nothing like your significant other to tell it like it is."

"I would be remiss if I did not, Martin." Sasha turned her attention to the yard just in time to watch Tristan, while chasing Maddox, trip over his own feet and proceed to front flip a few times. He ended up face down, and, before he could understand enough to let out a howl, Sasha had already made her way to his side. Her soothing influence brought calm to the boys and whisked them back inside.

Martin chowed through the last bits on his plate at a slower pace. The full belly and the recent events were weighing on his being. And

Perry could notice it.

"Uncle Em, I am really, really sorry. The police came, it was my fault. I should have never gone to that house."

"Oh Perry, no worries about that. Honestly if I were in your shoes, I guess I probably would have done the same. Can't fault you for trying to reconnect with Lucy."

"Promise?" Perry asked in a meek fashion.

"You got it kiddo. And besides, I gotta be a bit honest. I don't think that you were the reason that the boys in blue rolled up here."

With one eyebrow slightly raised, Perry gently prodded her uncle. "Oh, then continue, please."

"Thought that would perk you up. It isn't every day your old, dearest uncle is sought out by law enforcement. I am not sure if that makes you think any *more* less of me, but I figured I would come clean. I can trust you. I mean, who are you going to tell? The boys? They might be a little too little to truly understand. But then again, Tristan is quite quick. I always feel that he is destined to be a rocket scientist. Maddox, well…"

"Uncle Em, can you please get the train back on the tracks?" Perry interrupted playfully.

"Ehh, you know what? It probably isn't that interesting. Yeah, you wouldn't be up for it. I am sure your Aunt Sasha has some mean dessert inside. Maybe a slice of cake before bed?"

Perry shimmied herself closer to her uncle and tilted her head down to get a good stare eye to eye. She meant business, and Martin couldn't see a way out of it.

"Okay, no cake. That works for me. No go on the stalling," Martin mumbled. "So, you know how I had been trying to be a bit more active."

"Yeah, you have really taken it to your gut. At the pace you have been on, you will be nothing in no time."

"Well, I appreciate the noticing and the compliment. It does really make me feel energized and lively. That goes a long way with the two rugrats. But I digress. So, I have found the best time, and sometimes only time, to go out for a run is first thing in the morning. Before the sun even crests the horizon. I figure it is the best time to get my sweat on, not be run over by the horrible Jersey traffic, and not miss anything at home with the rest of the family asleep. I had been doing that for some months. The only thing out of the ordinary was how much I enjoyed it. I mean, how much I enjoy it. I still love the feeling."

"Then what?" inquired Perry.

"Hold your horses, I am getting there. So, the other day I was out there running. I was trying to get a good, solid time. It was a perfect morning for a good run. But as I went on, my time started to drop. Well, not that it got smaller, but it actually went up. My speed started to drop. That sounds better. Again, I digress. On my route, I was heading home on Main Street. I have run on that stretch of road dozens upon dozens of times. It passes by the woods in the middle of town before passing over Point Lake, right by that dance studio you mentioned," Perry nodded her head in agreement, and Martin continued. "Then it shoots right back home. I could probably draw the scenery settled in the early morning light by memory, that is if I had any artistic skills. I thought I might be pretty good after taking an art class in college, but I still ended up with a C, so it might not come out the greatest. And depth, that is a tough cookie to get. But seriously, I digress. This time on the run, something caught my eye. A light was shining through the trees, but it wasn't the sun because it wasn't yellow or orange or anything like that. And it was also in the west."

"Rise in the east, sets in the west," Perry said to herself.

"Exactly. And it was gone just as fast as I noticed it. But low and behold, a path shows up on the side of the sidewalk. I had never, in all of my runs, seen any type of opening. But there it was, clear as the dark morning. So, I went for it, got a bit back into the woods, and came across a huge, menacing looking fence. But that was not before I tripped and flew after my foot caught a root. I never saw the root before or after. But I was busted up pretty good. My knee got bloodied. My shoes were beat up. Like a trooper I got back up and went toward the fence. It looked like something out of an old monster movie, jagged wire hanging from the top. I figured I can follow it out of there. The lake would be someone to my left, so I started running. Not because I liked the pain pulsing from my joints, but because something was chasing me. When it caught me, all I could see was a blinding light. And it reeked of cinnamon. I could have sworn I heard someone, or something, speak. And as fast as it all happened, it was over. I made my way back home to clean myself off. That is when I realized the nuttiest thing. My knee was fine. Dried blood was still there, but no gash. Even nuttier? My shoes. They looked like new."

"What morning was this?" Perry asked inquisitively. Considering that all Martin had just revealed led Perry to not flinching a bit, he knew that she understood more than he could know.

"That'd been Wednesday, yesterday. When I got home, Sasha told me about you in the hospital."

Perry nodded agreeingly, encouraging him to continue. "Then what happened next?"

"The fact that you think there is more leads me to believe you know more," Martin responded. Once again, Perry nodded, but remained silent. "Well, this morning I ran out. I found a different path. I took it. But you know what the funny part is?"

Perry shook her head.

"Apparently that is called trespassing. Not just frowned upon, but technically illegal. So that is why the Five-Oh dropped by for a talk. It wasn't just exchanging recipes if that is what you were thinking."

"I wasn't. But could I ask you one question?"

"It depends, Perry. I got a question, or some questions, for you. I think we need to bring each other up to speed on things. You see, when I was down in the forest or portal or whatever the hell was down there, I had a nice conversation with the friends of yours."

Perry, not needing any further insight, interrupted, "I never meant for you to get involved. I thought this would be something that I could handle on my own. I really just wanted to help."

"What is your plan?" Martin interrupted this time.

"I... I don't know what you are talking about."

"You have never been a good liar. You have always been such an honest person. The thing is that I was told that something is going down. And it is going to happen soon. The other thing that I was told is that you are in danger. And that you have a plan. I am not too sure with all of this, but I am sure as shit sure that it makes sense to have a little help with all of this, you know considering the seriousness."

"It is complicated."

Slightly distraught yet not discouraged, Martin continued his plea, "Perry, you know I don't judge. I am the last one to pass judgment. I leave that to the big man. We are family. We are always in this together. I want to help. I can help. I just need to know what I can do to help."

Knowing that she wouldn't be able to hold it a complete secret for much longer, Perry sighed. "I understand your concern. It's just...I don't know. Complicated."

"Yes, I can imagine. From what I saw and heard, the truth would make a seasoned nun cry uncle. But you must know that you are not alone. I am here for you. I haven't told your aunt anything, and she is okay not knowing. Together we can get through this. I am not asking you to spill your guts, I just need to know what I need to know."

Slowly, Perry debated internally what she could and what she should tell Martin. At that point, Martin was sure that nothing could surprise him.

Settling on what her thought out words were to be Perry started, "The girl that had spoken to you, Ofelia, is not truly alive. But on the other hand, she is not truly dead. This is what she told me. I didn't come to that conclusion. The other voice that you probably heard is from the other side. I take it you made it through the fence?"

"Yuppers," Martin answered.

"That one is from beyond there. That thing isn't alive or dead either."

"So why you?" Martin asked despite having a bit of an answer from Ofelia.

"My best guess would be that we are kinda the same. Before she was put into that place, Ofelia was neglected and abused. It seems like we are kindred spirits. She reached out for help, and I figured I could."

"What kind of help does she need?" Martin asked directly.

"That is where it gets complicated. But I just need you to trust me."

Martin relented a bit. He sat back on his seat and stared up into the clear sky. If there were any doubts in his mind, they were now nonexistent. The gravity of everything was front and center in his mind.

"The only thing that is not sitting well with me was part of the conversation I had with that...that girl and the other thing. When I went back yesterday, they told me that you are in danger. Something is now out to get you. Something bad. And that you have a plan. She called it your sacrifice."

Perry looked Martin directly in the eyes, and stated bluntly, "There are bad people here, and there are bad people on the other side. There are times that we need to do something. I can be that person. I can make a difference in this world and beyond."

"Fair enough. Just always remember that I am here for you. I know you aren't crazy. If you were crazy, then I surely am getting fitted with the straight jacket along with you. You don't have to go through this alone."

"I know. I am sure I may need help, like a ride or something. I believe I have it all worked out in my mind, just hope everything goes well."

"And if it doesn't?"

"Well, let's just hope and pray it doesn't come to that."

"And that is exactly what we are in right now," Martin ended. The two of them cleaned up the rest of the dinner and made their way into the house as the sun started to set on Thursday. There was no further talk of any dreams or plans for the rest of the night. If things had gone the way Perry had planned them out in her mind, they wouldn't speak of things again, and that she would be fine. But as the best laid out plans throughout history have shown, nothing goes according to plan.

<h1 style="text-align:center">RUS 2</h1>

"So, what is the plan? How are we going to do this?" Rus urgently inquired from the passenger seat.

Alex didn't answer immediately. Once there was a break in traffic, he was able to maneuver their way onto Main Street. After Chief Williams had left the office after his unofficial, official break in the case, the two of them didn't have much of a conversation. Alex had decided it would be best for the two of them to sleep on it and reconvene in the morning, which is exactly what they had done. But as he had woken up in the morning, not much sleep logged with the thoughts of this day running through his mind, Rus found no answers with his boss. Alex had been decidedly more silent than usual on that Friday afternoon.

After the two were safely on their way, Alex opened a bit. "The thing with this is, I am not too sure a plan will help us."

"You mean, after the Chief of Police in town tipped us off to some inside information? Let us just roll up on this family, no invitation might I add, and start the conversation like, 'Hey so I heard through the grapevine that you guys are involved with some other worldly shit and we know that because your statement taken from the police, which the Chief himself couldn't wait a day to drop by our office and let that cat out of the bag?'"

"I wouldn't go that far," Alex calmly replied as he pulled the car from Main Street. "With a situation like we are currently involved in, it might be best to run this talk on the fly. No plan, just let things roll organically."

"Of all my time spent helping you out, working alongside you, keeping my feet on the pavement, the daily ins and outs, I never thought I would hear you say we are going into something like this with the plan of winging it. You really are on your way to the retirement community, aren't you?"

Alex chuckled a bit. "I guess you can say that. Seriously, I have never been good without having a plan. But I have always believed having a plan, and one that is not completely thought out, can lead down the wrong road."

"So where does that put us?"

Alex pulled over and threw the car into park. He looked over at Rus, and conceded, "This is your time. You are better at smooth talk than I ever was. This one is all you. I will follow your lead."

A bit flabbergasted, Rus took a second to let it settle in. While it was something that he thought would eventually happen, he never thought that Alex would relent on a case of this apparent magnitude. "Well, if that is the case, I figure we could run with something like we were investigating an open case, someone lost something in the woods, we heard through our sources that this guy was running through there. That is our in. You think that will work?"

Alex unbuckled and opened the door. "Well, it must. We are here," he answered as he exited the car.

Rus followed his boss's lead, leaving the car, then closed the door behind him. He leaned against the passenger side momentarily to gather all of his thoughts. While the time it took for Rus to roll through all of the scenarios in his mind, the whole situation brought him back to his high school days. He would do the same thing before each of his varsity football games. He was the first team, all-county middle linebacker, and he needed to know all of the possible outcomes that were before him as the heart of the defense. In his heart Rus knew he couldn't go through the myriad of possible outcomes, but the process of going through each different future helped to set his mind at ease.

Rus turned his head over to catch sight of Alex. "What do you know about this family?"

Alex shrugged, "Just from what I have come across in the past. Mostly, it revolves around Martha. She had come to the office a few times years ago, well before you came along. Her parents were involved in an accident, and the police didn't find anything suspicious. She couldn't accept that, she kept thinking something was being covered up. Maybe it was her way of coping with events. But I am no therapist. I had run into her brother, Martin, a few times while doing my diligence. He seemed to have dealt with the loss a lot better. Anyway, I heard she had a child, a daughter. I am not sure what happened to either of them as time went on. I never even caught her daughter's name. But, for the real reason we are here, Martha is Martin's sister. He is the runner, so to speak."

"Perrywinkle," Rus added.

"Excuse me?"

"The daughter, that is her name. After yesterday, I decided to poke around, gathering information, public and private sources. She would be thirteen years old at this point, extremely intelligent. A bit of a loner. Before you ask, I am not that far off from high school, so I still have connections."

"Well done, Rus."

Content with where his head was at, Rus strolled down the front walk, not realizing Alex was trailing behind him a step and a half. The two made their way to the house under darkening skies rolling into the area. Neither had been paying much attention to much of anything going on in the world outside of the non-discrete, limited square miles of land sitting in New Jersey.

A quick of the doorbell and the two detectives assumed

unassuming positions on the stairs leading to the house. There was some shuffling inside, and the door shortly opened.

The woman sporting blonde hair stood before them, holding what appeared to Rus to be toddler sized shirts with colorful stains in her hand. He pegged her in her early thirties, given the slight lines escaping the corners of her eyes and the responsibilities she clearly had borne. In the background, the sources of the stain started to become more and more apparent, with various objects being knocked to the floor and endless and innocent laughter echoing afterwards.

Before Rus could make his introduction and commence the first real job that he was spearheading, two rambunctious and energetic toddlers screamed through the foyer. Both were completely oblivious to the two of them at the front door, as they sprinted back and forth playing some sort of version of tag where the tagger needed to tackle the taggee. While keeping her attention on Rus and Alex, the mother of the two reached out without giving a glance and grabbed one of the two as they made their way back around. She was clearly an expert.

"May I help you, gentlemen?" the host inquired politely.

"Ma'am, sorry for bothering you, but the two of us are private eyes. We are currently working a case, and our investigation has led us here. Am I correct to assume you are Mrs. Shiner?" Rus started out. He could see in the corner of his sight that Alex was impressed with his opening. Hell, Rus could feel it inside of him. It was his time.

"Yes, I am. Who might you be?"

"I am Rus Brown, and this is my colleague Alex Peters," Rus pointed towards his boss without looking. Alex tipped his head as an introduction. "We run a little detective agency in town."

"Is that the same Peters that I saw a sign for down in town? In the same place as the diner?" she asked.

"Hamilton Square, home of Peters. Investigator. That is correct, ma'am." Rus replied.

"Please, call me Sasha. And if you," she pointed towards Alex, "are Peters, and the sign said Investigator, what does that make you?"

"Mrs. Shiner, that sign is in dire need of an upgrade, amongst other items around the office. Alex is officially taking a backseat in terms of his career and has groomed me to be in the driver's seat."

"I understand. But please call me Sasha," she pushed again.

"I will try, but my mother has always taught me to respect others and taught me with the wooden spoon to boot."

Sasha cracked a smile. Rus was natural at this.

"So, Russell. What can I answer for you?"

"Mrs. Shiner...Sasha. I apologize for interrupting. Please call me Rus. And this is not due to age or anything of that nature. My real name is Lazarus, but everyone calls me Rus."

"No need to apologize, my fault."

With the introductions aside, and the two detectives seemingly having made their interviewee comfortable, Rus continued onward with their discussion.

"Sasha, we just dropped by to ask a few questions of your husband."

"I am assuming this has some connection to why the police had just dropped by to ask a few questions of my husband yesterday," Sasha pressed.

Without a second thought, Rus responded, "Yes and no. Yes, because we received word that your husband had been found in a place he shouldn't have been. The good news with that is your husband is a fine and upstanding citizen and that the police have found no reason to pursue any type of complaints. No, because we are currently working a case that deals with certain missing items from a client. Nothing of true market value, so the police are not taking anything up, just filing the report. We have reason to believe that where the items in question are located might be in the area where your husband had jogged through in the first place. Considering that if we were to be found in that same plot of land, we would probably have had the same uncomfortable conversation. And in our line of business, we try with the greatest aplomb to keep on the good side of the law. It is good for business, to quote a phrase."

Rus couldn't glance over at Alex at that point. He was locked in eye contact with Mrs. Shiner. He had learned early on that trust can be easily conveyed by keeping unfaltering stares. But he could sense that Alex had taken a step back, both physically and within his own company.

"That makes sense. Unfortunately, Martin is out on a run right now. He probably should be back in a half hour or so."

Rus hit the first roadblock on his case. Time was truly of the essence. Whatever was on the horizon was imminent, and any delay could have drastic effects. While he really didn't grasp the true enormity of the situation, what had transpired between the two of them and the police chief made it clear that the level of shit they were going to enter was on the deep end of the cesspool.

Before he could manage the next step of the conversation, Rus noticed another set of sets watching him from deep inside the house. She was there, too. It was the niece, Perrywinkle. He could not turn away now, they had to delay.

"Well, given the clouds that seem to be rolling in, if I were a runner, I might notice and head on home," Rus threw out.

Without giving much of an opposition, Sasha replied, "Fair enough. If it is that pressing, you two are welcome to stay until he comes back. I wish to warn you that the odor might not be too appealing."

"Sasha, two little kids can create quite a stink. I have young cousins about the same age, and I am fine with it."

"They are actually okay. It is my husband that you will need to worry about when he returns," she explained.

Both Rus and Alex let out a courteous chuckle. Sasha had been quite proper in their limited interaction, but the slight at her husband seemed to be quite set up and tension easing. She even cracked a quick smile.

For the first time, Alex stepped forward a step. "Sasha, if it is okay with you, would you mind if we step inside until Martin returns. I am sorry, but I did feel a few drops fall."

"Of course, please come in." Sasha opened the door fully and gave them both a pass inside.

Rus stepped inside first, and found himself in a relatively put together house, considering the mayhem that was roaming around three feet off of the ground. The modest foyer led towards an opening, with a carpeted set of stairs stuck in the middle. Both sides of the stairway pushed through to the back of the house, with entertaining rooms on either side. The kitchen was found at the back of the house, set up an informal dining table with wooden chairs surrounding it.

As Sasha led the two of them into the house, Rus felt a warmth emanating throughout the inside. It wasn't as if the heat was on full blast, but more of a homey feeling. The walls were scattered with a mismatch of family pictures showing genuine enjoyment and growth throughout the years. It was quite an inviting and peaceful place.

"Please, feel free to make yourself comfortable. Do either of you want something to drink? Coffee, tea, water?" Sasha offered politely. To Rus, everything that she was was genuine. There was no energy wasted on any type of insincerity. It was a very rare thing to see at the time, and it was something that Rus hoped not to disrespect.

"Water is fine for me, Sasha," Rus answered. A quick nod from Alex, and she grabbed two glasses.

Rus got himself a bit more orientation with his surroundings. Around the dining table was a kitchen, living room for entertainment and a door opening up to the back. Beyond that there was a large wooden deck which pushed into a wide, green backyard littered with outdoor toys and games and a well-used playset, chock full of swings and slides. Rus smiled as he could imagine the two little rugrats spending endless hours running themselves rugged outside. The proof had shown through in the form of the most common paths that were taken had worn through the bright green lawn down to the earth. The scene brought him back to his youth, and even more warmth had come through.

As he was staring out the back, Rus felt the eyes on him again. It was not an ominous feeling, nothing making any hair spike up on skin. He pegged as a curious look. The source of the feeling was hidden in the living room, lying low on the couch.

"Here you guys are," Sasha announced, pulling Rus right back into reality, as she put the two glasses of water in front of two of the chairs. Feeling obligated to follow her lead, Rus found his way into one of the seats, with Alex close behind.

"So, Sasha, does your husband often go out running during the day?" Rus chose to break the ice with.

"Well, considering that the whole reason that brought you to our dining table this afternoon is that he was found to be somewhere he shouldn't have been before the sun had risen, I think you may know some of the answer," Sasha responded plainly.

Without missing a beat, Rus pushed forward, "Well, I have been quite an enthusiast of running myself. Ever since graduating school and taking strides towards my career path, I have had to make changes to my approach to exercise. I can relate to your husband. I often find myself changing the times that I can get out for a run. It definitely helps to keep things interesting and, well, you need to do what you need to do."

Looking as if he struck a chord, Sasha pulled back a bit, "I guess that makes sense." Rather than continue with the line they were currently embarking on, Sasha turned her attention to Rus's partner. "Is there a reason why you are quite silent?" she asked in a slightly rude manner. The whole running thing must be a sore subject to her, especially considering the police had stopped by yesterday.

"Well, Sasha, I have a lot riding on this case. In the end, if we do not close this case successfully, it might just cost me my retirement."

"That sounds serious. That missing jewel or whatever it might be surely must be something."

"To be honest, it isn't the money. This fine, young man is part of my retirement process."

Before they could continue their conversation, the door leading from what appeared to be from the garage swung open, and a man walked through in the hallway leading into the kitchen. His hair was a messy mop, and his shirt was soaked from the middle chest down to the bottom. After only a few moments, the slightly musty stench of exercise overtook the room.

The man paused once he saw the added company sitting at the dining table. His eyes went from Sasha to Rus to Alex and back to Sasha.

"Martin, this is Rus and Alex. They are from Peters, Investigator. I believe you have seen the sign."

Martin nodded, and a sight of better understanding came over his face. "I guess you guys are here to talk about what happened yesterday. I told the police everything that I could. I doubt they even believed me. Not sure what I can help you guys out with."

"You may be surprised. But we are very thorough according to our no-stone-unturned policy," answered Rus.

"Fair enough. Do you mind if I take a quick shower? I am sure your nostrils will agree."

Neither Rus nor Alex had to answer, just smiled. With that Martin hurried upstairs to retreat to the bathroom. Sasha, who had been standing in the middle of the kitchen, appeared to find the silence suspicious. She grabbed a few packets of assorted snacks and two water bottles and swung open the sliding door to the back deck.

"My apologies, the boys need a little outside time before the rain starts up. Whenever it gets this quiet inside, trouble is afoot. Martin will be down shortly. He doesn't take much time," Sasha explained. While it had only been a few seconds, the two boys, who were in undisclosed locations around the house, rampaged down the hallway, shoes in hand. They gave the two outsiders not a glance as they raced outside with their mother following closely behind.

Once they exited, the stillness came back into the house. Rus and Alex found themselves sitting around the table. Rus shrugged his shoulders and rose from the table. Just as he would do while waiting in similar situations on a case, Rus found himself looking around at the pictures on the walls and the details they often contain. More often than not, many things can be figured out by what a person hangs up and what they do not hang up on the walls. After slowly pacing around, he found the same thing that he had when he first entered: an innocuous and loving family. They had to have been if Rus and Alex were left alone inside their house after only a few minutes. If they had been a little bit less scrupulous and a little bit more devious, it could have been different. But this was Rus's lead, and he was trusted to prove himself. And he intended to do just that.

There was one common, uncommon commonality within the pictures that papered the walls. The majority of them contained not four family members, but five. While the extra member was not in every single picture, she was smattered throughout the family timeline, pre and post little kids. The one consistent part of each of her appearances was her glowing smile, genuine elation.

Rus felt the eyes back. As he peered into the living room, he found their origin. There she was, as far as he could tell the fifth member of the family unit was sitting on the couch. Her eyes were equal parts suspicious and inviting. Something about her expression showed more than what he had noticed in the pictures. It was an underlying level of distress and anxiety.

. *"This must be it, what the Chief had talked about,"* Rus thought to himself. *"This shit is getting real."*

The moments that passed in which Rus and the girl had locked eyes seemed to continue endlessly. The longer before he broke the ice, the worse everything would be. It may make her quite unnerved if he used her name. For the first time working as a detective, Rus felt sharp pangs of panic shooting through his body. This was his time.

"Good afternoon. How are you today?" Rus asked awkwardly.

Silence. Not even a blink. That was a swing and a miss.

"My name is Lazarus. But trust me, I haven't been raised from the dead. I can tell you that growing up with a different name wasn't the easiest. I go by Rus. But you can call me whatever you wish."

Still nothing. Rus could feel himself swaying nervously.

"Sorry, I am just a bit nervous today. This is a big chance for me. As long as I can remember, I had always wanted to be a detective. I guess it was because of my brother. He ran away when I was young.

I never really understood why, and really didn't believe what my parents told me. Anyway, I have probably bored you enough."

As Rus turned around, he made it a point to move slowly.

"I had the same thing. The name thing. It happened to me, too. My mom named me Perrywinkle. But she couldn't spell it in the hospital, so she made up something different. At least that is what I tell myself. I go by Perry."

Rus found his in, and it was the most obvious one.

"Pleased to meet you, Perry. I guess you could imagine why we are here."

"Yeah, but I don't think it has anything to do with that story you just sold my aunt," Perry replied with a smile on the side of her lips.

Rus let out a slight chuckle. The girl, as young as she is, was quite savvy.

"You got me. But it doesn't stop us from trying to get the information we need. We are here because, well, it isn't so simple. I have lived in this town my whole life, and things just don't add up. Something is just not right. And, right now, well it seems the craziness is going haywire. My boss over there, he has been through this kind of stuff before, and he is quite uneasy right now."

Perry shifted around uncomfortably on the couch. Rus didn't wish to push her further on the subject, but simply wanted to plant the idea.

"Anyway, we are trying to get as much information about what is going on at this point. Something is going to happen. Again, my boss has seen this stuff, and he knows how to help out. Just know we are here to help in whatever way we can." Rus handed over a Peters, Investigator business card towards her, with Alex's name crossed out and his own written hastily over.

In any other situation, Rus would feel uncomfortable handing over his information to a young girl. This had felt different. He felt impelled to reach out. And he felt she was relieved to an extent because the girl seemed to relax a bit. She sat there, an individual in desperate need of help or even a glimmer of such.

Rus gave Perry a muted smile, and, after she returned the favor, he returned to the dinner table. Steps could be heard from upstairs, and Martin returned down to the guests. The boys remained outside with their mother, with the threat of the rain now nonexistent.

"Alex, it has been a long time," Martin exclaimed and extended his hand for a friendly shake. "In any other time, I figure you would be back to talk about my parents and their cold case."

Alex returned his pleasantries, "You are smarter than people say."

"I wouldn't go that far. I see you got a new sidekick. Pleased to meet you, I am Martin if you couldn't tell," he finished by extending his hand towards Rus, who politely obliged. "What can I do for you today? Check that, what answers are you looking for?"

"I am not running this case, Martin. It is Rus's turn. Let him run the show."

"Fair enough," Martin replied while turning his head towards Rus. "Shoot."

"Well, we have reason to believe that something big is coming up. We have some ideas, been spit balling a bit. But in the end, we need a hot lead to help us out. That's why we are here. Our gut feelings are that you might be able to fill us in a bit." Rus had intentionally spoken a little louder than his usual inside voice. Again, he could sense Perry peering from the room adjacent to theirs.

"You want me to start from the top?"

"Not really. What I know and can tell, the majority of it is just freaky shit. What we would want to know is if there is anything beyond that. Like if you lived in that freaky shit all the time. It wouldn't be that freaky. And if it wasn't that freaky, what stands out? Does that make sense?"

Martin took a second and found himself settling into one of the chairs. The look that spread across his face announced that he knew what Rus was referring to. The look also showed that what was below the surface was troubling.

"The thing told me trouble came through, too. That big blue thing told me something dangerous managed to come over. I really don't get half of that, but that I believe completely. I mean, you are asking for trouble if you ignore the signs of trouble, right?" Martin nervously added.

"One hundred percent," Rus agreed. "Anything else? We would be greatly helped by crumbs and scraps at this point."

"Again, that blue thing said that whatever came through loves chaos, and you can't see it. It uses others to help."

The moment that Martin finished his sentence, Alex rose from his chair. It was enough for him, and Rus followed his lead.

"Well, Martin. We appreciate your time. Before the rest of the family comes back in, I think we should show ourselves out," Rus explained, taking the sign from Alex.

"Guess that is true. The kiddo cyclone is not something that you want to get caught in," Martin said. He was a bit still visibly unnerved.

As Rus and Alex turned to retreat out of the house, Rus caught eye with Perry, who was still sitting quietly on the couch. While Martin's eyes showed stress and nervousness, hers were bold and steady. Rus gave her a quick nod, which she returned, holding up slightly the business card in her hand. Rus smiled as he and Alex moved into the foyer. Martin slowly followed behind, not to be as cordial but to ensure the door was closed after they were out.

Once the two were walking down the walk, Alex alerted Rus, "This is bad. Real bad."

"Yeah, sounds like it. I never saw you up and leave like that before."

Alex paused his response until they were both at the side of the car. He looked around nervously as if looking for more answers to questions he didn't really want answered. "Listen, Rus. That thing Martin talked about. I am not talking about the blue one. That is something we don't need to worry about. This other one. That is the concerning part."

Rus leaned over the roof of the car to get closer. "So, what is the plan? You think this guy is telling the truth? Everything still seems so out of left field."

"I know Martin to be a very level headed guy. I believe what he says. You need to trust me on this. What he was describing in there, it is not good. The plan? Figure out who this thing is manipulating."

The level of craziness continued to pile up each day. This seemed to be mostly floating through Rus's head, not making any much sense. The week to that point had provided him with a completely different view on things, whether he liked it or not. At every turn, seemingly unrelated details around him bombarded his head. He could now see why Alex deferred to him on this one. If he could get this right, Rus would prove his worth to everyone.

"Seems like we have a lot of going-ons," Rus calmly added. "While not all of it makes sense, for Christ's sake, we have some dots that may connect."

The eyebrows perked up on Alex's face, "The car in the woods. We need to figure out who the hell that is."

MISSY 2

"Two whole *fuckin'* days, Tania. It took you two whole *fuckin'* days. I called you on Wednesday, it's Friday. I ain't the smartest person out there, but I can do some math," Missy yelled into the phone. She paused for a moment while her contact on the other end gathered herself.

"*I must apologize, Missy. Other things had come up and I couldn't make it over.*"

"That excuse is as flimsy as that brain you got sitting in your skull," Missy retorted.

"*Do you still need my help?*"

"What else the hell would I be callin' ya for? The goddamn weather report? Yeah, I need a hand, and I need it Wednesday."

"*It has been two days. Couldn't you do it yourself?*"

Rather than jump down her throat as she wanted, Missy held back. "Well, I been busy, too. Had other shit to take care of. I guess we are sitting in that same damn boat."

Sniffles came from the other end. "*Where are you now?*"

"My old man's place. You remember it?"

"Yes, I do."

"Perfect. Listen, we don't got much time anymore. We gotta act fast. Jus' get over here as soon as you can."

Sensing a slight break in their codependent relationship, Tania bothered not with pleasantries, but instead hung up. Missy could tell her simpleton lackey would be obedient this time. That was good. What happened the other night with those two pains in the ass rubes was one thing. The two of them could handle that. The next step of the plan that Missy checked off was a whole new level of shit. Missy needed to pull another into her red trail. Tania was perfect.

With the call ended, Missy replaced the headset back to the receiver. Even if she got over at breakneck speed, it would still be a few minutes. Missy had a moment to stop and think.

Missy moved into the living room, making sure not to disturb the now decomposing corpse of the serial toucher slunk into his favorite piece of furniture. There was a sofa sitting along the wall close to the television. She didn't recognize it, but its presence didn't surprise her. The fabric was laden with paisley and stains. No doubt it had a muskiness to it and was soaked with dust and critters.

"Good ole garbage day special. Oh, Reggie, you always were a tight ass," Missy reflected out loud. "But I sure as hell ain't a beggar."

Missy sat herself down in the middle of the sofa. She was correct about the condition of it because when she fully settled in, a plume of dust and filth was expelled up into the air. The few beams of the late afternoon light that made their way through the drawn curtains showed the denseness of the haze. It was a perfect time and place to plan out the next steps.

Missy brought her eyes up towards her handiwork still remaining in the middle of the room. Reggie still laid there, stiff as a board. The coagulated blood spray stained the area marking the event. The smell that the body let out stung the back of Missy's throat. But it wasn't appalling to her, it smelt to Missy of victory.

Missy stared directly into the open eyes of her once father and ever abuser. She was half expecting him to get up, with his pants still pulled down, showing his now rigor mortis hard member to the world, and approach her with the look that demented look he always had in his eyes after a night out with the boys. "So, you gotta plan?" Missy asked blankly.

From the Lay-Z-Boy, the stiffened, lifeless remains of Missy's father seemed to come to life. She focused hard on the details of his long dead face. A twitch of his eyebrow gave her pause. The movement was subtle but defined. At once, both moved up quickly, and returned to their place. Next up was his lower jaw, clicking downward opening even wider. The complete dryness of his mouth cracked as the tongue swiped back and forth over his lips. Despite not being of this world for days, Reggie's face was clearly coming back.

The lower jaw rocked up and down, and finally something came out. It was the unforgettable froggy voice. "Well, my dear, of course I do," the corpse responded, with the movement of its mouth matching the words as good as a subtitled foreign film. "You should not worry about that."

"Well, I figure we got a few minutes before Tania gets here. Despite all the shit she puts up her nose, seein' and hearin' you would drive her nutzo."

"Then I shall make this quick. Time is running short. We need to act. We need to get that girl. Stop her before she finishes helping that blasted blue beast."

"Yeah, yeah, yeah. I have heard this tons of times. But how the hell?"

"Yes, I understand. I think we need to go towards the portal."

"*Towards* the portal? You really think that is smart?" Missy questioned.

"Yes. I will be with you. You will be fine. We cannot let that blue monstrosity get anyone. Well, anyone that can help it. Do you understand?" the corpse with the newfound voice asked.

"Sure as shit, I think so. But if we go there, don't you think that someone might be there with us?"

"The girl is not an option. You are not an option. Well, for anyone else, I believe you know what you need to do. You have the power." As the body finished the final words, it found its way back to its normal, decomposing self. The moment it stopped moving, Missy heard a car pull into the driveway, and a door slam not long after.

Fully knowing that the moment when Tania would enter the house, it would either be a scream, collapse or upchuck, let alone any type of combination of the three, Missy should have told her to go around to the back door. The living room was the first place a person would see once past the front door. The last thing either of them would want is to attract any type of attention. Over the past two days, Missy had done the best to lay low from absolutely everything and everyone. To her surprise, not once did the phone ring. Good ole' Reggie was not that much in demand these days.

Missy spun around and tried to crack one of the windows behind her. The handle was half broken and cracked on the other side. Rather than get up to open the door, she pulled the handle off entirely, and, with a quick motion, slammed it to the bottom of the pane. The glass splintered, spidering upwards through the aged window. Luckily, it was only the handle that struck, and Missy came out unscathed. And the resulting opening would suffice.

With one eye peering out of the glass, Missy found Tania leaving her father's car. It was one of those ones with the fancy names that Missy was sure she had dealt with one of her temporary companions, or victims to be a little bit more accurate. Leather seats, all over the top amenities, all the things that make every single John Doe have a hard on when they see it drive by.

"Fuckin' John Does. They are all the same."

That was another thing in hindsight that Missy should have told Tania. A top-of-the-line car in a neighborhood like this is the same as someone outside screaming murder. It cannot be changed at this point.

"Hey, Tania. Go 'round back. That door is open," Missy projected outside. Obediently, her visitor didn't bother with the front, and circled around the house. She followed the same route that Missy had done two days earlier. It made her wonder if she had any idea what happened, the rage that flowed through her veins, and the thrill of success.

The gate could be heard swinging open from inside. Tania was clearly making haste getting into the house. As fried and absent as she could be, she was damn well obedient. And with her flaking off for two whole days doing only God knows what, she must feel extra guilty. And that would make her even more agreeable.

The back door followed closely behind the gate, and Tania was inside the house. Her face showed an unnatural level of worry, and that was before she could get her bearings on her surroundings. With a quick scan of the house, her eyes came down directly at the rotting lump of flesh seated in the middle of the living room. By the time the foul odor of decomposition hit her nose, Tania was already hunched over, stomach retching, and letting out painful gurgling sounds. To Missy's luck, the noises she let out were not going to cause any concern from the neighbors.

"Well, now do you get the hurry?" Missy asked plainly. "I ain't crazy. There was a reason for my call. And when we talked about a plan, I expected you to listen. Are you gonna listen *now*?"

Tania, rubbing the small amount of stomach acid that made its way out from her chin, couldn't get back upright, but was able to reply lowly, "Yes...I am sorry."

"Oh, no need to apologize. Past is the past. We can't go back. Hell, I wouldn't wanna. But now you are here, and we gotta talk this out."

Forcefully, Tania pushed her torso back up above her lower half. Her eyes found Missy, calm as ever, leaning forward, elbows on her knees, sitting on the couch. Missy could see the uneasiness in her eyes. She was very worried, and why shouldn't she be. Tania was always overly susceptible, and now was the time to exploit that.

"Come over here, and talk with me," Missy beckoned. By doing so, Tania would have to traverse by Reggie. That would help Missy's cause.

"But, but, well, Missy. Can we just go outside? I am sure the fresh air would help us think?" Tania pleaded.

Missy leaned back on the couch, causing more filth to escape into the air. "Well, that would be great, if the neighbors didn't like to snoop and gossip. The moment we said one *GODDAMN* thing, everyone would know," Missy explained. It really wasn't the truth by any means. No one had ever come slinking around the house that Missy could remember. But it was believable, and that was all that mattered. "Now, think about it. Look around. You are an accomplice. You will go straight to jail, no passing go, no collecting two hundred friggin' dollars, no matter who the hell your father is. The only way out of this is together. Me and you, kemosabe. Capiche?"

Tania, whose body was now trembling like a soaking child without a towel, could only manage to nod her head. The gravity of the situation was finally starting to sink down into her being.

"So, again, come on over, and pop a squat next to me," Missy ordered, moving over to one side of the couch to accommodate a sofa companion.

Rather than give any further resistance, Tania nervously started to make her way through the kitchen, towards the living room. Her eyes kept glued on the formerly blood-soaked father sitting as a statue in the currently crimson stained recliner. It didn't make her flinch at all as she stepped around the chair, placing her feet down softly and cracking the dried blood that had littered the shaggy carpet. With each movement, her face cringed even harder, and her upper body tensed up further. While the distance was mere feet, it appeared to take years from Tania's remaining life.

Finally making it to the couch, Tania paused a moment before seating herself next to Missy. The tension was palpable on her end, but Missy felt right at home. She still felt he was still around, her mentor's spirit hung densely through the atmosphere. Everything was going to be fine, all according to plan.

"Well, dear friend. There is a funny thing. What you have seen, you can't unseen. Not even for you and your messed up head. See, if you up and leave now this shitty scene right here, it will stay with ya. It will haunt ya. I figure you might have seen a dead body before, but I would peg it on an Oh-Dee. Not murder. Oh no, murder is a completely different game. Can't you just see the anger? The emotion?" Missy paused to let everything set in. "Yeah, I know you can, even with what you got left upstairs. This is a scene. Fuckin' a-mazin' if you ask me. But you know what the kicker is?"

There was an awkward pause while Missy allowed time to let Tania respond. Her eyes were fixated on Reggie's lifeless body. From their point of view, the jagged tip of the chef's knife glinted red in the late afternoon sun. Tania couldn't pull her sight away from the scene yet shook her head to push along with Missy's monologue.

"While you might be able to not remember what you are lookin' at right now. I doubt it, but as my father once said, 'Anything in hell is possible'. Kinda ironic, I guess," she ended the last syllable with a snicker. "Anyways, what will stay with you is the smell, the stench, the odor. It is the thing of nightmares. The moment you forget about all of this, you might be on a drive, looking for your next fix. It could be a nice hot day in June, and you pass one of them garbage dumps on the side of the highway. Ain't it strange how a rottin' dead body smells like trash sitting out in the sun? Well, when that smell hits your nose, everything'll come rushin' back. Hit ya like a ton of bricks square in the face. Sounds like a problem, right?"

At that point, the tears were dripping down Tania's cheeks. There was no bit of color left in her face. She nodded her head without breaking her staring contest with the subject of the hour.

"Well, here is the thing. I can help. Once we are all done with the plan, I got a way to make this whole thing disappear. Ain't that great?"

Another nod, no eye contact.

"Well, you trust in me, and I'll make sure that is what happens. Now we just gotta stick to the plan. You know, the one we talked about the other night. Tell me you remember?"

Tania nodded, but it was clear to Missy there was no clue about the plan. Missy knew it, too. She had no clue from the moment the phone rang on Wednesday. If she had a clear head, she would have been over a while ago. But Missy was counting on her friend's absent mindedness. In fact, the plan that she was referring to was never talked about. It was all in her head, but that would work all the same.

Well, I know you remember. It is only a few steps, so that nothing can go wrong. Even you'd not forget. We just first wrap this old guy up in the carpet 'round his chair. I can cut that up pretty easy, and that way, it'll be two pieces out, blood and all. We drop that bad boy into the trunk of my car, and I got some ideas on how we can pick up that big bastard. I got a sweet spot where we can drop him off at, and the cops'll never find him. We get back, put a match or two around the house, and hightail it off into the sunset in your ride. Presto, problem solved."

Missy couldn't hold back the smile. Some of the specifics were left vague and fuzzy, but for good measure. Missy couldn't rely on anyone else. It was just her and Erwin, and together they were going to get things done. Not a goddamn person was getting in the way.

PERRY 5

Not much more than a word was spoken between the Shiner family from the time the investigators left the house until past dinner. The boys ended up heading to bed a bit later than they normally would, with it being a Friday and their favorite cousin being around. Perry remained at her uncle's house and had planned to be there through Saturday for sure. Beyond that, it was up in the air.

Martin threw on a movie in the living room, one of those ones which claimed to be comedy, but was more of a bland series of disjointed jokes. Perry had seen some of those when she was over before, but nowhere else. The thing about them was that there was a distinct side effect once they were put on. It was a complete repellant to some.

Sasha, being one that was very good at picking up on the subtlety in things, retreated from the living room to parts unknown. While she didn't make much of an inquiry, Sasha could understand that things needed to be worked out. She placed a caring hand on Perry's head and gave her a smile as she left the room.

Once she was out of sight, a relatively awkward silence ensued. Both knew the movie was not really the focus of their attention. There was the conversation that both needed to be had, yet neither truly knew how it would end.

"So, you got that party tomorrow. Lucy's party, right?" Martin started them off.

"Yeah, it is at that dance place on Main Street," Perry replied, giving them both a start.

"Funny thing, I never saw you as the dancin' type."

"I will be there for Lucy. And for the cake, if I am honest."

Martin chuckled. "I knew you were raised right."

Perry didn't find much humor in his comment. It sounded like he was giving a little bit of maternal credit where it might not be due.

"Well, on that note, your mother called earlier," Martin pushed on. Clearly, he was trying to rip off the bandage quickly. "She expressed a desire to come with me to drop you off tomorrow. Maybe even pick you up. Seems like she misses you, I guess. I really couldn't say no."

"Actually, you could have. It is pretty easy. The word is only one syllable," Perry responded curtly.

Martin shrugged. "It always sounds that easy. Thing is that she seems like she is trying. She is your mother."

Not fighting the fight anymore, Perry let it go with a shrug of herself. "We all can try to do something. Next week, on my to-try list is to scale the Empire State Building, no harness. No harm in saying I am going to try."

"Har-de-har-har, dear Perry. All I am asking of you right now is to just give it a shot. She is your mother. But she is my sister. And if you don't know, I ain't got much in the way of family at this point. That is not changing anytime soon. I would like to see my sister happy again."

"When was she? Happy, I mean," Perry earnestly inquired.

Slightly caught off guard, Martin sat back in the couch, crossed his arms across his chest, and stared up at the ceiling. "Well, I guess it was before mom and dad. Your grandparents. Before they had their accident."

"The accident that she claims is a conspiracy?"

"I know what you are getting at, and all I gotta say is that everyone grieves differently. Events like that, they shape your life. And what shapes your life as much is right after, how you react. Me? I managed to get through it. I'll be honest, I went down that the-world-is-selling-me-shit-as-lies rabbit hole with her. But I came back up. My questions were settled. Hers, not so much. Maybe she just needs a hand to hold to get through."

"What about when I was born?"

"What do you mean?" Martin asked with an eyebrow cocked.

"Was she happy then?"

"Well, of course. I mean, you gave her another purpose."

"That doesn't really mean she was happy," Perry surmised.

Realizing there was no way down the road that would lead to anything pleasant, Martin shifted gears to a different subject. "There or here, it isn't at this point. That is up to you and her, keep me out of it. The bigger question is what the holy hell is going on, Perry?" he questioned quite directly.

"You know…" Perry trailed off. It was one of those moments in her life that she knew was coming, had time to figure things out, and yet still didn't know how to proceed.

"I don't know, Perry. That is why I am asking you. If I can help, I will do everything in my power to do so," Martin pleaded. The emotions wore through his face in a way that Perry hadn't ever noticed before.

Face down and bottom lip quivering, Perry couldn't hold it in anymore. It felt like everything was crashing onto her entire being. Rather than hold back any further, she let it out. If there was anyone that would understand it would be Uncle Em, and she needed an ally in this one.

With tears rolling down both of her cheeks, she felt her uncle put his arms around Perry, and held her tight. His grasp instantly calmed her and gave her the moment she needed to settle herself.

With her lips still twitching, Perry finally opened up, "I just don't know what to do. I just, I mean, I always could figure something out. Life has not been fair, but I always had a plan. This, well, this sucks."

"How much time is left?" Martin inquired earnestly.

"I don't know. A day maybe. Ofelia told me...you know, the girl in the woods. The waypoint would not be open much longer."

"You mean that crazy spot in the woods?"

"I guess. It seems deeper in the forest. Once that goes, if Ofelia didn't finish her part, she is gone."

"Well, you mean back where she came from?" Martin pointed out with eyebrow raised.

"Not really. From what I get, there is something on the other side. Kinda like her boss but just mean. It will torture her. It will drag her down. It will take her power."

"Yeah, that is mean," Martin added.

"Worst part? That other thing, you know that mean bitch that tried to end me?"

Martin nodded his head in agreement, not knowing who she really was but full well knowing the danger.

"Well, there is something attached to her. Helping her. Manipulating her. That goddamn thing will get the healing power that Ofelia has."

"That seems like that would be a nice combination," Martin joked. Her tears finally ended their descent. Her nose sniffled a bit as Perry tried to get things back under control. She sat up straight, no longer needing her uncle's comfort. "Yeah, you ain't kidding."

"You think that this part of the woods would open up again like this?"

Perry hadn't thought of it. In all the goings on that happened, it never dawned on her. But the answer was clear.

"Those guys that came over before, the detectives. The one of them seemed like he knew a lot more. He didn't speak much but I got a vibe from him. They were interested in your story, but they were definitely lying about their intentions."

"Do you think they know about it?"

Perry didn't miss a beat by replying, "Why else were they so interested in your crazy story when the police didn't bother as much? They must know. And if they know, then it must open up again."

"So if we don't make the girl with the healin' touch win her deal, then this place opens up again a year from now, and that other thing comes back through all juiced up with new found powers…"

"I don't even want to think of that," Perry interrupted.

"But we really gotta. You know, I was a Boy Scout. Be prepared and all that stuff."

"If all that happens, we are screwed. Royally. Well, I am screwed."

"Point taken. Let us not get it that far. How can we help the girl and the blue meanie?" Martin asked.

Perry paused. The hard part was finally there and explaining it would take her uncle past the point of no return. With a deep exhale, she answered, "Ofelia needs to bring a person back with her."

"Well at least it isn't that complicated," Martin nervously quipped. Before he could add any more levity to the conversation, he placed his face down into his open palms. The situation caught up to him and there was no joking any further. This time it was Perry placing her closest arm over her uncle's back.

"I hear you, Uncle Em. I got some ideas. We can figure it out."

From in between his fingers, Martin spoke, "What about offering up that crazy one to her?"

"It is either her or her friend, Tania. I know it is mean as hell, but I do not think either would be missed," Perry spoke with a discerningly low level of emotion given the words she said.

"This is *fuckin'* crazy, Perry. Are we actually talking about sacrificing a life for this shit?"

Perry lifted her head and locked eyes with him. "What I am saying is sacrificing a thing. No one is going to die. Whoever it is, they are just going for a little vacation for a while. And I know for a fact, no one is going to be looking for them."

"Okay, okay, okay. I gotta just go along with you on this one. How are we going to do it? When do we do it?"

"Soon. Probably tomorrow. Everything else is fuzzy. I do need your help, Uncle Em. And I need you to trust me on this."

"What do you need from me? Say it and it shall be done!" Martin performed his best genie impersonation.

"I need to talk to Ofelia. I need to figure everything out."

"What are you asking of me?"

"How much Benadryl do you have in the house?"

MISSY 3

With a sheetrock knife that Tania had found in the garage, Missy had cut up a large swath of the bloodstained carpet from the living room. She made sure to leave a bit of spray that had spotted around by the couch. To Missy, that was a trophy of sorts, a changing of the guard. As they rolled up the now severely stiffened corpse in the dated and crusty rug, seeing the remains of what she was able to do brought what her father used to call a shit-eatin' grin. Everything was coming together. It was just time to tie up the loose ends.

By the time the body was loaded into the trunk, the sun had already set on the horizon. The early summer night was falling down upon the earth. There was an odd peacefulness that hung throughout the air. Missy soaked it all in, while Tania seemed more distant as she was already positioned in the passenger seat of the car.

Missy walked around the car and found herself standing by the driver's side door. Before she could open and get the show on the road, she noticed him on the other side of the vehicle.

"My dearest Missy. I see that everything is going how it should," Erwin commented.

"Ain't leaving a goddamn thing to chance. Too much ridin' on this," Missy responded quite hoarsely.

"I am glad to see you taking this seriously," the ghostly figure responded. Despite not having even the slightest of breezes pushing through the atmosphere, Erwin's red mop was slowly free floating around.

"What other choice do I got?" Missy floated back its way.

"Everyone has a choice."

"Well, buddy. If you haven't seen it lately, I am in too deep now. A full barrel of shit deep."

"You can always repent," Erwin replied plainly. "But that is neither here nor there. Do you know what is going to happen next?"

"Yeah, yeah, yeah. I am headin' over to that spot where you came. Droppin' off the package. Then taking out the girl."

"There will be time for that tomorrow. It will be close, but what you need to do is head over to the spot now. I have a hunch that something is happening soon."

"You comin' with me? Sure as hell could use some cover with this boatload of police bait rollin' through town. Like how you got that fuckin' cop to not see a thing?"

"Do not worry. You need to go now." And with that Erwin was gone.

Before settling into the driver's seat, Missy took a moment to breathe it all in. The stagnant night felt like a perfect backdrop for the homestretch. There wouldn't be many more moments like this, without any tension. Despite what she had been through and the levels of callousness that had surfaced, Missy still felt quite uneasy with everything. She never had shown the traits that the typical cold-blooded killer exhibited. But then again, who really did when they were a cute single digit kid being constantly left alone in compromising situations, being verbally abused in public places by the assorted drunk family members, being the proverbial punching bag for all of others' life problems. In retrospect, Missy was surprised that a turn of events of this nature hadn't happened years ago. Even with that, there was also a part of her that just hurt.

"Time to stop heading down memory lane and get this shit show on the road," Missy proclaimed as she hopped into the driver's seat. Tania was in the passenger seat, belt already buckled. She crumbled over a bit, leaning against the window.

"What's a matter with you, sissy? Did flopping good ole Reggie into the trunk take too much out of ya? Didja hurt your back? Cuz I told ya to lift with your legs. Ain't you ever flopped a body in the trunk of a car?" Missy chuckled. It didn't elicit any response from the other seat. Maybe the whole ordeal was too much for her. Not everyone has the stomach.

Missy dropped the car into reverse and backed it out of the driveway. Before Tania lost what remained in her stomach while finishing the carpet rolling exercise, Missy grabbed her keys and switched the vehicles, putting hers in the garage. It might be a little suspicious rolling through in a top of the line, luxury vehicle lined without a doubt with traces of cocaine on all surfaces. It is always best to try to blend in a bit, which might still be hard driving around in a stolen, used Mercedes. Either way, Erwin was in her corner, he would clear the way.

As she spun the vehicle around and onto the street, Tania shifted back and forth, still not uttering a word. Her head bounced gently against the passenger window. She settled back into her slumped position next to Missy.

The car got going towards their destination, the next step in the plan. Missy figured it would only take five to ten to get to the woods. Might as well spend the time shooting the shit.

"Well, my dear Tania. Since we are both knee deep in this shit show, might as well just enjoy it. You know, crazy as this has been, you can't tell me it has been fun," Missy exclaimed with excitement. There was no response from her companion.

"Nah, can't blame you for not agreein'. Still taking it all in. Yeah, I was there once. Every little goddamn thing used to get to me. Every little time that voice on my shoulder would stop me, a piece of me died. And the craziest part? No one woulda blame me for doin' what I was doin'. The fuckin' *shit* I had to get through, jus to make it here."

Missy came to a four way stop. A red pickup truck was on her right and a white sedan in front. Both drivers looked pleasant enough, but neither could figure on going first. If it was a different time and place, Missy would have given both the finger and sped off. Right now, the last thing she needed was any unwanted attention. She politely flashed her lights quickly to help the two stragglers along. The sun was now completely set, and Missy waving them along would not have done much of a thing.

With the those two going along their merry way, Missy did the same, heading straight towards Hex Point. As she made her way through the intersection, Missy glanced over Tania's shoulder. All the anxiety was gone when she noticed him. He was with them. Not inside but around.

"Aww, is that the cat that got you all tongue tied? You notice my little friend?" Missy asked playfully.

No answer.

"You know what? Hell, I was the same, first time I saw him. You'll get over it. You'll be better once you finger that out."

Missy brought her attention back to the road. Tania must have finally kicked the shit. She was acting like a normal person, things were looking to affect her. Not good timing for a life change. But Missy had plans.

"So, guess, I'll be the entertainment for this ride. Nah, it'll be aight. We are almost there anyway."

Houses became more frequent and the side streets the same. They were nearly in town. He led the way, and Missy just followed his lead.

As they made their way onto Main Street, the town seemed to be in a lull of activity. Despite being an early Friday night there was quite an absence of people on the road. Stores were mostly closed for the night. And even with the weather being solid for an early summer night, there were no passersby.

"Well, well, well. Looks like everyone got the memo. Stay at home, ladies and gentlemen. Keep you kids home. Nothin' to see here. Move along ever'one," Missy spoke to herself.

As she went through the heart of town, the traffic went from slow to nonexistent. Over the bridge, the destination arrived on the left. Trying to stay out of anyone's attention, Missy put on her blinker and found her way into the same opening as she had not too long ago. She maneuvered deep into the forest, following the trail that seemingly opened in front of her. As the car bounced over each root and rock, both Tania and Missy jockeyed around in their seats. The last large bump in the trail caused Tania's head to rear back and strike the side window with a force that spiderwebbed the glass.

"Oh boy, that might leave a mark, there Tania," Missy quipped as she let out a quick chuckle.

Missy brought the car to a halt, narrowly avoiding a tree trunk in front of them. After only a split second, it continued on its way like a person crossing the street. Once it was out of the way, she pushed the vehicle further into the woods.

"You sure as shit weren't kidding that something was happening soon. This place looks like I got my vision from this one here," Missy said out loud, not caring that Tania could have heard.

The trunks continued to weave by each other, some expanding while others retracted. The entire scene appeared to be alive with alternating pulsation and conversion. It would make a normal person lose their sanity. Luckily for her, Missy was well beyond worrying about that.

As she meticulously made her way deeper, Missy paid great attention to the grave distractions coming from every angle. The root system pulled up and out of the ground, causing the slightly used, stolen Mercedes to rise and fall like a great ship traversing a sea storm. The rocking jerked both of them down towards the dash and back into their seats.

"Hold on to yer tits, Tania. The ride ain't over yet!" Missy yelled out, excitement pulsing through her voice.

Something in the distance finally came into view. It stretched for as far as Missy could see. Standing above the ground line, it looked like the fence around a junkyard. And she was heading the car right towards an opening.

"Guess we'll just drive this bitch right through the middle. Whatcha think, Tania?"

No response.

Missy pushed onward. While it seemed everything that surrounded the car was in a constant state of flux, the ominous barricade stood still like the mighty oak. Now she just needed to carefully maneuver a bit longer.

As the car began to enter the gaping entrance to the fence, the widest of trees slammed into the passenger's side of the car. The impact pushed the car up off its right tires. The airbags deployed, snapping both of their necks back to the head rests. Everything seemingly stopped, as the fraction of a second it took to cause major damage had nearly stopped time. Missy held tightly on to the steering wheel, trying desperately to avoid any further potential injury. Tania's head and limbs flailed wildly, as the car started its descent back to the ground. Missy tightened her grip and braced herself, as the tires both landed back onto terra firma. While the ordeal took only a second or two, it felt like a much longer time.

"Holy *SHIT*! Man, I never seen that until it plowed right into the damn car! Wow. Just WOW, that was some shit, Tania. Can't say I ever done that before. But sure as shit got my juices going!" Missy exclaimed, seemingly more excited that something like that happened to her rather than afraid that a tree with a four-foot diameter traveled over the ground and crashed into the front end of the car.

The Mercedes, now apparently out of commission, came to full stop shortly after making its way through the opening in the fence. On this side, Missy could see deeper into the woods, making out distant buildings in the distance, and with a lot less trees. The entire aura of the place was flipped on its head. An odd fog draped over the entire scene.

"Well, we ain't in Kansas anymore, ain't we, Tania?" Missy said as she put the car into park and opened the door. A heaviness held firm in the tight night air. There was an uneasiness that was there as well.

Missy got a look at her surroundings. Even to her, this place provided a level of creepiness that put goosebumps up and down her skin. The most unnerving part of everything was the complete silence that echoed through the area. A June night in New Jersey would have all types of insects and nightlife calling out to each other, let alone the noise interference the locals might add. Tonight, in this area, the void of sound was deafening.

"This is the place," Erwin said quietly from the other side of the Mercedes.

"No argument here."

"It will be tomorrow, here. We need to finish the job." With that Erwin was gone.

"Completely understood," Melissa answered. She peered deep into the areas that the Mercedes' headlights couldn't reach. No signs of life. No movement.

Then there it was. A hazy blue figure slowly came to sight. Was it a matter of the right place, right time? Melissa didn't care so much. She was here, and she was not alone.

OFELIA 2

An uneasy stillness hung gently through the night air. Momentary halts in the landscape near the waypoint made things easier to feel the other presence. Time was quickly running out, and they could feel it.

"*She will be here, right?*" Cobalt asked meekly.

"I believe so. Time is nearly out. We need to act fast," Ofelia replied, trying to quell the unrest within her enormous, blue corporal body. She wasn't truly sure if Perry would come. They had spoken at length at times how things would transpire, but now that the time was rapidly approaching. And it appeared that a fork in their road was presenting itself.

"*What if she doesn't come? What if we fail?*"

"We both know what will happen to us. The Sable is not the most judicial."

"*What will become of us?*"

"There will be no more us. No more of any of this. The end will be...well, it won't be pleasant. But worst of all. That red devil. The power. It will make it even more nefarious. That is the one thing that concerns me." Ofelia explained plainly, with pangs of pain reverberating through her voice. Throughout life and beyond that, Ofelia had met many of the worst people, things, and demons. She had made it through the other side every time. She had come and gone through the waypoint back to this place and returned with a job completed. She still didn't understand why the Sable gave her this job. Well, Ofelia had her thoughts. But the most precious commodity was the mere hours that remained.

Ofelia peered deep through the woods. She could make out the peaceful surface of the lake in the distance. Desperation was growing inside them. Something was amiss, but Ofelia couldn't figure if it was with Perry or something else.

Not but two feet in front of them, the air became overly heavy. A dense shadow formed in the middle of the forest, with a gentle breeze emanating from inside out. It grew out and morphed into a mass that reached down and touched the ground. Some of the heaviness that weighed upon Ofelia and Cobalt was lifted as the amorphous shadow figure melted into a more defined shape and size.

"Perry, we were beginning to worry that we wouldn't see you again," Ofelia exhaled with relief.

The shadowy figure with very distinctive Perry features took as much shape as it could. Where they were meeting wasn't a place where they both truly existed. But the figure was the same that had come in the past, the same that had bonded with them, the same that promised to help them through the worst. The sight, while not fully formed, was quite inviting.

"Sorry I hadn't come earlier. It is getting nutty, and I finally got some time," Perry explained.

"*Where is your body?*" Cobalt asked.

"With Uncle Em. It is in good hands. So, tomorrow is the day?"

Time within the waypoint was quite fuzzy. Things moved at a different pace and direction. What Perry called a day didn't translate exactly. Ofelia drew upon her days in Perry's shoes to understand.

"Yes, tomorrow is the end," Ofelia replied.

"Well, glad I was able to get over here again. So do you think the plan will still work?"

"*The drug addict is what you are referring to?*" Cobalt threw out.

"Yeah, her. Do you still think that she will do?" Perry asked earnestly.

Cobalt slightly shrugged its shoulders.

"I don't see why not," Ofelia affirmed.

The Perry figure nodded agreeingly. "Again, I will be close by tomorrow. Across the street, at a party. I am counting on you to have her there."

Ofelia, by way of Cobalt, returned the nod. "By us talking about it, she will be there. Erwin has always been close by when you are here. He knows. That means the others know. But you need to be careful. The one is unhinged and dangerous."

"Oh yeah, I had a close encounter with that one. Careful isn't something I am taking for granted," the shadow replied.

"And your uncle, he is reliable? Can he assist?"

"Already is. I filled him in. He is down to help. I didn't tell him all the ins and outs. If I did, surely, he would try to stop me."

"*He is a good man.*"

"Yeah, that is for sure. I always felt like he was my dad that I didn't have. He is a good man," the Perry shadow expressed, slightly sniffling.

"Family is what you make it," Ofelia added bluntly. "Family is what is around you when you need it."

The figure nodded again. "And there is something else. There were a couple of men that came over, asking questions about what was going on. I think they can help too."

"*Who are they?*"

"Their names were Rus and Al, I think. Rus was not very old. Al looked like he had been through a lot. And it looked like he knew a lot more than he was letting on."

"Al? Are you sure?"

"Or Peter. I'll be honest, didn't really have a connection like I did with Rus."

"*Alex Peters?*" Cobalt exclaimed.

"Yeah, that is it. I guess you two know him?"

"Alex is a good man. We know Alex. He can be a good ally," Ofelia explained.

"Good to know. I have Rus's contact somewhere around my body. I should make sure I hold onto that," the Perry shadow added.

Ofelia took a step back, and Cobalt followed suit. Their body language hung low, with many things weighing down both of their consciences. The end of the line was at hand. They both needed to make sure of things before they pushed forward.

"Perry, with tomorrow being the close, I need to reiterate something," Ofelia started. "You are a being that doesn't have to be involved. There is no reason for you to be doing this. This is not something you need to be included."

Perry didn't respond, the shadow shifted back and forth within the early summer breeze that made its way between them.

"You are risking so much. But you are not getting anything back. I just want to ask you again. Are you sure?" Ofelia pushed.

Taking a second to gather her thoughts, the shadow answered, "You are really me. I am you. If I can help you out, it could make one of us. I didn't have the support, neither did you. I guess you can say you are the same. It is something that you would do for me if the tables were turned."

The calming answer brought a smile over both Ofelia and Cobalt. Any friends during this time would go a long way. And someone like Perry would go even further.

As soon as the moment had arrived upon them, it was gone. They were not alone.

Rustling was audible in the distance. Beyond the barrier the trees were moving around randomly. The chaos that exuded the scene brought a tense feeling over them. But that is when they all saw the other figure come into sight.

The shape began to form with each distinctive step. The outline continued to sharpen as the being continued to make its way through the forest. The sound through the undergrowth made echoes through the area.

Before both of them, Ofelia and Cobalt in their forms and Perry in her more ethereal form, could make out what was in front of them, heading their way, the figure in the distance spoke out, "Well, it seems like a good ol' reunion of sorts here."

The figure continued to take shape as it approached them. A distinct female shape took hold, pulling something of size behind her. Whatever it was she was dragging along was of a size, but the figure seemed to effortlessly make her way through the woods onward.

"Oh, please don't mind me at all. I will be in and out before you can ever realize. I am only dropping off a package. Setting it free out in the wilderness, so to speak."

Ofelia could feel the other side to what lay in front of her.

"I mean no harm. Just a passerby meandering through the beautiful night."

Ofelia could now feel the smile ominously hanging in the dark. This was not good. Not good for anyone.

As the figure got closer, she saw something that made all the alarms ring off loudly in her head. Before her was the one that Erwin was controlling. And they were both together.

"Oh, I am sorry. I did not formally introduce myself. You may call me Melissa," she spoke softly.

Ofelia shot a glance at Perry. The look of abject horror that hung across her semi-formed face was an obvious indication of despair.

As Melissa made her way towards the lot of them, the package that she was dragging behind her became quite apparent. It was a lifeless body. She was pulling it over the vast root system, holding both ends of the jean ends folded into her two hands. With each pull, the limp body bounced around peacefully on the ground. Leaves, twigs and the like were caught up in what appeared to be once well-kept blonde hair. Every time Melissa traversed the forest floor, the body's head knocked against each floral flotsam and jetsam that scattered around.

Now fully into focus, Melissa continued, "I have heard that if I leave something in this place, it might not ever be found."

Melissa stopped near the foot of all of them. Without much effort, she yanked the corpse from behind her and dropped it squarely in the middle. While it didn't make much of an effect on Ofelia, outside of the potentially senseless loss of life by the inevitable red terror that was tormenting them all, the sight of the body caused what was left of the figure within the shadow to not resemble Perry in the slightest.

"Oh, this one? She finally outlived her usefulness. That is the thing with people. They tend to keep going even though there is no point. But you see, we have a destiny. We are the ones that will help usher in change. We will be beautiful and wonderful."

"*You will bring hell and chaos,*" bellowed Cobalt

"Yes. But aren't both the same? Isn't there an unadulterated peacefulness and beauty in chaos? It is something that is pure. There are not many things in this world that can be like that. Why shouldn't we all embrace it?"

Melissa looked down towards the body on the ground. Almost on instinct, Ofelia and the shadowy form of Perry followed suit. With a swift kick to the corpse's head from Melissa, all of them could see the cause of death. The handle of a kitchen knife was planted deeply into the right side of the young girl's neck. From how it appeared, it must have been relatively quick and painless, if ever such a thing could be possible. Blood had long been coagulated up and down her neck. Not much else was out of place. Before the end came calling for her, the girl must have trusted this Melissa more than what was good for her.

With her focus downward, Ofelia didn't see it coming. Before she could react, Melissa had thrown out her hands violently towards Perry. Despite Perry not truly being there with them, Melissa was still able to grab hold of her. The calm and vicious nature of her actions was both terrifying and explosive. The shadow figure that Perry had been communicating through writhed in pain. Melissa's face did not change as she wretched down, trying to extinguish the glimmer of hope that Ofelia held dear.

"Stop, stop! *Erwin!*" Ofelia screamed. Melissa did not stop.

Instead of heeding the warning, she increased the force, and hunched over the shadow. The lower halves of her arms disappeared into the billowing, black mist that was writhing around, desperate to leave this plane.

"I am just…," Melissa started, pushing the Perry mist around, attempting to end this unsightly battle before things could get any further.

Without any more thought, Ofelia, with Cobalt's help, lounged directly into Melissa's midsection. As soon as they made contact, the bond between Erwin and his connection was severed. Her hands came back from the black shadow, and Perry was gone.

MARTIN 6

"This is wrong," Martin said aloud to himself. It wasn't much more than a whisper, considering the last thing that he wanted was to wake the boys or even attract his significant other downstairs. "This is wrong as *hell.*"

Martin was kneeling on the living room floor next to the body of his loving niece. She had been lying down for not more than ten minutes at that point. Alongside her were the instruments of the night: a half-eaten jar of peanut butter, chunky upon Perry's request and a half-drained bottle of allergy medicine. At first, Martin was quite skeptical of the whole thing. With each of his objections, she had the equal and opposite answer. The peanut butter would send her into a mild case of anaphylaxis shock. It wouldn't kill her but would make the next few days damn rough. The knock off brand allergy liquid, cherry flavored of course, would help twofold. Number one, it would help to counter her reaction. That was a plus. The other reason was as concerning as the peanut butter. With enough of a dose, Perry would be sent to sleepy time. Put those two things together, and she would float around in a more ethereal form, visiting the being in the woods. If Martin hadn't had an encounter of his own, he probably wouldn't have played along. Then again, Perry was never a kid to make up stories, even though she had every right and reason to do so while growing up in her broken home.

For the first minutes of the whole ordeal, Martin watched intently as Perry twitched and slowly jerked her limbs while laying on her back. It reminded him of the way his boyhood mutt of a dog used to sit in the summer sun, trotting away in its own personal dreamland. At one point, all movement had stopped. Her left eye cracked up, revealing a pale white from behind. Perry turned her head, first to the left and then to the right, but back again straight up. Her limbs started up their chaotic movement, causing static build up and discharge on the floor rug.

"Jesus, she must have found her. Perry must have gotten there," Martin continued his whisper.

Then it was over. Perry's body laid eerily still. There was absolutely no movement. Martin struggled to see her chest expand and contract. It was there, but it was faint.

Five minutes passed. Still nothing. No arms. No legs. Even Perry's left eye was now completely shut. The pangs of panic had built up through his stomach and into the back of his throat. The uncertainty of the whole ordeal felt like it was killing him.

Just as the absence of movement came upon Perry suddenly, what happened next was both unexpected and horrifying. The skin around her neck got pushed in, causing Perry to begin writhing around violently. She couldn't move her head at all. The flesh around her neck began to form and take shape. Martin could see two imprints of hands gripping her throat. There was not a soul there with them, yet something unseen was trying to choke the life out of her. The veins bunched up at the base of her head. Nothing was flowing. Something was killing Perry.

Martin started to panic. He was not prepared for this. What possibly could he do? He sure as hell couldn't enter that same hypnotic trance that she was under and beat the shit out of whatever was on the other side. At least he didn't believe he could.

Rather than continue one further second, and risk losing Perry to her tormentor, Martin grabbed both of her shoulders. He gave her a quick and forceful jolt back and forth. He didn't want to inflict any more damage at all. But as sure as the sun rises in the east, Martin wasn't going to let her perish.

Just as Perry's face morphed from a red hue to the alarming slight blue, Martin tried one more time. Rather than try to force whatever was attacking her away, he leaned down next to one of Perry's ears. Different tact sometimes works.

With a soft tone, Martin whispered into her ear, "Come back to me. Come back to your family."

The moment he finished his plea, Perry popped up into an upright position. She desperately forced all the air she could down into her lungs. She gasped and brought her own hands up towards her neck, checking to see if her attacker was still around. Finding nothing but herself, Perry put her hands on her knees, and wept quietly.

"Thank you, Uncle Em. I mean, *Thank you!* I was in big trouble. Things went wrong. All sorts of wrong. But then I heard you. I heard you calling me back. And I am here," Perry sighed. "I don't know how it happened, but I am here."

"What the *hell* happened? Did you talk to her? Was she the one that was trying to...kill you?" Martin rambled off.

"Oh no. It wasn't Ofelia. But we were not alone. She came. I mean, they were there."

"What did you call her? The she-beast?" Martin attempted a little humor. It didn't register with Perry.

"Yeah, her and the other thing. The red thing. They were one. They call themselves Melissa. I just...I mean, it was too much."

"And she...er, they grabbed you?"

"Yeah. I wasn't really there. But it didn't matter, that thing grabbed me. I could feel the pain. All I could feel was the heat of the attack. My god, I never want to feel that again."

"Amen, little girl."

Perry lowered her head down, bringing her knees up to her chest, and rested her weak neck on top. The tears pushed their way down her cheeks, making her skin glisten in the light. What could be next?

"Our plan. We gotta get a new plan," Perry started. She didn't look towards Martin but kept going. "Our plan is toast, Uncle Em. Melissa was in the middle of the woods. She was dragging.... the knife...she...they murdered Tania."

Martin gasped. That was the easiest ticket to ending this whole bat shit craziness that they were knee deep inside. She was the most vulnerable and could have solved their problems.

"Yeah, it sucks. And tomorrow is the day. I could sense it. We gotta figure this out and get it done tomorrow. Less than one day. We gotta get someone else to Ofelia. If she fails, and this red pain-in-the-ass comes back even more powerful, it could just be all hell loose. Not hell, but chaos. The thing is terrible."

"Someone else…"

"Don't think less of me, Uncle Em. We gotta get a bunch of someones there. Tomorrow. We don't have time to come up with a new plan. We just gotta act. Think on our feet."

This was the time that it hit Martin. He pulled his own knees into his chest and began to quietly sob.

"Someone is going through that waypoint tomorrow with Ofelia. We have to make sure of that."

ALEX 3

Deep down inside, Alex knew the day was today. He had found himself in situations like this one many times in his lifetime. They always seemed to follow the same pattern. The air was changing. Any other resident of the town should be able to figure out things were amiss. It wasn't completely obscure. Then again, not many of the townsfolk were as observant as he was. That is what made Alex a very fine career.

This time was different. As he had called it in his mind, this closing had different implications. Alex had seen firsthand the turbulence that some of the souls that came through the various town's waypoints could cause, even outside of the times that the jet black being made its way over. He also had seen the good that they could accomplish, including curing old Mrs. Rafferty's stage four lung cancer. The doctors still can't wrap their minds around that. On the other hand, those doctors were earthily. But all that might not matter in the slightest if the dice don't roll right.

Alex, despite knowing that the end of something was nigh, sat back in his chair and placed his heels on top of his desk. He took a moment and looked at his office wall. Through all his years being a P.I., he really didn't have much to show for it. Sure, there were the many different connections that he helped to foster over the years, and with that came certain perks and amenities. What he did have were his memories. Some of them were laid out, a bit haphazardly throughout the years, on the floor next to his desk. But his favorites, and most important ones, were hung onto the wall closest to his desk. A fair number of them were of him and Marianne. The early times. The fun times. The what-could-have-been times. Then there were those of him and Rus. The wise times. The teaching times. The what-the-future-holds times.

All that was nice to reflect upon. But Alex was waiting for this time. Not exactly how he imagined it, but deep down inside, he knew it was it. Once all this craziness finally subsides, the keys to the farm will be handed over to his soon-to-be former partner. He wasn't one to ride off into the sunset so to speak, he felt that would be leaving Rus high and dry. As nutty as it was, it felt like when they made it over to the other side, this would be Rus's float or sink moment in his life. Alex Peters would be officially retired.

"I kinda like the sound of that," Alex thought to himself. *"We are in the home stretch. Once I get through this, I will rest."*

Feeling a bit more content and determined, Alex rose to his feet. He stretched his arms up over his head, getting a good wrench on his back. One of the side effects of the clock kept pushing ahead, but something that he had grown to live with. Twisting back and forth to relieve the rest of the pressure build up, he found himself staring out his window, over Point Lake, and into the restricted woods. The lake was overly still for a June day. Alex couldn't find a single ripple disturbing the glassy surface. Even with that, the trees slowly rocked side to side as if a constant breeze was pushing through. The mismatch that his eyes were obvious and telling.

Alex pulled up the bottom sash of his window. He wanted to let a bit of the outside inside. The moment it hit the back of his throat he knew. It was time. Well, the clock on the wall read a quarter to eleven, but the case was rapidly closing. He needed to get Rus on the way, sooner rather than later.

As he went to close the window once more, Alex's eyes caught his safe. He took a pause to think about it. A gun in this situation might not have any effect.

"That one will work on anything from here, not there. I am not sure it would help." That thought didn't stop Alex from struggling inside for a split second. Not only had he only brought it on a case a handful of times, but he also never shot it outside of the shooting range. This time seemed different than anything he had ever experienced. Finding the key in the top drawer of his desk, notwithstanding the lack of creativity for hiding places, he unlocked the safe, flipped the lid and pulled out the sidearm. He made sure the safety was still on when he placed it inside the holster, also found in the safe.

Placing the effects on the desk, Alex fumbled to find his phone in his pocket. It was time to move, and Rus needed to get a move on. As he pulled it out, a quick, forceful gust of wind shot through the window and knocked it out of his hand. It landed right next to his gun on the desk.

Alex turned his attention back to the window. He placed his hands on top and began to push the lower pane back in place. Something across Point Lake caught his eye. Even from this distance, he could make out two somethings on the other side of the water. What wasn't there a moment ago, two large things bobbed up and down in the lake near the shoreline. The various colors that shined off them in the light made it clearly apparent.

"Holy shit. Those are bodies," Alex exclaimed to himself. Without even thinking, he swung on his holster and grabbed his phone. It didn't take long to sort through his contact list before he came to Rus's number.

A few rings after hitting dial, Rus picked up.

"Where are you at?" he asked.

"I am at the office. It is happening. It seems like it is going to be a rough go of it. Are you still available?"

"Bossman, I have to see this one through." Rus replied without much hesitation.

"Sounds good. Get over here as soon as you can. I am not sure how much time is left."

The line went dead. Rus already hung up. Alex purposely held back the sight of the two bobbers holding spots in the lake. He didn't want to plant that visual in Rus's head at this point. Surely, he would hear about it later, but adding that factor to the mix might be too much for the poor guy at this point.

Now with the resounding alarms ringing through his head, Alex tried to take a moment to calm himself down. His next moves were critical, and the last thing he needed was a misstep.

With his gun on his side, Alex threw over the sport jacket he had perpetually hanging on the back of his chair. The last thing that he wanted to happen in this situation was to be running through town, with the locals seeing an armed non police officer acting potentially frantic.

Without thinking, Alex bent down to his office phone, and hit the speed dial button at the bottom of the list. Rarely was that the case, but he had reached out for less serious things. This was needed.

The phone rang three times. It always rang three times when he hit the ultimate button on the speed dial. At the end of the third ring, the other side picked up.

"Mr. Peters. What can I do ya for?" the other line responded.

"You know I wouldn't be calling you like this if it wasn't serious," Alex opened.

"Oh huh. I got it, Alex. What do you need from me?"

"Time," Alex answered.

"I'm listening."

"An hour or so. After that, you are free to do your job."

"Of course. But I must know why I am going to hold back the whole force for that amount of time."

Alex sighed. The point of no return was here for him.

"Chief, the woods are closing. Whatever is here is going back."

"This has happened plenty of times before and both of us know it. We have been through this same thing many times. What is different, Alex? I am serious," Chief Williams inquired.

Another sigh. Alex could hear from the Chief's tone that he could sense there was trouble. Alex never really showed any bit of exasperation in this voice.

"That dangerous one that we know is lurking around town…"

"Melissa Simpson," Chief interrupted.

"Excuse me?"

"You didn't hear it from me, it is an open investigation."

"Understood," Alex agreed.

"She is quite unhinged from what we figure. We checked her old man's house. We couldn't find anyone home, but the garage door was wide open. Back door wide open."

Alex cringed. "I think I know where you need to look. Someone is floating on the other side of Point Lake."

"Jesus, Alex. So, you are asking me to hold back when there is a body floating in my town?" the Chief pushed back.

"No, that is not what I am asking. I am asking you to turn away for about an hour when there are two bodies floating in your town."

"*Shit, Alex!*" Alex could sense Chief Williams running his offhand through his hair, considering the proposition given to him. A few tense seconds passed while Alex held his breath. "You know this is a huge ask of me, right?"

"Chief, I completely understand. The thing is it is the last ask."

The breathless pause was now taken from the other end. "Does that mean what I think it does?" the Chief asked earnestly.

"This is it for me, dear friend. I am stepping away from the game."

"Well, I figure you can consider this will be your first retirement gift, Alex. We will catch up later."

With that, the line went silent. With the quick little conversation, Alex just bought some time before the police would intervene. It wouldn't be too long, but from the looks of it, it shouldn't take long.

MARTHA 2

It had been a few days since Martha last saw her daughter. It was another one of those many times in her life that Martha relented and had her brother and his wife take charge. She was sure that they knew what she was doing but didn't care in the least. Perry seemed to cool off and get through things after a little drop in with her good ole Uncle Mart. He always had a way to connect to people. Maybe it was his goofiness. Could be the rare times he got serious. Martha could never put her finger on what her brother had that she didn't, but in this case it didn't matter. She wanted her daughter to work through it.

But something told her that today was different. Today it was Martha's time to step in as the mother. It was a predictable pattern, but she could tell that Perry deep down appreciated it.

Martha had gotten up that day with the rise of the sun. Her head seemed to have gotten rid of its recent state of fogginess. This mourning period of the year has been slowly passing, and she started feeling a bit more in control of things. On a Friday night in the summer, Martha would be at some point dropping by all her local hangouts, but not this one. This Friday night, Martha pulled out the

Book.

The Book bordered on an obsession. Over the years, she clipped newspaper blurbs, took notes of things she saw, and put together the missing links of a hazy memory. If she had a spare room in her house, Martha had no doubt that the entire area would be lined with string and post-its like some of the old detective movies had shown. But, for her, the strings and post-its were the Book. She had connections and references through what used to be a simple black and white composition notebook. It had been many years since she had any new entries in it, but it was all the same for her. Losing her parents in such an unsolved way clearly was not going away in her mind any time soon. Martha would find the answers, and she knew they were out there. With all the dots that could be connected, there always was a gaping hole in her thoughts. And it always felt like Mart knew more than he was letting on.

With a clear head, Martha packed away the Book back into the bottom drawer of her nightstand. The sober mind made maneuvering early in the morning quite a breeze. The only downside was that Martha could not turn off her locomotive speed thoughts.

"So, yeah, the cops found the car. That cannot be argued," Martha started with herself as she brewed a cup of coffee. "Was it their car? What did the police report say, the VIP number was the same. Or VIM, I always forget what it is called. I remember that one officer explaining to me that each car had a unique number and it matched what their car was."

Martha always found it odd how far back she could draw from her memory banks when she wasn't in full blown self-medication mode.

"So yeah, they found the car. It was right there near that lake near Mart's house. That is a whole 'nother ball o' wax. I know I am not that far, but I couldn't live that close to where they had their 'accident'," Martha continued, even making air quotes even though she was the only person in her house.

"Maybe there is something about that place. Some kind of clue hiding in plain sight." Martha paused for internal deliberation. "Yeah, that could work."

Today was the day that Perry's friend Lucy was having a birthday party. And after speaking with Sasha, regrettably, on the phone the other night, the kicker was that the party was to take place at that little strip mall of stores in Hex Point, right across the street from the lake. Two birds with one stone; reconnect with Perry via motherly care and a bit of investigation. It was her weekend off from work, and, hell, maybe she could get some more details out of her brother. It was worth a shot.

With the quick productivity in the morning, Martha took the time to settle down into her thoughts. The party was in the afternoon, and it was only ten. She would probably leave shortly and show up a bit early at her brother's house. Would Perry object to her mother helping to drop her off at a party? Probably not.

The sobriety that had infected her brain left Martha with a bit more thinking power. The near endless fog that she tried to meander through was the norm and a bit of comfort. Being able to think about stuff, and about everything, was always an odd sensation.

"Come clarity," Martha whispered to herself, before grabbing her effects and heading out the door.

She made it over to Mart's house. As Martha approached the front, she could hear the boys out back.

"If the twins are playing in the backyard, Perry is probably with them," Martha thought. And she was correct.

Martha helped herself inside and found her brother in the dining room. He was sitting at the table, literally twiddling his thumbs.

"Why, hello sister. What can I do for ya?" Mart asked without looking up.

"Well, I just figured I would come over. It has been a few days since we spoke. I hope we can all catch up. Maybe move forward a bit."

Mart looked up and caught her eyes. "Are you good?"

Her brother was well accustomed to the cycles Martha invariably went through. She couldn't hide it. "I guess so. I pulled out the Book last night."

Mart nodded and rose from his chair. His face showed Martha that he was on the same page.

"I just wondered if I could stop by early, and just...chat," Martha trailed off.

"Just chat? That doesn't sound like my sis, no not at all," Mart added as he started to meander around the dining area. His steps made him over to the sliding glass door to the back. All appeared accounted for, so he returned over to Martha. He led her over to the living room to have a seat on the couch.

"Listen, sis. I don't know what you want me to say. There is nothing to say that hasn't been said," Mart whispered sternly to her.

Head cocked to the side, Martha pushed forward. "Mart. You and I know that you are a shitty liar. You always have been, and you always will be. I am not saying that to get you pissed. I am just stating a fact. And you are now looking me in the eyes, and lying to me."

Mart, clearly being called out, placed his head down into his hands. He rocked his body back and forth in place. Martha had seen her younger brother act like this in their youth. He did the same thing the day that their family dog ran away. He last did it the night their parents had their little 'accident'. Mart was hiding something from her.

"What is it, Mart? I am your sister. Why are you hiding something from me?" Martha pleaded.

Mart just kept rocking his body. He started slowly shaking his head. *"Keep turning the screws, he will relent,"* Martha thought to herself.

Martha reached out and put a loving hand in the middle of his back. He instantly stopped moving and raised his head out of his hands. There were tears slowly pushing down Mart's cheeks.

"Mart. I am your sister," Martha repeated. "I am your older sister. I know I have had a tendency to go off the rails sometimes. I can't deny that. The parents...well that hit me hard. I think that is obvious. If there might have been any details or hopes that I could have clung to, maybe things would have been different for me."

The last sentence got Mart right in the side. He reached out and grabbed Martha with both arms, holding her tight. It was another thing that she hadn't felt from him since the parents.

Mart pulled her closer and brought his face towards her ear.

"It is the woods. By the lake. The detective we hired seemed to be very cautious there. He always seemed to know more than he let on."

Martha felt somewhat vindicated of her borderline insanity. She wasn't wrong. But she could have kept on the screws, digging into her brother for not letting her know for how many years. Instead, she let him keep going.

"And then the other day, he shows up. Here. Asking questions about that place. What I know for sure is that there is some sort of portal there. I really don't get where it goes, and, at this point, I really don't care. What I care about is that Perry is mixed up in all of this shit, and something is going to happen today."

Even if the rest of the family didn't come in, that was all that Martha had to hear. Vindication was achieved, now she needed to protect her daughter.

The boys sprung through the back door, mud from head to toe. They were followed by Sasha, who gave Martha a nod and a wave acknowledging her existence. Perry was the last to come in. The moment the two saw each other, Perry stopped walking.

"Well, I need to get these little guys a good wash. Don't you have Lucy's party soon, Perry?" Sasha asked.

"Yeah, not too long," Perry answered, without taking her eyes away from Martha. Sasha escorted the boys to the bathroom for a good scrubbing.

Rather than wait for her daughter, Martha rose to her feet and slowly made her way over. Perry didn't run away like she had done sometimes in her youth. She always had a keen understanding of her mother's current mental state. Perry was always the brightest.

"Perry. I just wanted to drop by to see you. It has been some time. Things are better."

Martha caught Perry shooting a glance towards her brother. Upon seeing his rosy cheeks and red eyes, Perry would know exactly how the conversation went. She couldn't hide that but hoped her daughter would be agreeable.

"Well, that is good," Perry responded flatly.

"I was hoping that I could go with you to help drop you off at the party. Maybe we can catch up?" Martha put it out there.

Perry shot another glance towards Mart. There was a heightened level of concern in her face this time.

"Not sure how much there is to catch up on. It has only been a few days."

"Well, I am your mother. I just want to help."

Perry relented. What she did next caught Martha completely off guard. Perry lunged at her, grabbing her by the torso. She squeezed in a loving embrace. Martha squeezed right back.

"*Something bad is going to happen,*" Martha thought.

ERWIN 1

The force was getting greater with each of the moments that walked by. Every single second tried to pull him back. The waypoint was only going to stay open for a short period of time. Erwin would be damned if he didn't ruin someone's day.

Cars passed by, completely unaware that he was standing a mere foot away from the main street. Everyone was simply and ignorantly going about their day. Having such a great amount of anonymity brought a smile to Erwin's faded face.

"Just keep on doing what you do, people. I will be gone shortly," he said to himself through his jagged grin. "Oh, but I will be back. And it will be glorious."

Erwin chuckled as he finished. The other times that he decided to be as brazen as he was generally didn't turn out very well. Then again, he was never the one with his back against the wall. Rather, Erwin was the opportunist. Always had been. That is how he liked it.

With his flowing red locks swaying against the wake of traffic, Erwin stood patiently despite the clock seemingly gaining steam. It was patience that had helped him throughout his time. What else could he do otherwise? Each part of his plan was well thought out, another one of his calculating traits, and moved along as he had wished. There hadn't been a single hiccup. With most of the time he had crossed over from the Souls to the land where he once truly roamed, Erwin had seen his fair share of problems with his plans. It was normal with the person he picked to help out. He had seen his fair share of failures. It was quite surprising how undedicated people could be. But in the end, those that backed out, and invariably found themselves on the wrong side of the law. And who was going to believe the ghostly, red-haired figure that came from the trees was coercing them to do it?

"Just another day in paradise, I guess," Erwin softly spoke, watching each car pass. He had positioned himself in front of the last parking spot off the road. He needed it clear. Anyone that thought they found a little meaningless treasure as they were running behind whatever trivial task they had to complete would be seeing a completely nondescript sedan. A plain, slightly rusted white sedan of no particular origin sat there as long as Erwin wanted the sight to be seen. Of course, it would be slightly crooked within the spot, as most parkers tended to leave their vehicles. It was best to not stand out when the plot was murder.

"Devious is what they call me, right?" Erwin asked. He had heard it on occasion before on both sides of the waypoint. "Well, that means I am doing something right. My reputation precedes me. Well, who am I to disappoint."

The only thing standing between himself and success was a mortal. She hadn't been strong enough at certain times, and Erwin had to step in. That was really not his preference. It was always easier to pull strings from the shadows. Someone else would always take the blame for his actions. Deep down inside, Erwin knew his captives were aware that in the end, they would be the scapegoat. They would be the ones locked up. They would be the ones on trial. They would be the ones to burn. Considering Erwin couldn't truly do anything, but his persuasion, well, that was one of the best in the business.

Erwin scanned both ways, with the patience slowly fading. He hoped that she would stick to the plan. She had been getting reckless lately. In the end they were still on track. Erwin never really thought of removing the friend from the equation. He did enjoy the amount of torture and stress that he was able to put down upon her. Yet, in the end, the friend would have become a roadblock at some part. Maybe she was right to put her knife through her neck. Maybe it was a bit too late. Or maybe it was a bit too soon. Another person within his flock could have been a help at this juncture. But then again, another person romping around could mean another person that the blue bastard could take back to the Sable.

As the waypoint force pulled ever so slightly harder on his chest, Erwin found the girl strolling down the sidewalk. The nonchalance in her stride made him cringe. Down at her right side, she was holding a towel clearly wrapped around something. And that something was glinting in the midday sun.

"*Sonaofabitch,*" Erwin muttered. The level of brazenness was at an all-time high. There were times where Erwin surely wanted to go full off the hinges, but that would hurt the plan. Nothing could hurt the plan. Not even this girl sauntering down the heart of this town with not only a knife in plain sight, but the murder weapon. If the police or even a curious bystander might come across her, the plan would be ruined. Not that Erwin really cared what happened to her. She could spend the rest of her days in whatever hellhole of a prison. It didn't matter much to him. When all is said and done, that is probably what is going to happen to her anyway.

Erwin shifted his focus from the mirage of the parked car and onto the girl's side. If anyone were to notice her as she made her way through the intersection and towards where he was, they would now see a bookbag on her side rather than a jagged knife wrapped in what is most likely a blood-ridden towel. He was careful not to draw any attention towards himself or the now empty space in front of him. As good as he was, Erwin couldn't properly multitask. But the worry was for nothing, as the drivers and passengers that moved by hardly took notice of the shadowy figure hanging out in front of the strip of assorted stores. Not even ghosts are that audacious to be loitering in the place of the local teens.

Within a few moments and smile packed steps, the girl was right by Erwin's side.

Grin still muttered across her face, she started, "Was a-matter? Didja miss me?"

"Please be a bit more discreet for me, okay?" Erwin answered, pointing down at her side.

Sensing his tone, the girl rewrapped the surprisingly clean blade. Erwin was expecting to find parts and evidence of the horror scene that was the front seat of the car. Again, this girl shocked Erwin with the level that she had descended. If this was before his unfortunate and equally fortunate time at the lab, he could see the two of them being very close. Friends, even. But even that was a stretch for him.

Now that the weapon was out of the open, Erwin returned his attention to the vacated parking spot. It wasn't a moment too soon either, as a pickup truck that was lumbering down the street started to brake, the driver clearly scanning for an easy end.

"Are you ready?" Erwin asked.

"Shit, ready as I'll ever be. I'm all ramped up," the girl answered.

"And the plan?"

"I'mma mess that thing up good. Finish the job, ya' know."

Without acknowledging her response, Erwin continued, "When she arrives, it will inevitably be just her and her uncle. I will release the spot in front, they will take that, I am sure. He won't be able to see in the back from there or through the windows. And the front door…"

The girl reached into her jeans pocket and retrieved a few small, metal items. Seeing that she held up her end, Erwin once again scanned the traffic. Not finding anything either way, he took over the girl. One of the many skills that he mastered in his other life revolved around doors and the locks they contain. In a matter of seconds, the deadbolt switched positions. Erwin exited and put up the parking spot closed sign.

"…is locked," Erwin continued. "Now, you need to hide out by the back door. Again, do not bring any attention to yourself. I will be close by. When the time comes, I will make sure that no one sees you or anything you are doing."

"Aye, aye! *Captain!*" the girl responded, while dropping the towel to the ground and using the jagged knife in a makeshift salute.

"Enough of that," Erwin barked. "It all ends here. She cannot leave here alive. If she dies here, not a soul will be going to the other side. If no one goes to the other side, I get that blue bastard's essence. And if I get that blue bastard's essence, then I can be nearly unstoppable here. Make sure it all happens. If it doesn't happen just like that, then you can kiss your ass goodbye."

The last tone made a good impact on the girl. The second that Erwin finished his last word, she was already rewrapping the knife, collecting herself, and heading around the side of the building.

Erwin retreated a bit, stopping at the corner of the wall. It gave him enough sight to watch for incoming. The shuffling that he heard coming from the other side of the building had stopped. The girl must have found a good spot to hide out, without major detection.

"And with the trap set, we shall wait, like the greatest of hunters," Erwin whispered to himself. "And before the blood dries on the sidewalk, it will be time to tie up the loose ends. You will be kissing your ass goodbye."

PERRY 6

Once she saw her mother in the living room, a knot formed in Perry's insides. She had a plan with Uncle Em. While it wasn't bulletproof, at least it was a plan. Today was the day of Lucy's party. Missy or Melissa or whoever the hell she is would be there. Not really sure where, but Perry had a strong inclination that the she-beast would make one final push. She was out to get Perry. The way that she changed from fizzle-haired nutjob to the well put together sociopath gave Perry pause. What Ofelia had informed her about the other thing from the other side was troubling to say the least. This girl was crazy and unhinged, but with the other thing, the red thing, she was on a whole different level.

Perry looked at her mother's face as they exchanged a few lines and could tell that they wouldn't be able to leave her behind. Whatever inspiration that she had got recently has brought her here, and she now was a wrench in the cogs. A source of complexity. Things could go awry with just Uncle Em and Perry, but her mother was quite a wildcard.

So, Perry grabbed her and hugged her. It wasn't as much a hug as it was an embrace. It was a genuine moment between the two, something that rarely had happened over the years. Perry couldn't really say when the next time this might happen ever again.

Seeing that it was inevitable, Perry didn't push her mother back on joining them. She just had to adapt. The plan would have to keep moving on. Somehow, someway that bully had to go back through to the other side.

Perry followed the two as the time had finally come to get a move on. They made their way out the front door and into Uncle Em's car. Perry took the backseat, letting her mother and mother's brother sit in the front. The entire time the two had been going back and forth, talking about things that happened or didn't happen in the past. Perry couldn't focus or even try to look like she was paying any attention. Clearly, she had other things on her mind. More important things.

It was not long before Uncle Em maneuvered the car down Main Street. It was a clear and beautiful summer Saturday, and the traffic was clogging up everywhere. People were all out and about, going to attend to their these things and their those. For an occasionally sleepy, anonymous town, Hex Point was alive with life. Maybe that would work in Perry's favor. Or maybe not.

As both Uncle and mother started getting a bit heated and emotional in their conversation, Perry started to scan the area. Every single parking spot in front of the small strip of stores was completely full, even the handicapped spots at the end of the building, where the dance studio was. It wasn't surprising, but Perry was hoping to have a drop off spot close to the party. It would be easier to get in and out. Less chance of a surprise.

Perry glanced across the street and found the diner Uncle Em liked had a line out the door. People were waiting as far as a few more store fronts. She was quite fond of the pancakes there. Once all of this was settled, Perry was pretty sure she could convince her uncle to swing by. He typically needed just a flimsy excuse to stop by for a good old diner size gorging.

The sun was shining bright and caught Perry off guard. She raised her hand to block some of the rays. In doing so, she caught sight of the windows above the diner and its neighboring stores. She had never noticed the offices and apartments that sat above before. The first window, directly above the diner, was where she saw him. Perry locked eyes for the briefest of moments with the detective that had stopped by Uncle Em's house the other day. In that briefest of moments, she could have sworn he nodded.

"Okay, another one in our corner," Perry mumbled under her breath.

"Not sure what you said back there, but we are here," Uncle Em. "And look, we got ourselves some front row parking." He slid the car into the only open space

Alarm bells rang in Perry's head. The level of anxiety and the tightness of her stomach's knot grew much tighter. A few meager seconds before, the entire line of spots was filled. Perry didn't notice any car exit. Something was amiss. They were definitely not alone.

Before she could react, the car was in park, and Uncle Em was twisted around towards her.

"We got your back," he said.

Her mother turned around in the same fashion. "I am glad I came over this morning, honey. Something inside told me to get up and get my shit together."

With that Perry cracked a smile. She could feel it, too. It did feel different. Something was there.

Perry opened her door and hopped out. While it wasn't a pep talk a grizzled high school varsity coach would give before homecoming, Perry's anxiety was tempered a bit. It was good to have her mother there, even though the plan might be out the window.

With a new hitch in her step, Perry headed towards the front door. She could see through the foyer and into the main lobby. Balloons and streamers adorned the walls. Everything was pink. Lucy was like that, she was a girly girl through and through. With the short-sighted hiccup that was the misguided friendship excluded, she was always there for her, and she was always consistent. All things considered, of course.

Perry reached out to open the first of the glass set of doors, but found it locked. And it wasn't just jammed or stuck like some of the old store fronts around town can get. This was deadbolt locked. No way in on this route.

A few inches above the handle there was a single piece of paper taped to the inside of the glass. Perry found it quite odd that she hadn't noticed it as she drew closer. But something like that, she chalked it up to nerves.

Door is broken, needs to stay locked. Please use entry in back.

Sorry for the inconvenience,
Management

Perry peeked in through the glass doors. She could make out foot traffic in the front of the studio. Amongst the clutter of sneakers and extra bags, she spotted a rung of keys half hidden.

"It is time," Perry muttered under her breath.

She turned around and found the eyes of her family still seated in the car. She nodded towards them. Both nodded back in concert. They were ready.

Perry started to make her way towards the back. The shortest way around was following the outside wall of the dance studio. That was the quickest and the most obvious. Before she got to the corner to head out of sight, Perry instead turned around and went what her grandfather, as Uncle Em would tell the story, would call the short cut. This route would give Perry a bit more time to get settled. It was also not the quickest and most obvious way. What sat in waiting behind the studio certainly would be hoping she would go around that side. Whatever was left in her control, Perry opted to execute.

Next to the dance studio were a few assorted other locales. There was the Hex Point Post Office. The good, old neighborhood drug store was next to that. Perry noticed the name always changed. A vacant location came next, littered with FOR RENT signs. The bagel shop was the last in line, and the other building corner drew near. Without hesitation, Perry shot to the side of the building.

She kept her eyes on the ground as she went along, looking for anything that might help her. The concrete sidewalk was littered with garbage cans and other refuse. Nothing really to note. As she approached the last turn, she spotted a pile of trash on the ground. It appeared to be a load of trash from a home improvement project. Most likely left there by a do-it-your-selfer who didn't want to dispose of his handiwork properly. To one a hopefully disposed pile of materials but to another a glimmering light of hope.

Perry reached down and pulled out the one thing that she had eyed. It was a three-foot-long piece of copper pipe. Light enough to swing but solid enough to inflict some major damage. Feeling a bit more confident, she flipped it around in the air and caught it with the same hand.

Once she rounded to the back of the building, Perry started to scan the area. Nothing out of the ordinary. Assorted dumpsters lined the back, next to the rear doors for each store. It was a sight that a person would see thousands of times and not give another thought. The problem here was that there was a predator somewhere.

Perry continued down the back, maneuvering around each garbage dumpster. Each time she passed one, she took a quick glance at the wall. It was an easy hiding space for any surprise. Each time she looked, Perry gripped the pipe tighter.

As she approached the rear of the dance studio, Perry spotted her. There, in broad daylight, was Missy peeking around the other side of the building with her back towards Perry. The little bit longer of a trip had surely given Perry the upper hand.

She tried, with all effort, to rush Missy while she had the moment. Perry focused her energy to close the gap between the two. As she was within a stride, a breeze pulled through her body. The split-second shift threw Perry off ever so slightly. Once she was within reach, Perry swung the pipe with both hands. The hit wasn't a direct hit as she wanted. The calculated breeze pushed her off aim. The pipe glanced off the back of Missy's head and found itself bouncing into the brick-faced wall. Perry's hands burned at the vibration feeling and fed all the way up to her elbows.

Missy grabbed her head, taken completely off guard. She crouched down and pivoted around. The look of shock on her face read that she was on the defensive. If it wasn't for the other thing that was clearly around, Perry would have cracked her skull. It was a shame that she didn't because Missy was able to get herself together rather quickly and lounged at her.

Perry swung the pipe again. This time wasn't a success as Missy simply raised her arm and deflected the swat with a towel she was holding in her hand. Her other arm reached out and connected with Perry's chest, knocking her to the ground. Her head bounced from hitting the concrete, causing a daze to come over Perry. It was panic time.

With Perry down on the ground, Missy hovered over her, placing one of her bulky feet directly on her chest. She shifted her weight to try to push the air out of Perry. The she-beast leaned over, causing Perry to lose her breath.

"End of the line, you little dumb *bitch*," Missy sputtered, as she pulled out the knife that was hidden within the towel. "I'm gonna like seein' you bleed out."

It was the point that Perry's instincts kicked in. At one point during school, Perry had been taught how to get away from an assaulter. One of the best pointers that she could remember was that no matter the person, a kick to the crotch was always effective. Perry raised her left foot as hard as she could straight upwards. She connected with Missy and was surprised when she didn't feel anything of the masculine variety. It was well placed, and stunned Missy. She dropped down on top of Perry in agony. Perry quickly shoved the moaning body off her. Once she was free, Perry got to her feet. Escape was the plan of action, and Perry knew exactly where.

Around the building, the short way this time, Perry bolted. Her legs were filled with adrenaline. It made the pain that was emanating from the back of her head dull. The warmth that trickled down through her hair gave her a slight pause. But it was only a slight hesitation. The plan was afoot. One way or another, Perry and friends were going to get Missy to cross through that portal before it closed. From the looks of it, that time was rapidly approaching.

Without looking both ways as she had been taught many times over growing up, Perry sprinted across Main Street. Traffic be damned. Luckily for her those vehicles that were in their lanes had seen her in time and braked. Horns rang out, as Perry got into the far lane. Once she hopped onto the sidewalk, she turned her head back. There she found her uncle and mother already out of their car and making their way to the road. She couldn't see Missy, but she did hear another pair of feet slamming against the road. Missy was following. In the restricted woods. Where the portal was. When Perry brought her attention to the woods, she found an opening the size of a dump truck sat on the other side of the concrete. Beyond there, she could see the trees were not slowly moving around. They were shaking violently.

"There isn't much time left," Perry stated aloud when she entered the forest.

ALEX 4

The car horns rang outside. Alex didn't need to look out to know what was happening. He knew it was happening, only he hoped it wasn't too late.

Alex, making sure his gun was firmly in its holster, ran towards the stairs and made his way down and out of his office. He could have sworn he missed a step or two, but it didn't matter in the end. Time was of the essence.

Alex slammed the door open and made his way around the complex. The line spilling out of Morey's littered the walk-in front of the building. Alex zigged and zagged through the soon to be patrons before he could get a hold of the situation.

Once he was clear of the growing throng of people, Alex could see what was unfolding in front of him. The Shiner girl had just made her way into the woods. She appeared to be running with a purpose, but he couldn't see anyone chasing after her.

As he made his way over the Main Street bridge over Clarks Run, there is where Alex spotted it. There was a car stopped in the middle of the street, with its driver's side door wide open. It was Rus's car.

He must have made his way over in record time. It was not surprising as the kid was one helluva listener.

Alex picked up the pace and got over to the other side of the Lake. Assorted bystanders were out and enjoying the beautiful weather, making Alex move around, even hopping onto the street to make his way.

A strange thing happened as Alex approached the edge of the woods. A clear path gaped on the side of the road. Something he had seen before, but it had been a while. It was an invitation to join the party.

The trail inside led Alex deeper towards the restricted area. It had been a long time since he had made his way to these parts, but all the memories that he had here came crashing back. He could count on one hand the number of times that he had found himself in this otherworldly place. And it always seemed that each and every time that happened, it was not a pleasant experience.

Once the smells of the spot entered his nostrils, all of Alex's failures came to the forefront of his mind. He was always so diligent on his cases, his personal ones. He was always drawn to this place as a child, and it was at an early age came to the realization that the fantasy here was not completely welcoming. So many times when the air went thin and something breached this world, Alex was able to find out a way to keep it under control. There were only a handful of people in the area, and the world for that matter, that knew of his exploits. Hell, those that knew really didn't understand what was going on and what he was actually doing. All they knew was that he, for one reason or another, was saving a lot of people from whatever crawled out from the other side. But there were times that Alex was caught off guard or just simply unable to get the job done. That was when the bad things happened. Whether it was the little Randolph boy that ended up looking like he went through a meat grinder or the Shiner couple that went AWOL near the Lake or even the formerly cheerful Evelin O'Brian who had not been able to speak after stabbing her throat so that she wouldn't be able to repeat the horrors she endured. When the waypoint eventually closes, certain unspeakable sights would leave, but the aftermath was always irreversible.

Alex tried in vain to push out the failures from his mind. The focus was on saving the girl before the Crimson and its lackey got to her. If he failed, she would be gone in one way or another. This was his last case, and he didn't want anything to end like this.

Alex did his best to force his way deeper into the woods, despite the demons holding him back. The sounds that were reverberating from beyond the hellish gates that he knew for a fact lined the area not far from his pace put him pushed it from brisk to breakneck. The noises alternated from a low frequency whirring to what Alex could only describe as jagged nails on a chalkboard. They were down to the final minutes. The waypoint was on the precipice of collapsing. By the way it appeared, no business was finished. Nothing like waiting until the last minute.

Alex was finally within sight of the outer fence. The twisted metal that draped from the top swung rhythmically side to side. The uprights and links, long rusted open from neglect and otherworldly forces, rattled with the ground. While the chaos that the area had in his life, Alex found the scene consistent with the other unfortunate times he found himself there.

Then he saw them. What Alex saw made him tighten up every muscle in his body. His feet stopped right away, causing his body to trip and stumble. Alex was able to get his balance before he hit the dirt.

Perry had her back against the fence, trying desperately to push herself away. She had her arms raised, trying to protect herself. There was a stream of blood running down the side of her face, emitting from a gash on her forehead. Above her, looming and poised to strike, was the Simpson girl. She was the one that the Crimson was controlling. By the light of the sun that made its way down to the forest floor, a shimmer reflected into his eyes. She was grasping a large knife. It was an overly large kind and being held with the blade down. The girl was preparing to bring it down onto Perry. It was nearly game over.

What happened next, Alex could never understand. He never questioned his actions. It was what made him as successful as he had been. If he could go back, he wasn't sure what else could have been done. It was the scene that he would relive each night as he lay sleepless in his bed for the remainder of his life.

Alex reached to his side and pulled his gun out of its holster. With one quick motion, it was up and aimed at its target. Without any hesitation, Alex squeezed the trigger. The gun was obedient. A bullet found its way out of the chamber and exited the barrel.

Time began to slow down in Alex's mind, with confusion setting in. The vulnerability of Perry was obvious. But the vulnerability of the girl was odd. For as cunning as that red devil was, it seemed too easy. And it was.

As the bullet made its way towards its target, the Crimson appeared. The flowing red hair was the most obvious sign. It had materialized right in Alex's line of sight. When it made its way from a shadow to a mist to a full form, he could no longer see his bullet's target. Alex could feel his heart drop. This being was baiting him into a trap, and now it might be too late for the lot of them.

Just as Alex thought his bullet would strike the being, the red devil pulled to the side. As it moved over, his heart completely fell out of his body. It was hiding a person. That person was also running to help. That person was also trying to fix the wrongs and help the rights. That person was also in the wrong place at the wrong time.

Alex didn't notice the red devil slink away into the shadows. That was no longer a concern of his. The bullet struck its victim's back, and he fell instantly to the ground. Alex didn't need to know who it was and where it hit. All he knew was that he was being played, and he had lost.

Alex stumbled his way over in disbelief. He rolled the body over to its back. Alex held him up in his arms. The warmth of the blood soaked through his clothes. As he started to openly weep, he felt Rus let loose his final breath.

MARTIN 7

With his sister by his side, Martin sprinted across Main Street. He didn't even notice the cars swerving out of the way with horns blaring coming from either direction. The only things that he could hear were the sounds of his shoes slamming on the pavement and the frantic breathing from his sibling. His peripheral vision went black. The only thing that was in his focus was the ever-widening opening of the forest.

Martin made it to the other side of the street in a few strides. Without hesitation, he left the safety of the concrete and entered into the unknown. A quick glance back, and Martin found his sister not that far behind. She had instinctively followed him into this place. The moment that she had crossed over, Martin watched as the opening quickly closed shut, with the thickets and brush shifting around back to their normal positions. Once it was clear that they may be a bit over their heads, he brought his attention back to in front of him.

The trees in front of Martin seemed to convulse each time a foot landed on the ground. The interweaved roots pulsated upwards and ebbed back down. The frantic and chaotic nature of nature pushed his nerves up a few notches. It was clear the time was at hand.

As he got further and further, the gigantic fence came into view. The hulking presence was all too familiar. What wasn't all too familiar was the other scene that seemed to be unfolding in front of him.

It all happened so quickly. It was hard for Martin to process. On one end of the sight was that menacing bully of a girl. She was standing in a prone position, looking like she would attack at any minute. Beneath her was the more troubling part. Perry was in an extremely vulnerable spot, back to the fence and on her ass. The look of fright was plastered across her face. On the other side, Martin found Alex Peters with a body in his lap opening weeping. Something had just happened, but it seemed like it wasn't completely done.

Martin ran right past the spot where Alex was on the ground. For him, there was no time to waste. The distance between himself and that Missy girl was about ten yards. Martin felt the stride running through him as he hit the fastest pace he had all year long. The time it took to cover that distance was over in the matter of a few steps.

Once he was close to Missy, Martin lowered his shoulder, leaned forward and pushed his body through the air with all of his force. With her arm lifted slightly, he made contact with the exposed section of her rib cage. What Martin failed to recognize was the large kitchen knife that was grasped in Missy's right hand. As he passed by it through the air, part of the blade peeled across the side of his face, letting go mercifully near his chin.

Martin felt the bony part of his shoulder dig into the sensitive spot in Missy's ribs. The warmth from his face didn't seem to matter. He could hear an audible snap as he pushed all his bodyweight down on top of her as they sailed down to the ground like a pair of uncoordinated dancers. As they touched back down to the earth, Martin leaned onto her side, trying to disable the aggressor. Her limbs flopped around awkwardly, with the weapon flailing around in the air. Despite being caught completely off guard, the girl maintained the grip on the weapon.

Both were stunned after they came to a full stop. There was a moment when everything in the woods had stopped. Not just the two of them, but the trees, the ground, the leaves. Everything was completely and utterly still.

While the moment felt like it would last forever, it was only a few seconds later when Martin could hear the audible sobs coming from behind him. There were rapidly approaching footsteps not far from his spot as well. The steps didn't last very long, and Martin brought himself from his back to a prone position. There he found Martha with her arms wrapped around Perry, trying to bring her to her feet. Both had looks of shock on their faces.

Martin looked to his side. He was surprised to see the knife by his side, without its owner near it. Upon a quick closer inspection, the blade was both snapped at the tip and caked with blood. The most distressing part was the handle was no longer gripped tightly.

Missy was on her feet and was fleeing. Given her aggressive nature, it caught him by surprise. By the time Martin was on his feet, she was already making her way back where the trail opening had previously existed.

"*ALEX!*" Martin yelled out, hoping to shock the detective back to reality. "*SHE IS GETTING AWAY!*"

Alex slowly pulled his head up from Rus's side. His eyes were welled with tears. It was bad. From the look of him, Martin could sense that they all were not coming out of this the same. And maybe not at all.

"*SHE NEEDS TO GO THROUGH THE PORTAL! AND THE FUCKING THING IS CLOSING!*"

Something broke through this time. Alex understood something. Enough to place the body of his former partner down delicately and rise to his feet. By the time Alex began to run, Missy was a few yards away. Despite the fact he was decades her elder, the man was still fleet a foot.

Even if the thickets were not in her way and the forest had been open for her, Missy wouldn't have made it. By the time she was closing in on the outer edge of civilization, Alex had grabbed the back of her shirt. With one fluid motion, he wrestled her to the ground and was able to get his knee planted into her lower back. Missy squealed in agony. Martin had half a mind to run over to Alex's side and place his knee on her upper neck, but remembered she was still needed. If they couldn't send her back with Ofelia, then that other thing would win. It would become more powerful. And if that was the case, the next time that thing came back, it would be worse. Much worse.

PERRY 7

Everything that had just happened had become a blur in Perry's mind. In one moment, she was fighting off Missy behind the dance studio, and now she was being held by her mother, leaning up against the ominous, rusted fence. She took inventory of the things around her. The shock and speed of the happenings made her confused about the scope of what was going on.

Besides the embrace of her mother, which Perry could even feel the warmth radiating from her which was soothing, there were other sights that made her worry. Not far from where the two stood together was a body. It was slumped over on its side, blood saturating throughout its shirt. Without getting any closer, she could easily see that it clearly had no life left. In the distance, she could make out three figures. As far as she could tell, two of them were on either side of the other. They were leading the other. Leading the other back towards where Perry and her mother were. Leading her.

Perry glanced up at her mother quickly. Then she looked back at those that were coming closer by the step. She could make out the figure on the right was Uncle Em, having a slice across half his face.

On the opposite side, with the entire right side of his face stained with blood was Mr. Peters, the detective. It was then that Perry's heart dropped. The body on the ground…

"*RUS!*" Perry screamed.

Martha pulled her tighter into her chest, trying to calm her down. It did just the opposite. Perry pushed away as hard as she could and found herself running towards Rus's lifeless body. She bent down and rolled the body over to make sure. It was unmistakable. The man that was chatting with Perry in her Uncle Em's house a day ago was now dead. He had seemed charming and relatable in the short time that they were there. And now he had gotten involved and was an innocent causality of this whole mess. Because of Perry.

"No… I can't…please don't be…," Perry couldn't continue. Even though she had no idea what really happened to him. She was cowering before her attacker during what must have transpired occurred. Looking at his final state, all she could figure was that it wasn't a knife that caused his final end. It was a clean bullet hole that had torn right through where Perry had countlessly placed her hand while reciting the Pledge. At least he didn't suffer.

Before she knew it, her mother was by her side, trying her best to console her. The thing was that Martha hadn't done much of consoling her daughter over the years, so, while it felt genuine when she rubbed Perry's back, it was forced and awkward. She was trying to make up for the times that she had missed with Perry, but it just wasn't the same as being there for her through all the rough times.

Perry cried. The ordeal had finally gotten to her. A less strong kid would have broken a long time ago, but not Perry. It took another person to die for her to crack. Her tears ran down her sweaty cheeks and dripped onto the ground.

"This is all my fault…," Perry choked out. "I just could have…I mean, if I would have…oh…shit…." She placed her hands into her palms and let out a sob. It was a long time coming. The air couldn't get into her lungs quick enough, as she let go.

Martha stood dutifully by her side. She looked as if she really didn't know what to do and how to react. It was really the first time she put forth the effort and was there for Perry.

Perry tried to pull back and get herself under control. She never wanted the world to see her as vulnerable. She never felt she was at her best letting emotions out. She never liked the feeling, but it was unavoidable.

Perry made some long snot sniffles, trying to pull back in the mucus that had found its way out. When she got the rest of the snot to hold off its march outward, it dawned on her.

She picked up her head and found her mother's eyes. The epiphany that she had been looking for came to her.

"We need to bring him past the fence. We need to bring him inside."

Martha was a bit shocked by her response. She looked over to the place she found Perry in peril. She pointed over towards the spot, confirming what Perry had said.

"Yes, over there. But look past it. Look further," Perry added.

Martha obediently complied. She had to place her hand over her brow to shield the sun. Her head bumped back in astonishment. Beyond the fence, between the trees, past the ruins of a past time, there it was. A light, flickering yet steady, shone through. The colors flashed across the spectrum. Its size grew and shrunk with a lifelike pulse. It was otherworldly, yet natural. It was the crossover, the waypoint, and it looked like it was in its finale.

Both grabbed each side and began to drag the body over the forest floor. Despite Rus being a stout, strong young man, the two Shiners were able to pull him with quite ease. It must have been the adrenaline, but the two of them made their way faster than Uncle Em and Mr. Peters dragging Missy kicking.

The moment that they pulled the body through the menacing gates to the other side, the entire landscape changed. Perry felt like she had walked into a movie. The wild forest was a well-trimmed and maintained complex. Buildings were strewn across the land. Each one had a scientific yet crooked feeling. Shadows of beings were traversing from one to another, without any notice of the two of them. The ground was beaten down and trampled by the years of feet following the same paths back and forth. When Perry looked behind them, the fence was nothing more than a brick wall and wooden fence.

Both took a moment to try to orient themselves. The light of the portal was nowhere to be found. The world that they found themselves could have been across the world or within a different decade. All seemed lost.

As hope sank to the lowest part of Perry's body, a familiar voice sounded out.

"Perry, you are here," it said.

She recognized it instantaneously.

"Ofelia! Oh, Ofelia, where are we?" Perry asked.

A girl, shorter and appearing to be younger than the Shiner daughter, ran from the rear of one of the laboratory looking buildings. A worried look was struck across her face.

"It is almost time. You shouldn't be here!" Ofelia exclaimed. "If it closes when you are here...No, you need to leave!"

"Not yet," Perry answered. "We are bringing the girl. We are here to finish the plan."

"Oh, thank god. The last thing I wanted to do was face the Sable. That thing is not very kind. Where is she?"

"My uncle and another are bringing her here. But before that, we need your help."

Ofelia looked down at Rus. Instantly, she understood.

"I can see what I can do. Time is running out. I am not sure if I have enough power left."

Ofelia bent down at the side of Rus. She placed both hands on top of his chest. The blood still hadn't coagulated yet, as Ofelia's hands smeared around. She closed her eyes, lowered her head, and began to speak words under her breath. Perry could not make out anything that she was saying, but it did not matter. The more that Ofelia spoke and rubbed, the more hope came back into Perry. The hope that things wouldn't continue down the turn that they had. That there was a light at the end of this tunnel.

Ofelia stopped completely. She put her mouth next to Rus's right ear and whispered. From one moment the body was devoid of life and the next shivers ran down its sides. The body began to convulse, starting as light movements and moving up to full body shakes. Incoherent babbling could be heard. The eyelids flickered with life. And as quickly it started, the body went limp. Seconds passed with unnatural silence and stillness. Anticipation was high for something to happen. And without notice, something did.

Just as a person that had thought they experienced an earthquake in the middle of the night, Rus popped upright. The initial look on his face and eyes was a blank and disturbing one. Despite the body sitting upright on the ground, it didn't appear that there was any life inside. Ofelia leaned over, and placed her hands over both of his ears. With a deep breath and a forceful exhale by the little girl, the body of Rus shocked back to reality. His hands reached up and grabbed both of Ofelia's arms. His head swiveled around in utter disorientation. His breathing became rapid and confused. His face creased and twisted in ways that Perry had never seen before.

Rus looked around at his surroundings. It appeared everything around him was causing even more confusion. That was until he saw Perry.

"What…. wha happened?" he managed.

Perry shot over and grabbed a hold of the virile young man. She squeezed him tightly. Rus didn't return the favor, but that was fine with her. His shirt was still fully blood soaked, but the hole that cut Rus's life too short was no more.

Moments passed, and Rus put an arm around Perry. It was a connection between the two, and not just because Rus was good with words.

"We must continue. I have no more energy left. I cannot help anymore," Ofelia said plainly.

Rus perked up at the ethereal little girl. Anyone around could see his mind connecting the dots.

"So, am I…"

Ofelia came to his side and looked him in the eyes.

"Yes and no. We can discuss it at another time. For now, you and the others need to bring the bully to me."

Realizing that everything was not over yet, Perry popped up to her feet. She found her mother drifting around the space, inquisitively looking around. It didn't last too long as Perry started sprinting back out of the unworldly world, Martha followed right behind.

ALEX 5

Alex couldn't figure what was pulling him down more. The heaviness of his heart from the events that befallen him. Or the trashing, little devil that he and Mart were trying to drag back through the woods. She kept twisting, and wrangling, and doing anything to escape their grip. Luckily for him, Mart was no slouch. The handle they had on her was good enough to bring her unwillingly towards the waypoint.

"You guys ain't getting away with this. Manhandling a little girl. You bunch of *fuckin'* perverts. Why dontcha take your turns with me before you sacrifice me!" Missy screamed out. She tried to swing one of her heels from front to back. It just grazed the size of Alex's leg.

"Listen here. If it wasn't for you, Rus would still be alive. It is completely your fault. And I don't care what the hell happens to you when we get you to the other side," Alex frustratingly exclaimed. He gave her a shove, forcing what balance she had left off.

"Oh, you sick, old man. Jus because your little boytoy got killed, doesn't mean what happens next will make anything better!"

The last part struck a tone with Alex. Not that he had any type of feelings like that towards Rus. But part of her was right. By offering her up to whatever might be on the other side would not right the wrongs. But it might soften the blow.

"Well, I will take my chances," Alex shot back.

The two of them did all that they could to keep Missy from trying to escape. The hardest part of it wasn't holding her tight, it was trying to keep the obscenities and vulgarities out of his head.

"You lost! Don't that hurt? You didn't win and you *SHOT THAT FUCKIN' KID!*"

"Keep it together, Alex," Mart encouraged. "She means nothing. She is a bat shit crazy loon and doesn't know what she is talking about."

Missy could do nothing but laugh. It started out low but rolled into a roaring, ominous cackle. She let her body go limp, as it appeared that she could not fight the two teeth and nail and let out a horrifying howl at the same time.

"Oh, YES, I DO! OH, MY GAWD! YOU TWO ARE SO *SCREWED!*"

The moment that she finished the last syllable, her body fell to the ground, right out of Alex and Mart's grasp. In an instant, she felt like she weighed three times what she really did.

Both not fully knowing what happened, the men took a step back, surveying what had just happened.

Missy stood back up from the ground, only it wasn't her. At least it wasn't just her anymore.

"Gentlemen. While it has been a pleasure, I must bid you adieu," the being had spoken ever so eloquently. While her facial features could still be seen, it was no longer Missy. To Alex, he knew what was happening. It was both of them. The Crimson had taken over.

With a swift, roundhouse swing, the new Missy knocked both onto the ground. Alex could only watch in horror as it walked straight towards the collapsing waypoint. The thing was going to cross over with the Missy body. It would be game over if that happened.

As the thing walked ever so confidently away from them, Alex could see she was fighting it. That devious being had a plan all along, and everyone was its pawns.

For a second or two, Missy was able to break away from its grip. Just long enough to turn around and catch Alex and Mart in the eyes. The look that stared back at them was one of abject horror. She knew now what was in store for her, and it appeared too late. But too late for her was also too late for them.

The Crimson regained control. It looked back at them, with a coy smile creeping across its face.

"The game is now over," it said as it turned back around.

Alex shot a glance at Mart. He was in the same predicament. But were not able to move, either due to the shock and gravity of what was happening or something paranormally worse.

As the new Missy reached the edge of the waypoint lights, Alex could hear evil laughing and blood curdling screams concurrently.

OFELIA 3

Perry and her mother didn't make it out to their world. Once they were on the precipice, something entered. Much to Ofelia's dismay, the worst-case scenario came through.

The bully came through, but she wasn't by herself. Alex and Martin were not alongside her. Erwin was there, and he was in control.

The moment the monstrosity entered, Perry and Martha stopped in their tracks. The combination of Erwin and the girl spotted them and shot over to the spot where they were frozen. With a quick spin of its arms, mother and daughter went flying through the air. Perry landed on her back and rolled up against a tree while Martha crashed down on her shoulder. A loud crack rang out through the forest followed by an agonizing scream. Something snapped.

With a huge and devious grin, the duo looked directly towards Ofelia.

"Well, hello, my dearest Ofelia. Pleasure meeting you here today," it kept its hellish smile on its face.

"What are you doing, Erwin?"

"Well, I think I am doing exactly as you think I am doing."

Ofelia watched as the being started to make its way towards one of the closer research laboratories. With each step, she could see two faces. The more ethereal one had the smile. Red, flowing hair draped down over its features. The other one had a look of utter horror and appeared to be screaming out. But there was nothing that could be heard. It was doubtful she knew exactly what was in store for her, but it was evident she understood it wasn't going to be pleasant.

With a sense of urgency, Ofelia ran as fast as she could, trying in vain to cut off the route that Erwin was currently on. Once she came near him and her, she tried to separate the two. She clutched and pulled at the air. Nothing was working.

With a quick backhand hit to her head, Ofelia went down in a heap. "Well, dear. It looks like you are flush out of power," it surmised.

From behind where Ofelia had landed, rapid footsteps echoed through the still air. Erwin and his captive looked up to find the resurrected man on a mission to stop everything from happening. Rather than continue to gloat on the potential success of its plan, Erwin pulled himself and the girl as quickly as possible into the laboratory. The second that the door slammed shut, the entire building started to glow and shake. The surrounding ground began to tremble and growl. The body that was referred to as Lazarus Brown only a few minutes ago was not able to intercept Erwin and his plot.

Everything went still once more, but the light grew in intensity, to the point everyone around had to shield their eyes. And just as quickly as it started, it stopped. With the light finally receding, Ofelia and everyone else could see what had happened. There was a large empty spot in the land where the laboratory had been. It was now gone, engulfed by the waypoint. And with it was also any hope. The Sable was not a very understanding being, rather quite a malevolent horror. It was the first time that Ofelia had failed it, and now the bill was coming due.

Ofelia stood up, finding Perry by her side. She tried to give an embrace, but it didn't work. As Erwin had said, Ofelia no longer had any powers in this place. She used the last of them to bring back the soul from the depths. Now she had to limp back through to the other place with her tail hung between her legs.

The worst part wouldn't be what happened to Ofelia when she went back. It would be when Erwin returned. He would be unstoppable, and chaos would reign.

MARTHA 3

Martha was able to pull herself up. Despite the confusing and frightening events that had just transpired, she could not focus on anything around her. The throbbing agony of her right shoulder clouded everything around her. It lay down limp at her side, sending unending pain back up. With her left, Martha was able to hold the useless arm up to a point where some of the pain abetted.

The forest around her, and all the random buildings and people, appeared to be slinking back to where they had come from. Things looked to be coming to an end. And by the looks that Martha could get of her daughter and that other girl, it didn't seem very promising.

Martha started to make her way over. Each time she placed weight on her right foot, there was the shooting pain again. She could have just sat back down and been done with the whole damn thing. But it looked like this was one of the many times that Perrywinkle needed her. And she stopped counting how many times that she was not there for her. Martha had to come through for her at least once.

With that motivating her, Martha trudged along. Her right foot went from bearing the slightest of weights to being drug behind her body. In any other circumstance, Martha would have tapped out, thrown in the towel, or just plain forfeited. But the stakes were much greater than herself.

The closer she got to her daughter, the more excruciating the pain became. Her entire body felt aflame. In the end, it really didn't matter. It felt like the culmination of something, but it was actually reassuring.

As she approached, Martha found the terrain turned rocky and jagged. Before the tears welled in her eyes, she made it next to Perry and the other girl.

"Am I too late?" Martha asked, feeling the dour moment.

The two of them looked up at her, surprised by her presence given the fall that had befallen her.

"She is gone. Missy is gone…," Perry trailed off.

"So, that is it?" Martha asked earnestly.

"She was the plan. She had to go. But now she is gone."

Martha was quite confused. Things just didn't really make total sense. The answer seemed out there, just had to find it.

"Where did she go?"

"She went through to the other side," Ofelia answered.

"So doesn't that count?" Martha questioned, more perplexed.

"No. Erwin...that other being...took her back with him. The Midnight Sable tasked me to come back with a soul from this side. It is in control on the other side. So, I will be going back, empty handed so to speak," Ofelia explained.

Martha looked at the little girl. With each second that passed, her body began to become ever more translucent. It wouldn't be long now.

Martha then looked at Perry. It was all clear, and it was time to step up.

"Well, then. I don't think there is anything else that can be done."

Martha looked back at Ofelia and then to Perry again and back to Ofelia once more.

"I will come with you."

The stillness reappeared. The breathlessness invaded.

"Wha...what?" Perry spoke softly. It wasn't as much a question as it was a statement.

"If someone doesn't go with you, that thing will come back. And with more power? Then I should go," Martha reiterated.

The shock covered Perry's face. Her mouth was agape. Her eyes were stuck open.

"Listen, Perry. I haven't been the greatest of mothers. Hell, I haven't been even the most adequate of mothers. I haven't been there when you needed me."

Martha put her hand under Perry's chin. Her eyes were slowly dripping down her cheeks.

"It's true, I haven't been there. I have been distracted, stuck in the past."

Martha looked at Ofelia this time.

"I think there is something on that side. Answers. Do you understand?"

Ofelia nodded, yet added, "Just know, it will not be easy. There will be pain."

Martha nodded back.

"Well, I am probably due for that. I have caused much pain to you, Perry. I have failed you."

Perry openly wept. She grasped onto Martha's side and squeezed tightly. She didn't fight back. Martha held her back.

"Perry. You...you deserve better. I can't fix the past. I have too many distractions, too many questions unanswered. You will be better off this way."

Perry kept squeezing tightly. There wasn't any objection from her.

Martha held her head down onto her daughters. She pulled herself even closer and brought her voice low.

"You have found a home," Martha whispered.

Perry broke down. Martha could feel her tears soaking through her shirt. It was the first real moment they had had together in the longest of times.

"Time is up," Ofelia interrupted. "If you are true, then we need to go."

Martha nodded affirmingly. She pulled back ever so slightly, and Perry looked up. Martha kissed her on the forehead and let go. She took a step back, giving Perry a look, before she took Ofelia's hand and headed towards the closest building.

MARTIN 8

It had been over a year since everything happened. All things considered, it appeared that the healing time might have been finally settling in. Nothing could change what had happened to them, and, looking back, Martin wasn't very sure there was anything else that they could have done. In a way, it seemed to him that everything had occurred the way it did with some sort of purpose. Like it was written in the stars. Part of him knew better, but the other part really didn't know. In the end, he just tried to take each day as it came.

It was a beautiful early autumn day outside. The sun was out, but it wasn't too hot. The wind was blowing slightly, but it wasn't too cold. It was the perfect atmosphere, for a party, for a family get-together. Guests were beginning to arrive. The twins were turning seven, which Martin really couldn't grasp how quickly the time had been travelling. It really did fly when the kids were growing like weeds.

With Sasha having everything preplanned and set up to the best of her abilities, Martin was left to escort the kids outside. Both Tristan and Maddox didn't need much convincing once they heard their cousins out on the deck. The hard part was making sure they didn't tumble down the stairs as they hauled ass around the house and out the back door. Sasha was there to open the screen door so that they didn't run right through the damn thing. She was the greatest at anticipating the chaos brought by those two little rambunctious balls of energy.

Martin followed the hallway to what used to be his office and the spare room. The door was mostly closed, but he could hear music coming from within. There had been days and even weeks when the only thing he could hear was echoing silence. The music was a warm and welcoming sight.

He rapped on the door slightly, but not enough to have it open any more. Within a few seconds, it swung open fully. Perry stood behind. She had been wearing a new glow to her that Martin had never seen before.

"You all good?" Martin asked.

"I have seen better days," Perry wisely replied.

Martin gave her the eye. Perry couldn't hold it in and giggled.

"Yes, I am good. Thank you for asking."

"Ready for the party?"

"Not really." That was an honest answer for all that Martin could tell. Today marked the first time that she would be around the more distant family in a very long time. There would be questions. There would be concern. There would be awkward times.

"I gotcha. I understand. But take it like this, kiddo. It's all a part of healing."

Perry nodded in agreement.

"You are right," she affirmed. "I guess even a blind squirrel finds a nut every now and then."

Martin let out a bellowing laugh. When Perry was shooting out quips, she seemed to be in a good space, especially in her head.

"Well, on that note, let's beat feet and hit the street!"

Martin led her out of the recent office yet newly bedroom to the hallway and down the stairs. The voices and sounds of the party were echoing around the house and up to them. Before getting to the bottom, Perry stopped and took a seat on one of the stairs.

"Uncle Em…"

"Yoooooouuuuuu rannnnnnnnnggggg?"

Much to Martin's dismay, the reference flew way over Perry's head.

"Not sure what you are talking about, but rather than hurt your feelings, I will move along."

"Fair enough."

"Do you think…I mean, do you think there was anything else I could have done?"

Martin put his head down a bit. "Perry, honestly?"

"Yeah."

"Not a goddamn thing."

"Yeah?"

"Yup. Here is the thing. Whatever happened, happened. Can't change a thing. My sister…I mean, your mother. This whole thing, well it was like an awakening for her. When she thought there might be a chance of a chance, well she ran with it."

"What do you think?"

"About what?" Martin asked.

"About your parents?"

"Well, I am not completely sold. I came to grips with the fact they weren't coming back. Sis? Not so much. Did I think that there might be more? Yeah, part of me. I am not going to lie to you. But the thing is, there were other things that pushed me forward. I met Sasha, I had the twins, you know?

Perry shrugged, "Yeah, I guess I can see it."

"And, the thing is, there was a part of me that could get why she did what she did."

Perry went silent. Everything had taken time to set in lately. That was completely understandable to Martin.

"I hear him sometimes."

"Excuse me?" Martin questioned, perplexed.

"Rus. Sometimes at night, I hear his voice."

"Really?"

"Yeah. But I think it is okay. He is still out there."

"What about your mother?"

Perry put her head down. The answer was clear and evident.

"No."

Martin put his arm around Perry. He pulled her close and squeezed tightly. He could feel her heartbeat.

"Perry," Martin pushed onward. "You mother was...is trying to get through to the other side of the tunnel. Gonna try to find the light."

Perry kept her head up, yet still started to cry. Martin could tell that it wasn't the usual kind. It was hope.

PERRY 8

The tears continued to flow. Uncle Em had already left for the party festivities in the backyard. Perry was alone at the base of the stairs, with only her mind to comfort her.

Many different things could have occurred, and the outcome could have been completely different. While Uncle Em thought it was destiny, Perry knew better. The number of moving parts had constantly worried her, but, in the end, the stress was all from naught. In the end, all the pawns moved to their respective squares just as they should have. When she took a moment to reminisce, Perry couldn't help but smile.

The events that transpired, in the order that they had to, were still a blur in her mind. From the first time she met Ofelia to the last moment that she was standing in the grounds of the waypoint, the entire ordeal seemed one continuous part in time. The few memories that were imprinted on the inside of her skull were directly after getting roughed up by Missy. The first time that is. It wasn't the first time Perry made her way through the ether to visit the restricted woods, but it was there and then that the plan was born. The plan between herself,

Ofelia and Erwin. Erwin got what he wanted, bringing Missy back with him. Who knows if he was telling the truth about his reasons for having her at his disposal, but Perry really didn't care. Ofelia made it back with her mother, that is what mattered to Perry.

There was a part deep down inside that felt for her mother. She could only imagine what was happening to her on that side. From her conversations with Ofelia, and Erwin to a lesser degree, it didn't seem like a very inviting place. Constant pain and torment. Not like the Hell she learned from her books and studies. More like a place overrun by a tyrant. Perry could understand how living in a place like that could bring pain and suffering.

Maybe her mother would find what she was looking for there. From what she heard, it was possible that her parents really were stuck on the other side. That thought helped to ease any heartache on Perry's end. But now, none of that mattered. All that did was that Perry was together with her family finally.

ABOUT THE AUTHOR

Maggie King is the author of the Hazel Rose Book Group mysteries. Her short stories appear in various anthologies, including the *Virginia is for Mysteries* series, *50 Shades of Cabernet*, *Deadly Southern Charm*, *Death by Cupcake*, *Murder by the Glass*, and *First Comes Love, Then Comes Murder, and Crime in the Old Dominion*.

Maggie graduated from Rochester Institute of Technology. She is a member of Sisters in Crime, James River Writers, and the Short Mystery Fiction Society. She has worked as a software developer, retail sales manager, customer service supervisor, web designer, and non-profit administrator. She has called New Jersey, Massachusetts, and California home. These days she lives in Richmond, Virginia with her husband Glen and mischievous cat, Olive. All these jobs, schools, and homes have gifted her with story ideas for years to come. www.maggieking.com.

Connect with me
    Facebook: facebook.com/maggiekingauthor
    Instagram: instagram.com/maggiekingauthor

Sign up for my quarterly newsletter at maggieking.com for news, views, and giveaways.